Full Moon Rising

by
Carol Hall

Cover art by
Brenna Paradinovich

This book is dedicated to everyone who loves werewolf stories and has lost many a nights sleep wondering if one was just outside your window.

Prologue

The tiny cabin was set back in the woods far away from prying eyes. The path to get to it was tangled with briars and tall weeds. Thick, heavily leaved trees formed a canopy over the dirt trail almost obscuring it from view. It would be almost impossible to find if you didn't already know where it was.

I already knew where it was. I had been there several times before.

As darkness fell across the sky, I made my way down the path. An eerie fog was slowly rising from the damp earth, swirling around my feet.

I stuffed my hands in my pockets and hunched my shoulders up under my ears trying to ward off the chill that suddenly filled the air.

I was close. I could feel it.

A tiny yellow glow flickering through the trees up ahead warned me that I was almost there.

As I stepped out of the dark woods that surrounded the cabin, I could see that a candle had been lit and set in the front window. Normally this would have been a welcoming sight, but not tonight. I was here for a purpose, not a friendly visit.

I shook off the unpleasant feeling I always got when I came here and crossed the small yard to the front door.

Taking a long, deep breath, I blew it out between pursed lips trying to gain my composure. The reason I was here had not been an easy choice to make, but I finally gave myself over to the darkness inside me and ventured out here hoping to find the help I needed.

I knocked three times and stepped back. Somewhere in the distance I heard an owl hoot. It was a lonely sound that seemed fitting for this place.

The door squeaked as it swung part way open.

"Come in," said a crackly, old woman's voice.

I pushed the door open a bit more to allow enough room to squeeze through the opening.

I realized as soon as I walked into the room that the old woman had not gotten up out of her chair to open the door for me. I turned around and watched as it slowly closed on its own.

Turning back to the woman who was sitting in front of a small fireplace, I cautiously approached her.

"It's me," I said. "Do you remember me?"

She sat quietly with her back to me looking down at her lap at something she was holding in her hands.

"Of course I remember you. I remember everyone who has ever come to see me."

"I need your help," I said.

Slowly getting up out of her chair, she turned to face me. Her wrinkled old face and long, silver, unkempt hair never ceased to make me feel uneasy and a bit scared.

She stuck out her hand and dropped what she had been holding onto a table that sat behind her chair.

A dead crow with one of its feet cut off lay dead and stiff where she dropped it.

A shudder ran through me, but I made no bones as to what she was or what she did. That's why I came here. I needed her kind of help.

"What do you need?" she asked me, walking over and grabbing a small jar off a shelf next to the fireplace.

Opening the lid, she reached her gnarled fingers inside and took out a pinch of its contents. Leaning over the fire, she threw what looked like crushed green leaves into the flames. Sparks flew up the chimney and a strong, sweet aroma filled the air.

Placing the jar back in its place, she turned to look at me again.

"Well?" she asked, staring at me. "What do you need?"

The smell from whatever she threw in the fire made me feel a bit lightheaded and dizzy. I blinked several times and cleared my throat.

Finally finding my voice, I stuttered, "I...need you...to make...make me into...a...a…," I couldn't bring myself to say the word.

"A what?" She was beginning to lose patience with me and I was afraid she would tell me to leave, so I quickly blurted out, "A werewolf."

She narrowed her eyes and looked hard at me. "A werewolf, huh?"

"Yes, ma'am," I said. I could feel my knees start to shake and my palms were getting sweaty.

"Why do you want to be a werewolf?" she asked quietly.

"I want to hurt people who have hurt me," I said.

There, I admitted it.

The old woman slowly paced the small room, rubbing her chin between her thumb and finger.

"I suppose I could help you with that," she finally said. "For a price, of course."

"I brought it," I said.

"Good, good." Excitement laced her words and she rubbed her hands together in anticipation at the gift I brought her. Money was of no use to her, so I brought her the one thing she couldn't get living out here all alone.

I pulled a small pack from my shoulder and unzipped it.

As I reached my hand down inside to pull out the offering, she rushed over and grabbed the bag from me and gently placed it on the table.

"Is it small?" she asked, as she spread open the flaps and peered down inside the bag.

"As small as I could find," I said.

A soft mewling sound came from the bottom of the pack. A wide smile spread across the old woman's face as she slowly and gently lifted out the tiny, black kitten.

"Boy or girl?" she asked, as she snuggled the kitten under her chin and stroked its soft fur.

"Uh, I don't know," I said. "I didn't ask. I just picked the smallest one."

The pet store I found the kitten at hadn't told me whether it was male or female. They just gladly accepted my money and handed over the tiniest, blackest kitten they had.

"No matter," she said. "Spook can be a name for either boy or girl."

I just nodded and watched as she laid the kitten in a small basket and placed it next to the fireplace. I knew she wouldn't hurt the kitten. She was just lonely and wanted the companionship.

After she made sure the kitten was comfortable, she turned back to me. "Payment accepted," she said. "Now, are you sure this is what you want? Cause once it's done, there's no undoing it."

"I'm sure," I said.

I had spent a long time trying to decide if this was the way to go and finally I knew that it was. I wanted to hurt those who hurt me, who made me feel so worthless and despised. I wanted them to pay for what they had done to me.

"Then let's begin," she said.

I pulled out one of the chairs that sat around the table and took a seat. I knew this would take a little time, so I made myself comfortable.

As she scurried around the room gathering up the items she would need, I looked around the small cabin.

Dried herbs of many varieties hung from nails in the low hanging rafters. Jars and jars filled with things I didn't want to know of lined shelves on one side of the fireplace. Feathers, rat tails and rabbit feet were piled up on another shelf by the door.

The cabin only had one window which made it feel like being in a cave. The whole place smelled like dried grass and sweet flowers. Not an unpleasant smell considering that brews, potions and any number of other unspeakable things were cooked up in here.

The single room cabin boasted only one small bed placed in the far corner and a single rocking chair in front of the fireplace and the small table I was now sitting at, but for a small, old woman living out here alone, it was all she really needed.

Finally having placed all the needed items on the table, she began measuring out ingredients into a small cast iron pot.

I picked up a beautiful purple flower with a long green stem that she had laid on the table along with all the other ingredients. Turning it over in my hand, I asked, "What is this?"

She quickly snatched it from my hand and began cutting it up and dropping it into a mortar. As she smashed up the flowers and leaves with the pestle she said, "Wolfsbane. Poisonous, but necessary for the potion."

"Poisonous?" I asked. "Will it kill me?"

She looked up from her grinding and for a moment didn't say anything. Then, as she dumped the pulverized plant into the pot, she looked at me. "Turning into a werewolf will make you only half human from now on. The other half will be wolf. So I guess, in a sense, half of you will die."

I let those words sink in. I was only going to be half human. Was I ok with that? If that's what it took for me to get my revenge, then yes, I was, indeed, ok with that.

I watched as she dumped several more ingredients into the pot and stirred them all together.

Lifting the pot off the table, she took it over and hung it on a hook over the fire.

"It will have to cook for several hours," she said. "Make yourself comfortable while I tell you how to take this potion and what you can expect from it."

I leaned back in my chair and listened intently to every word she said.

As the potion cooked and she continued to talk, I began to feel a bit drowsy and lightheaded. The smell from the potion was intoxicating. A smile stretched across my face as I realized I would soon be getting the revenge I so desperately deserved.

Some time later, I awoke with a start. I must have fallen asleep at the table while she cooked the potion.

I glanced around the room and saw her sitting in her rocker in front of the fireplace stirring the contents of the pot.

"I'm sorry," I said, feeling ashamed that I had fallen asleep on her. "I didn't mean to fall asleep."

Without turning to look at me, she said, "You didn't have a choice. The herbs and stuff I put in the potion would have knocked you out anyway. It's suppose to be that way. You will need your strength when you drink it, so resting before hand is always a good idea."

"Oh," I said, feeling that it was an inadequate response, but not knowing what else to say. "Is it done?"

"Yes."

I sat up straight and waited while she carried the hot pot back to the table and set it down.

She reached behind her and pulled a large wooden mug down off a shelf and set it in front of me. "You will have to drink all of the potion. Every drop. Do you understand?"

"Yes," I said, feeling a bit nervous. "Do I drink it all at once?"

"Every last drop," she said, ladling out some of the hot, steaming liquid and pouring it into the mug. "You're not going to like it. It will burn your throat and your stomach will feel like it's on fire, but you have to keep drinking till it's all gone, you understand?"

"Yes, ma'am," I said. I was willing to do whatever it took. I reached for the cup, but she grabbed my wrist.

"Not yet," she said. "You need to hear it all. It will give you the worst headache of your life. It will feel like your skull is being split in two."

This was beginning to worry me a bit. Would I survive the transformation? Would it be too much to handle? Could I stop before I finished drinking all the potion and walk away?

"Anything else," I asked, as my voice broke over the words.

"Your body will react violently to the potion. Your limbs will twist and jerk, your body will contort in unnatural ways."

I stared at her like she had lost her mind. "So, it *is* going to kill me," I said.

"I warned you it would be hard. Very hard. But if you want it, then you'll have to earn it."

"How long will this transformation take?" I asked.

"Only moments," she said.

I let out the breath I didn't even realize I was holding. "Well, then, that doesn't seem too bad. I can handle it if it's only for a few moments."

"It will be the longest few moments of your life," she said, dropping the ladle back into the pot. "Remember, you must drink every last drop in order for it to work."

"Ok, I'm ready," I said, not feeling ready at all, but just wanting to get it over with.

She handed me the mug and I lifted it to my nose. Sniffing it cautiously, I was surprised at the pleasant smell it had.

Tipping the mug up to my lips, I drank down the full amount in one gulp.

Suddenly, my throat felt like someone lit a torch in it. My stomach seized up on me and I bent over in such agonizing pain I didn't think I could bear it. My eyes began to water so bad I couldn't see out of them. Tears streamed down my face and snot poured out of my nose.

She handed me the mug filled to the brim again and told me to drink it. I reached out my hand for the mug, but the pain in my body was so horrific, I didn't know if I could hang on to it.

"Drink it," she demanded.

I lifted the mug to my lips and gulped down the contents as quickly as I could. My head felt like it was going to explode. The pain behind my eyes was excruciating. My limbs began to twist in odd directions and I screamed in pain.

One more time she dipped the ladle into the pot and shoved the mug toward me. "Last one," she said, unsympathetically.

I reached for the mug just as my body bent over backward and twisted sideways at the same time. It began to convulse and contort in ways no body was meant to bend. The pain was unbearable. I couldn't handle this degree of agony. I wanted to give up. I wanted to die.

She grabbed up the mug and walked around the table to my bent and twisted body laying on the floor. Every muscle I had was seized up. I couldn't move. My mouth was gaped open, so she poured the rest of the potion down my throat.

Hot liquid fire flowed through my veins. My bones felt like they were being crushed in violent ways. I could no longer see out of my eyes and a loud roaring suddenly filled my ears.

Just when I thought I couldn't take anymore pain without dying, everything suddenly stopped.

I lay on the floor panting and sweating profusely. My face was covered in tears and snot. My arms and legs were laying at odd angles at the sides of my body. My back was rigid and I had soiled myself. But I was alive.

My body began to relax and the pain slowly ebbed away.

I was afraid to move. I was afraid to breath.

Then suddenly a warmth spread through me. A pleasant warmth.

I felt my strength returning, but much stronger than it had been before.

My eyes were clear. I could see better now than I ever could before in my life.

The roaring in my ears stopped. My hearing was so much more acute now.

I felt like a new person. A new and improved version of my old self.

I got up off the floor and wiped my face off on my sleeve and straightened my clothing.

The old woman was watching me. Her eyes narrowed and she walked over to me. "How do you feel?" she asked.

"Like a brand new person," I told her.

She nodded her head, but didn't say anything else.

"When will I turn into a werewolf? The next full moon?"

"You read too many books or watch too many movies. The full moon has nothing to do with you changing. You will change when you choose to."

"You mean, I can control when I change?" I asked.

"Yes," she said. "When you want to become the werewolf half of yourself, just imagine that you are the werewolf and you will change."

"Can I turn back into my human self whenever I want, too?"

"Yes, but be careful with how often you change. If you change too often, you will eventually become more werewolf than human. Choose wisely how often you change."

"Thank you again for your services," I said to her. "I knew I could count on you."

She nodded her head and opened the door for me to leave. "Remember, the only thing that can kill you is silver. Stay away from silver at all costs."

I stepped out into the early morning air. I had been here all night. I sucked in a lungful of the cool, fresh air and realized my sense of smell was greatly intensified. I could smell the earth, the trees, and…animals. I could smell deer, squirrel, raccoon and I knew what they were by their smell.

I stepped onto the path that would lead me back to my car which was parked a long way off on a service road that wound through the forest.

I felt so alive. So free. So new. I felt invincible.

I couldn't wait to use my new gift. People were finally going to pay for what they did to me. Oh, how they would pay.

Chapter 1

Taryn Givens was running late. This wasn't exactly the example she wanted to set for the people who worked under her. Just because she was the sheriff of a small town didn't mean she could relax her standards or shirk her duties.

Grabbing her mug of coffee, she raced out the door and slid behind the wheel of her car. Hastily fastening her seat belt, she threw the SUV into drive and took off down the road.

With her coffee cup held tightly in her left hand and the steering wheel in her right, she glanced down at the clock on the dashboard.

8:15 a.m.

She was already fifteen minutes late and it was still going to take her another fifteen minutes to get to the station.

Stepping on the gas, she rounded a curve in the road just as a vehicle whipped out in front of her from an old abandoned service road that cut back through the woods on the left hand side of the road.

She swerved to the right to avoid hitting the car and slammed on her brakes, throwing the coffee cup up into the air. Coffee splattered down the window and door and sloshed down over her left arm and into her lap. The hot liquid caused her to gasp as her car came to a screeching halt.

Throwing the car door open, she jumped out of the car and began wiping the hot coffee off her clothes to no avail. Her shirt and slacks were soaked. Grumbling to herself, she saw that the car that had pulled out in front of her had pulled over to the side of the road just up ahead of her.

Grabbing her gun and fastening it around her waist, she walked down the road toward the car.

As she approached, she saw it was an older model ford that was so badly rusted it was almost impossible to tell what color the paint job was. Red? Orange? But she knew exactly who the owner was.

Benji Willis.

Benji wasn't known for being too bright. In fact, if a decision had to be made, he usually made the wrong one. At twenty eight years old, he still lived at home with his mother and couldn't seem to hold down a job. Most folks around town considered him useless and worthless, but Taryn knew he was harmless, just a bit rough around the edges, was all.

She walked up to the window and leaned down to look inside.

"Benji," she said, a little irritated. "What are you doing? You almost ran me off the road."

"Sorry, Sheriff Givens," Benji said, looking sheepish. "I didn't see you coming."

"What are you doing out here this early in the morning and what were you doing up on that old service road?"

"I was hunting squirrels," he said.

"Squirrels?" Taryn asked, clearly not believing him.

"Yes, ma'am. You know how much my mama loves her squirrel stew."

Taryn couldn't help but chuckle at this. Gertie Willis was known around town for how much she loved her squirrel stew.

"Yes, I do," Taryn said. "But why were you out here hunting them?"

"There's more of them out here in the woods than there are around our property."

Gertie and Benji lived on the outskirts of town near the old cemetery. Though they didn't have a big place, it did butt up against the woods which meant that there should have been plenty of squirrels around there making Taryn question again why he was out in the middle of the woods hunting for some.

Taryn looked in the back seat of Benji's car, but didn't see a rifle or gun.

"How are you killing them without a gun?" she asked him.

"I don't need a gun," he said.

"You don't shoot them?"

"No, ma'am. I just sit real still and wait for them to come near me, then I grab them and..."

Taryn cut him off before he could finish. "I don't need to hear the details."

Still feeling a bit suspicious, she looked back toward the trunk.

"Would you mind opening the trunk for me and showing me what you caught?"

"Sure," Benji said, swinging the car door open and stepping out.

He was tall and lanky with greasy, dark brown hair that hung down over his eyes. His ripped up jeans and stained t-shirt looked like they had seen better days and his boots were coming apart at the soles. Taryn noticed that he smelled like sweat and earth.

They walked to the back of the car and Benji inserted his key in the keyhole behind the license plate and popped the lid open. Inside were five squirrels, gutted and laying on a garbage bag.

"Five, huh?" Taryn asked. "That's enough for a good size pot of stew."

"Yes, ma'am," Benji said, shutting the lid again. "Is there a limit on how many squirrels you're allowed to kill?"

"I don't believe so," Taryn said, chuckling. "You're mama is going to be real happy with you for bringing those home to her."

"I sure hope so," Benji said, lowing his head. "I broke her lamp last night playing with the dog and thought this might make it up to her."

Benji slid back into the driver's seat and shut the door.

"Am I gonna get a ticket for pulling out in front of you?" he asked, nervously.

"Not today," Taryn said. "But from now on, watch what you're doing. Look both ways before you pull out of a road, ok?"

"Yes, ma'am," Benji said. "Thank you."

"Oh, and Benji…," Taryn said. "You may want to consider getting a new car before long. I don't know how much more glue and duct tape it's going to take to hold this old rust bucket together."

Benji looked shocked.

"Oh, no ma'am," he said. "This car's still got a lot of miles left in her."

Taryn just laughed and shook her head.

"If you say so," she said. "Have a good day, Benji, and tell your mama 'Hello' for me."

"I will," he said, as he turned the ignition over and revved the engine.

Taryn watched as he pulled out onto the road and drove off.

As she turned to head back toward her car, a creepy feeling came over her. She scanned the woods around her, but didn't see anything or hear anything out of the normal.

Shaking off the uneasy feeling, she climbed into her car and headed for the station.

~~~~~

Switcher's Hollow, West Virginia was a small rural community that sat along the banks of the Ohio River, boasting only about fifteen hundred people.

Taryn was born and raised here and couldn't imagine living anywhere else.

At thirty five years of age, she was one of the youngest sheriffs the town had ever seen, but she loved her job and took it seriously. It wasn't easy being a female sheriff with two male deputies under her command, but she managed to gain their respect and they all got along well.

As she pulled up to the station, she flipped her visor down and took a quick look in the mirror at herself. Her short, curly, brown hair was a bit mussed up since she hadn't taken the time this morning to do much with it since she had been running late. Her uniform was beginning to fit a bit snug since she put on those extra twenty pounds over the winter, but she wasn't too worried about it. Divorce could cause any woman to overeat and she'd always been told she was cute, even with a few extra inches around her middle.

Her thoughts reflected back to her ex-husband for a moment. Rhobby had been her high school sweetheart. They had married right out of high school, but over the years they had grown apart, and eventually, Rhobby had found comfort in another woman's arms. Taryn had tried to forgive him, but her heart couldn't let it go, so she filed for divorce a year later. That was nine months ago, but it felt like a lifetime.

Shaking the thoughts from her head, she slid out of the car and walked into the station.

"What happened to you?" Troy Garrett, one of her deputies, asked.

"Got ran off the road by Benji," she said, looking down at the coffee stains on her uniform. "I was holding my coffee cup in my hand and sent it airborne when he pulled out in front of me."

"That idiot's going to kill someone one of these days the way he drives," Cheryl Clark mumbled from her seat at the front desk.

"He's harmless, guys," Taryn said. "Albeit, a little misguided."

"Misguided, my foot," said Ron Thompson, the other deputy. "He's a nuisance."

Taryn just shook her head and walked back to her office.

The station was small. Aside from her office at the back, the building only consisted of the front entryway where Cheryl's desk sat and a small room next to her office where Ron's and Troy's desk were located. A small coffee area and the bathroom were situated in the corner of the entryway.

Slipping into the chair behind her desk, she riffled through the papers that were stacked there.

It was going to be a slow day and Taryn was glad of that. That was one of the things she loved about Switcher's Hollow. It was boring. Nothing much ever happened here. In fact, their local paper, Hometown Happenings, was usually only a couple pages long, highlighting local businesses and an occasional local event. Nothing news worthy hardly ever happened here.

The phone on the corner of her desk began to ring and she reached over and picked it up.

"Hello, Sheriff Given's," she said.

"Hey," said an all too familiar voice. "Can we talk?"

"Rhobby, I'm at work," she said, gritting her teeth. "Can this wait?"

"I...well...I was wondering if I could come by later?"

"Why?"

"I...just...want to talk," Rhobby said.

Taryn closed her eyes and took a deep breath. It was hard to tell him no. Whether she wanted to admit it or not, she was still in love with him.

"I get off at six," she said, letting out her breath.

"Do you want me to grab a pizza on my way over?" he asked. "I know if I don't you'll just open up a can of soup or something."

"Pizza's fine," Taryn said, resignedly.

"Great," Rhobby said, a lift in his voice. "I'll see you around six thirty."

"Fine," Taryn mumbled. "Oh, and grab a bottle of pop while you're at it. All I've got at home is water."

"Pizza and pop, got it," he said.

Taryn hung up the phone and felt a slight headache building behind her eyes. It's not tears, she told herself. It was just tension from the near accident she almost had on her way to work this morning, that's all. She was done shedding tears for Rhobby. Goodness knows, she had shed enough of them.

The day seemed to drag on forever. Six o'clock felt like it was never going to arrive. She didn't know why she wanted the day to end so quickly. Was it because she was anxious to see Rhobby? What else could it be, she thought ruefully.

Taryn had sent Ron and Troy out to handle a domestic dispute and she worked on some reports that she had put off till she could no longer ignore them.

After filing them and returning to her seat, she glanced at the clock again.

Ten till six. Finally.

Shutting down her computer, she grabbed up her purse and headed for the front room where Cheryl was busy popping her gum and filing her nails.

"Life in a small town," Taryn said as she pulled up a chair in front of Cheryl's desk. "It's a rather cushy job when all you have time for is doing your nails, huh?"

Cheryl looked up at her with a bored look on her face. "I think I'd rather be in a big city where I was constantly answering the phone and taking calls about shootings, car wrecks, burglaries and muggings. At least it would be interesting."

"Speak for yourself," Taryn said. "I much prefer the long, boring days where nothing happens. Makes me feel a lot safer at night."

Cheryl was fresh out of college. Taryn had no idea why she had come back to Switcher's Hollow when it was so obvious she hated it here. She had asked her many times, but all Cheryl would say was "I didn't have anywhere else to go." Taryn knew that she had studied accounting in college and had graduated with honors, but for some reason, had never pursued a career in her field.

Taryn looked at Cheryl now. She was of medium height and build with dirty blonde hair and hazel eyes. Though not a beautiful girl, she was attractive enough to turn the heads of some of the local boys. Taryn knew she had dated a few of them, but nothing serious ever came from any of the dates. Not wanting to pry, Taryn had never asked her why.

"Well, time to close up," Taryn said. "It's six o'clock and I'm ready to get out of here."

"You and me both," Cheryl said, with one last pop of her gum.

Ron and Troy had not returned from their call out, but Taryn knew they would just go home when they were through, so she locked up the station and headed for home.

The drive to her house was a peaceful one. After her divorce, she had purchased a small two bedroom house on three acres about six miles outside of town. It wasn't much, but she could afford it. It was cozy and comfortable and that was all she needed. Something small that didn't require a lot of upkeep. Working full time with a lot of overtime, she didn't have the time or desire to do a lot of yard work or gardening, so even though her place was clean and kept up, it wasn't fancy.

As she pulled up into the driveway, she noticed that Rhobby wasn't there yet. Just as well, she thought. That would give her time to change out of her uniform and do a little picking up around the house before he came.

She didn't know why she worried about it. Who cares what he thinks of her place. It was hers. She could do with it whatever she wanted and it was none of his business. Not anymore.

She had just finished washing up last nights dinner dishes when she heard his pickup pull into her drive.

She opened the front door for him just as he stepped up onto the porch.

"Hey," he said, as he lifted the box of pizza for her to see. "Pepperoni with mushrooms and jalapenos. I know that's your favorite."

She held the door open as he stepped into the living room.

"Just set it on the coffee table and I'll grab a couple of plates and glasses," Taryn told him.

She was amazed at how at ease he seemed in her house. Like he belonged there or something.

Shaking the thought from her head, she carried the plates and glasses in and set them down on the coffee table and watched as he dished out a couple of slices onto each plate.

She poured the pop into the glasses and sat back on the couch and waited for him to say something.

Picking up a plate, he eased back on the couch next to her and handed her a plate.

"I'm sorry, Taryn," he said, softly. "I really screwed up."

"We've been over this, Rhobby," she said, taking a bite of her pizza.

"I know. But I…,"

"What? You what?" Taryn asked. "You want another chance?"

"Well, yeah," Rhobby said. "I'd like to talk about it."

"You cheated on me. You hurt me really bad. What am I supposed to do? You walked out on me and left me to deal with it. Now you want to come back?" She could feel her anger rising, as well as all the pain. "I tried to forgive you, remember? I stayed for a whole year, but I just couldn't trust you wouldn't do it again. I just don't want to be hurt again, Rhobby."

"I know," he said. "I messed up real bad. It was just that you were working so much and I got lonely. I messed up."

"Nothing's changed," Taryn said. "I still work a lot and always will. It's part of my job."

"I know that, but I've changed. I can handle it now."

"Really?" Taryn asked, unbelievably. "Because I have a hard time believing that. After awhile, you will get lonely again and find another woman to comfort you...again."

"No, I won't," Rhobby said, reaching over and laying his hand on her knee. "I really am sorry. I won't do it again. I promise."

"What ever happened to Norma Sue, your girlfriend?" Taryn asked, pushing his hand off her leg. "You get tired of her, too?"

"She moved back in with her mama," Rhobby said, looking down into his lap.

"And?" Taryn asked.

"She dumped me. Said her mama didn't approve of me."

"Get out," Taryn said between gritted teeth.

"What?" Rhobby asked, stunned. "Why?"

Taryn jumped up off the couch and stormed over to the front door and threw it open. "Get out!" she shouted at him.

"Taryn, what's wrong? Why are you kicking me out?"

"The only reason you're here is because Norma Sue dumped you and you can't stand to be alone, so you figured you'd come grovelling to me and I'd take you back."

"No," Rhobby said, getting to his feet. "That's not it at all."

"Out, now!" Taryn felt tears stinging her eyes, but she held her ground. "I want you out of my house now!"

Rhobby stepped out onto the porch and turned to say something more, but Taryn slammed the door in his face.

Leaning her back against the door, she heard his truck start up and pull away.

Hot tears streaked down her face. Anger and pain welled up inside her. How could she have been so stupid as to think that he had changed. That maybe he really was sorry. Well, never again. She wouldn't fall for his sweet talk ever again.

Chapter 2

Taryn was wrapped up tight in her blankets looking out her bedroom window at the trees swaying in the breeze. She had opened her window to let the cool summer breeze in and now she was glad she had. Her eyes were hot and swollen from crying and her hair was plastered to her head from the effort of shedding so many tears.

As she released one last sob, she thought she heard a noise somewhere outside. The hair on the back of her neck suddenly stood on end.

Sitting up in bed, she stared out the window and listened for the noise again.

There it was.

A howl.

A deep, long howl.

A wolf? There were no wolves in West Virginia, were there?

Staring out the window, she thought she saw movement out in the trees that lined the back of her property.

Crawling out of the covers, she walked over to the window and peered out into the shadows and darkness of the woods.

Nothing moved. No more howls.

She stood there for several moments, but nothing more was heard or seen.

Closing the window and pulling the curtains closed, she crawled back into bed. The red digital numbers on her alarm clock read 11:31 p.m.

Snuggling down into her covers, she pulled the blankets up over her head and went to sleep. Morning was going to come early and she didn't want to be late to work again.

~~~~~

The moon was high in the sky. A cool breeze blew across my hot, fevered skin from the open window in my bathroom.

It was time. Time to try out my new gift.

Standing naked in front of the mirror, I close my eyes and picture myself as a wolf. A huge, strong wolf.

At first, I feel nothing. Was this working? But then...was that a twitch? Yes. My hands begin to twitch, and then my feet.

Long, thick, black hair begins popping out all over my body and I can feel my insides shifting, adjusting to my new forming body.

Looking down at my hands, I see long, black claws starting to extent out of my fingertips. Longer and longer until they are long enough to rip and tear flesh from bone.

A giddiness comes over me. I am changing. I am changing into a huge, monstrous wolf. My time for revenge is at hand.

Suddenly a sharp, bone cracking pain spreads through my body. I cry out in excruciating pain as my legs begin to extent and contort. My knees buckle backward like a dog's. My feet stretch and bend into paws.

Crashing to the floor, I lay helplessly as my body begins to jerk and writhe as it changes form.

My arms are now covered in thick black hair and begin to grow long and muscular before my very eyes.

My face explodes with pain as my nose stretches out to a long snout. Razor sharp teeth drop down from my bleeding gums.

My ears stretch upward and extent from the top of my head.

Finally the transformation is complete.

I lay on the floor panting, trying to catch my breath.

Standing up, I look into the full length mirror that hangs behind the door.

I do not recognize myself. Fear grips my heart for a moment until I realize this is what I wanted. This is what I went out to see her for.

Staring at my new form, amazement and wonder fill me.

The most terrifying, huge, black, savage looking werewolf with long limbs, sharp claws and razor sharp fangs stares back at me.

Terror. I am terror of the worst kind. I represent death. A horrible, painful death.

Throwing back my head, I let out a howl that would send chills through the toughest of men.

Flexing my arms and stretching my back, I burst out the bathroom door and race through the house.

The front door is no match for me. With one powerful jerk, I rip it from it's hinges, showering the ground outside with splintered wood.

I feel powerful. Invincible.

I bolt from the house and take off running at full speed. I can't believe how fast I can move.

The smells. Oh, the smells. I can smell everything. Animals, earth, people.

I can hear everything. I hear the small woodland animals scurrying across the ground. I hear squirrels cracking open their nuts. I hear cars in the distance. I can hear my own heartbeat pounding in my chest.

I feel so alive. So incredibly aware of everything around me.

I run through the woods with unbelievable speed and accuracy. I am able to see and maneuver around trees without any problem. I can feel the cool, damp earth beneath my running feet.

As I run, I realize I am close to her *house.*

I stop.

I throw back my head and let out a long, mournful howl.

I cannot hurt her. *I will not hurt* her.

I know I am very close to her *house. I must not be seen. Not yet. Not by* her.

Racing off, I know who my first target will be. I know who is first on my list.

Saliva drips from my fangs at the thought of my first kill. Excitement races through me. Finally, I will have my revenge.

His place isn't far from here. I can be there in minutes.

I'm primed and ready.

Let's go.

~~~~~

It was just past midnight.

Frank Forrester tossed and turned in his bed. It was going to be another sleepless night.

Throwing the covers back, he slipped from the bed and made his way downstairs to the kitchen.

The old farmhouse he lived in just didn't feel much like home anymore now that Velma had passed. The big, rambling house felt empty and sad now.

Reaching into the refrigerator, he pulled out a bottle of water and pulled out a chair at the kitchen table and sat down.

From where he sat, he could look out the large dining room window across the front lawn and into the barnyard. The barn sat just off to the right with the doors facing out into the pasture. The cows were stuffed away in the barn for the night, so the pasture was empty except for the silvery moonlight that shed it's milky glow across the ground.

At one time, this farm had over a hundred acres, but over the years, he had sold off most of it, only keeping ten acres for himself. It was just enough to raise the few cows he had left.

Being in his late seventies now, he was almost ready to hang up his hat and be done with farming. It wasn't much fun anymore without Velma anyway.

He leaned back in his chair and rubbed his large, round belly with his meaty hand. His old, blue, striped pajamas were getting to the point that they barely stretched over his girth. Velma had warned him to lay off the cakes and cookies, but since she was gone, they had become his comfort food.

As he sat there sipping on his water, a movement in the shadows near the barn caught his eye.

Squinting, he leaned forward in his chair to get a better look.

"Probably just those stupid kids from next door," he said out loud.

Frank had always hated kids. He and Velma never had any due in part to the fact that he had no use for them. He was known for being mean and nasty toward any kid who ventured onto his land. Rumor had it that he fired buckshot at a young boy years earlier who had stopped by inquiring about a job. Frank chased the boy off and warned him never to return unless he wanted another round of buckshot fired at him. No one knew if the rumors were true, but all the kids in the area were warned to stay away from Old Man Forrester's Place.

A dark shadow crossed in front of the barn doors as Frank was craning his neck to see.

"Stupid kids," he grumbled as he threw back his chair and stomped over to the coat closet and pulled out his shotgun.

Slipping into a pair of muck boots, he shoved the gun under his arm and stepped out the door into the front yard.

"I see you, you little devil," he yelled across the yard. "Get out of here!"

He stood still for a moment waiting to see if he heard or saw any more movement.

Nothing.

"I'll pepper your rear end with buckshot if you don't get out of here, you hear me?"

Nothing.

Grumbling under his breath, he stomped off toward the barn.

The moonlight illuminated his path enough for him to see where he was going. It wasn't a full moon, but it was bright and white nonetheless.

Nearing the barn, he thought he heard a shuffling movement coming from around the corner of the barn.

Raising the shotgun, he pointed it in that direction.

"I hear you," he yelled.

He opened the gate that led into the pasture and walked over to the barn doors. The cows had began to make a lot of noise and as he reached the doors, their bellowing got louder and more insistent.

He knew the noises his cows made and he recognized the bellowing as a sign of fear.

What had gotten the cows so scared? Kids wouldn't set them off that way.

The hair on the back of his neck began to stand on end and sweat broke out across his brow. His heart started to pound and fear welled up inside him. Whatever was out here wasn't kids.

He was just getting ready to take a step back toward the house when something stepped out of the shadows on the other side of the barn.

Moonlight fell across the most terrifying monster Frank had ever seen. An enormous beast with long, black hair, muscular limbs and a long snout with drool dripping from its jowls.

Red piercing eyes narrowed as a low, rumbling growl escaped from its throat.

Frank didn't have a chance to turn and run. The creature lunged at him, digging it's long, dagger-like claws into the flesh of his back, knocking him to the ground.

As Frank screamed in pain and terror, the beast sank his teeth into the back of his neck and ripped the flesh from his bones.

Frank could feel the white hot pain as blood gushed down his neck and across his face.

The beast swung it's massive arm, and digging its claws into the flesh on Frank's back, ripped a chunk of skin off exposing bone and muscle.

Flipping him over with one powerful swipe of its arm, the last thing Frank saw before he drifted off into blackness was the beast staring at him with the most piercing, evil, red eyes.

~~~~~

The kill was still fresh. Hot blood coats the inside of my mouth, dripps from my claws and runs down the backs of my arms.

I feel powerful.
Revenge is sweet.

Stretching to my full height, I throw back my head, arch my back and let out the longest, deepest howl I could.

It's my first kill. Frank Forrester will never shoot me with buckshot again. The external wounds may have healed, but the humiliation and emotional pain never did...until now.

I look down at what used to be Frank Forrester. Satisfaction like I've never known fills me.

It was too quick. I killed him too quick.

No worries. It was, after all, my first kill. I was anxious, excited. I will be more in control next time. Slower.

I lope off into the woods feeling good.

I wait till I am home to change into my human form again. I didn't want to take the chance of someone seeing me.

I stand in front of the mirror in my bathroom again. I stare at the person I see.

Somewhere deep down inside, I know I prefer being the wolf. The wolf is who I really am. The wolf is who I was meant to be.

Chapter 3

Taryn woke up at 6:45 a.m. according to her alarm clock.

Rolling out of bed, she quickly got dressed and headed for the cup of coffee she knew was waiting for her in the kitchen.

Glancing out the window, she noticed dark clouds moving in. Small droplets of rain were beginning to splat against the window.

As she sat drinking her coffee, she remembered the weird howling she had heard last night. She knew she hadn't dreamed it, because she hadn't been asleep yet.

She would mention it to Ron and Troy today at the station and see if they've heard anyone talk about hearing or seeing a wolf in the area lately. And if they hadn't, then what could it have been?

Downing the last of her coffee, she grabbed up her gear and headed out the door.

She pulled into her parking spot at the station right at 8:00 a.m.

Looking around, she noticed that Cheryl, Ron and Troy were already there.

"Great," she said to herself. "I'm not late today, but I'm still the last one here."

Dashing from the car to keep from getting wet in the now downpour of rain, she threw open the door and stepped inside, shaking the water from her hair.

"It's going to be a dismal day today, huh?" she asked Cheryl, as she walked over to the coffee bar to pour herself a cup of the hot liquid.

Cheryl looked up from the magazine she was reading and nodded.

"Any calls?" Taryn asked.

"Nope," Cheryl said. "I don't know why you ask every morning. There are never any calls. This is such a boring little town."

Taryn smiled at her, "Just the way I like it."

"Whatever," Cheryl drawled.

"Where are Ron and Troy?" she asked, noticing they weren't at their desks.

"I don't know," Cheryl said, sounding bored. "They said something about donuts."

Taryn's mood suddenly perked up. Donuts? From Pandy's Pasteries? Oh, she sure hoped so. It was a local bakery that served the best donuts Taryn had ever tasted.

Just as she was heading back to her office, the front door opened and Ron and Troy came in carrying a pink box with white flowers imprinted on it.

"Uh, boys?" Taryn said. "I need to see you in my office. Now."

Ron started to set the box down on Cheryl's desk, but Taryn stopped him.

"No, no," she said. "Bring that with you."

Ron chuckled as he opened the box and held it out toward Cheryl.

"Hurry up and grab a couple," he said. "Otherwise, they may never make it out of Taryn's office."

Cheryl and Troy laughed as Cheryl pulled out a couple of chocolate glazed donuts and laid them on a napkin on her desk.

Everyone knew Taryn couldn't resist a donut from Pandy's Pasteries. Ron always made sure he bought a dozen when he brought them into the station. Two each for Troy, Cheryl and himself and six for Taryn.

"Close the door, please," Taryn said, when the two men had entered her office.

"Wow, I didn't know the donuts required such secrecy," Troy said, laughing.

Taryn pulled out the chair behind her desk and took a seat, reaching into the box of donuts and pulling out a crème puff.

"Have a seat, boys," she said, stuffing a large bite into her mouth.

"What's up, Boss?" Ron said, a frown creasing his forehead. At forty two, he was young looking for his age. His short, dark hair and brown eyes made him very attractive, but Taryn knew he wasn't a playboy. He was devoted to his wife, Carolyn and their three boys.

Troy on the other hand, was short and stocky with blond hair and blue eyes. He had a slightly elevated opinion of himself, but everyone knew he had a hard time keeping a girlfriend. At thirty eight, he had never been married, but had had plenty of girlfriends. Taryn thought that perhaps that was the problem. Troy thought he was too good for just one woman. He wasn't currently dating anyone, and Taryn figured it was probably because he was running out of choices in this small, rural town.

"Have either of you heard anyone mention anything about seeing or hearing a wolf in the area?" Taryn asked them.

"No, I haven't," Ron said. He looked at Troy questioningly. Troy shook his head.

"Why?" Troy asked.

"I heard a strange howling last night and thought it might be a wolf," Taryn said.

"Uh, Taryn," Ron said. "We don't have wolves in West Virginia."

"I know that," Taryn said, sarcastically. "But I heard something last night that sounded like a wolf or a very large dog or something."

"Does Frank Forrester have a dog?" Troy asked. "He lives just down the road from you. Maybe you heard a dog at his place."

"No, I don't think so," Taryn said. "At least, not the last time I was down there."

"No idea, boss," Ron said. "Probably just a stray or something."

"Yeah, probably so," Taryn said. "Thanks anyway, boys. Now get to work."

The rain had picked up. Taryn could hear it pounding on the roof overhead.

Rain usually meant accidents. For some reason, whenever it rained in these parts, people forgot how to drive. She knew it was only a matter of time before a call came in about a wreck.

Shortly before noon, Taryn heard a knock on her door. *Well, here it is*, she thought, glumly. *The first wreck of the day.*

"Come in," she called.

Cheryl opened the door and stuck her head in. "Someone's out here to see you."

"Who is it?" Taryn asked.

"Lester Flynn."

"What does he want?" Taryn asked.

"You need to come out and see him," Cheryl said, biting her lower lip.

Lester Flynn was the groundskeeper at the Switcher's Hollow cemetery. It was rare that he ever came into town, so the fact that he was standing in her station made Taryn a little uneasy.

Walking out to greet him, she saw that he was distressed and upset about something.

"Mr. Flynn, what's wrong?" she asked, as she rushed up to him.

"It's Frank. Frank Forrester," Lester said, his bottom lip quivering. "He's dead."

"What?" Taryn asked, shocked. "What happened?"

"Don't rightly know, ma'am," Lester said. "Looks like he was mauled by an animal or something. He's tore up pretty bad."

"How did you find him?" Taryn asked.

"I went over there this morning to get my fresh quart of milk and when he didn't answer the door, I assumed he was out back with the cows. I walked back to the barn and I saw him laying there on the ground. Or what's left of him anyway."

Ron and Troy came over to see what was going on.

"You want us to go check it out?" Troy asked.

"I'm coming, too," Taryn said.

Turning to Lester she said, "Lester, go home for now, ok? I'll send Ron and Troy by later for a statement."

Lester nodded, but continued to chew on his lower lip.

Taryn reached out and squeezed his arm. "It's ok, Lester. We'll take care of it. You just go home and relax. I'll be in touch with you soon."

"He's tore up real bad, Sheriff Givens," Lester said, beginning to sob. "I ain't never seen anything like it."

Lester was as old as the hills. No one knew for sure exactly how old he was, though. He'd been taking care of the cemetery for as long as people could remember. To see this frail old man so worked up tore at Taryn's heart.

Turning to Cheryl, she said, "Cheryl, why don't you drive Lester home and sit with him till one of us can get out there. I don't think he's in any shape to drive."

"Sure," Cheryl said, gently taking Lester by the arm and leading him out the door.

"Just take his truck," Taryn called after her. "I'll pick you up later and bring you back here to get your car."

Cheryl nodded and guided Lester to his truck. As soon as they pulled out, Taryn turned to Ron and Troy.

"I hope this doesn't have anything to do with that howl I heard last night," she said.

"I guess we'll find out," Ron said.

The drive out to Frank Forrester's was a somber one. This was the part of the job Taryn hated. Frank had no living relatives. Velma had been all he had and since she passed, Frank was left all alone. The county would probably end up taking care of Frank's funeral and undoubtedly, he would be buried in the local cemetery.

As they pulled up to the farm, the rain had slacked off enough that Taryn didn't need her umbrella. Grabbing a rain slicker instead, she stepped out of the car.

The smell of cow manure and hay was thick and heavy in the damp air. The rain had caused the ground around the barn to be turned into mud and sloshing through the thick, gooey mess made Taryn realize she should have grabbed her boots before heading out here. The smell of the farm was so pungent, it made her glad she didn't live any closer than she did. The five miles that separated his place from hers spared her from having to get a whiff of this place every time she stepped outside.

As they reached the pasture, Taryn saw the body of Frank Forrester laying face up on the ground just outside the barn doors.

Horror struck her as she neared the body. Blood was everywhere. It had soaked into the ground around him and covered almost every inch of his body. Frank's neck had been ripped out, the skin and muscle torn away clear down to the bone. Deep gash wounds covered his chest. The flesh torn and ripped so deep, it exposed his innards. The thick, metallic smell of blood permeated the scene. Flies had already begun to swarm over the body as the temperatures outside heated up.

Ron reached out and touched her arm as she leaned in for a closer look.

"Boss, don't," he said.

"What could have done this?" Taryn asked, aghast.

Troy stood off to the side. Taryn heard him gag.

"Troy, if you're going to toss your cookies, please do it over there somewhere," Taryn told him, pointing to the other side of the fence. "We don't need you muddying up the crime scene."

Troy coughed a couple of times, but didn't walk away.

As the three of them stood looking at the body, the medical examiner pulled up and made his way up to them. Taryn had put a call in to him as soon as they had left the station.

"Dr. Middleton," Taryn greeted him as he approached.

"What have we got here?" Dr. Middleton asked, as he approached the body.

"That's what we're hoping you can tell us," Ron said.

Dr. Middleton was the only medical examiner in the area. Having been at the job for over thirty years, he had seen a lot of terrible stuff. If anyone could shed some light on what happened here, Taryn knew it was him.

"Looks like an animal attack," Dr. Middleton said. "Although...," He stopping half way through the sentence.

"What?" Taryn asked. "Although, what?"

Dr. Middleton leaned his tall, lanky frame over the body and scrutinized the wounds with his eyes narrowed. "Doesn't look like any animal attack I've ever seen before. But I won't know anything until I get him into the lab and run some tests."

"It wasn't a bear or a bobcat?" Troy asked.

Both bears and bobcats were known to be in the area. It wasn't uncommon for smaller livestock to be killed by one or the other, but it was rare for a human to be attacked by one.

"I don't want to hazard a guess at this point," the doctor said, checking the body's temperature and carefully examining the wounds as best he could. "Let's wait till I do my examination and I'll give you more information then."

"How long till you can tell us something?" Taryn asked.

"A day or two, at least."

Taryn looked around the ground for any possible footprints, but the only thing she saw was cow tracks.

"Can you at least give us a time of death?" she asked the coroner.

"Judging by the temperature of the body, I'd say sometime late last night or early in the morning."

An ambulance pulled up just as Dr. Middleton finished his initial exam.

"Just in time," he said, as he waved the EMTs over to the sight.

They pushed a gurney up as far as they could to the body, but stopped just outside the gate to the pasture.

Dr. Middleton reached for the body bag and stretched it out on the ground next to the dead body.

As the EMTs lifted the body onto the body bag, Frank's head rolled to the side and almost separated from the body. A thin strip of skin and sinew the only things holding it on. His glassy eyes were still open, staring blankly at nothing.

"Good merciful heavens," Ron gasped. "What animal is strong enough to almost sever a man's head?"

Dr. Middleton reached down and maneuvered the head back against the shoulders and quickly zipped the bag up. "Get him out of here, boys," he said to the EMTs.

Taryn couldn't breathe. In all her years of being a sheriff, she had never witnessed such a gruesome sight before. She had known Frank. He was her closest neighbor. To see him dead, torn apart in that manner, was almost more than she could take.

Stepping back, she gulped down several lungfuls of air before she could compose herself. White, hot tears stung her eyes, but she dashed them away before joining Ron and Troy again.

As the gurney was rolled away, she stood looking down at the ground where the body had lain. It just didn't make sense. If an animal had been prowling around, how come Frank hadn't shot at it. He wasn't afraid to fire his gun at anything. It was almost like he was taken by surprise. But that didn't make any sense. Frank was keen on carrying his gun with him everywhere he went and shooting at anything that came onto his property uninvited.

Leaning down, she picked up the double barrel shotgun off the ground next to where the body had lain. Opening the barrel, she noticed that both shells were still in it. So, he had not fired it.

"Ron, Troy," Taryn said to the two deputies. "Scour the area and see if you can find any prints, hair or anything that might tell us what kind of animal this was."

"On it, boss," Ron said.

As the two men headed off toward the barn to check the area, Taryn followed Dr. Middleton to his car.

"Sir," she called to him, just as he was getting ready to slid into the driver's seat.

"Yes?"

"Is there anything you can tell me about what happened here?" she asked him. "Off the record."

"Taryn," he said, looking down at his hands. "Whatever did this was no bear and no bobcat. I don't know what did it, but whatever it was, it was big and it was out for blood."

"Is it normal for an animal to kill something, then just leave the body without eating it?"

"No."

"Could it have been a wolf?" she asked, tentatively.

"A wolf? No, Taryn. There are no wolves in this area. You should know that."

"But could one have come into the area?"

"I'm a coroner, not a wildlife biologist. I don't know the answer to that," he told her kindly. "Why are you asking about wolves?"

"I thought I heard one howling last night outside my bedroom window."

"Hhmmm, interesting," he said. "I will let you know what I find once I do my examination. Until then, just sit tight. I'll let you know something just as soon as I figure it out."

"Thanks, Dr. Middleton," Taryn said.

"Give me a day or two and I should have some answers for you," he said. He slid into the car and drove away.

Taryn made her way back to the pasture just as Ron and Troy were finishing up.

"Anything?" she asked them.

"Nothing," said Troy. "Not so much as a hair."

"Ok, boys," Taryn said. "Let's wrap it up and go talk to Lester."

Lester's place was right across the road from the cemetery. It was a small, one room shack that he had lived in since he was a small boy. The tin roof and wood siding were slowly decaying to the elements and the windows rattled every time the wind blew, but he could not be talked into moving to a safer place. This was his home and he would probably die here.

As they pulled up into the yard, Taryn noticed that he had not mowed his yard in so long that the weeds were growing up the side of the house and across the stoop that led to his front door.

Stepping over the tangled foliage, she knocked gently on the door.

Cheryl opened the door for them and let them in.

The smell that greeted them when they stepped inside was not what Taryn had expected. Instead of smelling like rotting wood and dirt, it smelled pleasantly of honeysuckle.

A candle sat on the only end table in the house and next to it was the couch where Lester was sitting. Taryn assumed that was where the honeysuckle smell was coming from.

"Hi Lester," Taryn said, as she took a seat next to him on the moldy, green and orange flowered couch. "How're you doing?"

Lester just stared at his lap and nodded.

"I know this is hard for you, but we need to ask you a few questions. Is that alright?" Taryn asked, quietly.

Lester nodded again, so she motioned for Ron to get out is pad and pen and take notes. Troy stood off to the side and just watched.

"Can you tell us if you saw anyone or anything when you went up to the barn?" Taryn asked.

"Nothing, but Frank laying there on the ground," Lester said, barely above a whisper.

"No animals?"

"No."

"Did you hear anything unusual?"

"No," said Lester, still looking at his lap.

"Is there anything you can tell us that might help us figure out what happened?" Taryn asked.

"All I know is, I went there to get my milk and I found Frank laying in the pasture all tore up. I didn't see anyone or hear anything other than his cows mooing in the barn."

"Ok, Lester," Taryn said, reaching over and gently laying her hand on his arm. "Thank you. If you think of anything, just give me a call at the station, ok? You have my number, right?"

Lester nodded.

"Do you need anything before we leave," Troy asked him.

Lester just shook his head.

They all got up to leave when Lester suddenly got to his feet.

"Wait," he said. "I did hear something last night, though."

Taryn turned to look at him. Dread beginning to fill her. She knew what he was going to say before he said it.

"What did you hear?" Ron asked.

"A wolf howling," Lester said. "Yeah, I heard a wolf howling."

Chapter 4

Taryn sat up in bed that night unable to sleep. Lester had said he heard a wolf howl the night before. The same night she had heard it.

Could a wolf have killed Frank Forrester? He was a pretty big man. A man who wasn't afraid to use a gun. If a wolf had been prowling around his property, he would have had no problem shooting it, yet his gun had not been fired.

"There are no wolves in West Virginia," she said out loud, trying to calm herself down.

A feral dog. That's all it was. Dog's have been known to kill people, especially if they have been mistreated. But could a dog do that kind of damage to someone? Frank's throat had been ripped out. The claw marks on his body were deep. Fatally deep. A dog's claws just weren't long enough to do that.

Giving herself a mental shake, she slid down into the covers and pulled them up over her head. She hadn't opened the window tonight. It was too chilly, she had tried to tell herself, but if she was being honest, she knew it was because the whole Frank thing had freaked her out a bit. Even though she was an adult, she still got scared being alone at night sometimes. It was on nights like this that she wished Rhobby was still around. Well...almost.

The annoying buzz of the alarm clock squawking next to her ear let Taryn know it was 6:00 a.m.

Reaching over and slamming her hand down on top of the small plastic box didn't give her much relief. It continued its buzzing until she punched the little button that turned it off.

Grumbling, she threw the covers off and swung her legs over the side of the bed, sitting up. A deep yawn escaped her lips as she stood and looked around the room.

The sun wasn't all the way up yet and the room was cast in long shadows.

Glancing at the window, she couldn't help but feel a little uneasy. The curtains were pulled closed, but she still felt as if something could look in at her.

"Stop being ridiculous," she mumbled to herself. She walked to the end of her bed and yanked the curtains open and looked out.

Trees were swaying in the early morning breeze and splashes of pink, orange and yellow streaked across the horizon. It promised to be a beautiful day.

"See? Nothing there," she said as she made her way to the bathroom to get ready for work.

She didn't know why she was letting that wolfish howl get to her. She had lived in the country her whole life and had never been afraid before. Why was she so on edge now? It was that howl. It still gave her the creeps when she thought about it. It just seemed so eerie, so unnatural.

Shaking off the feeling, she quickly got dressed and headed for the kitchen.

Coffee cup in hand, she stepped out onto her front porch and sucked in a long, deep breath of fresh air. The rain yesterday had washed all the dust and dirt out of the air leaving a clean, sweet smell. She loved the way it smelled after a good rain.

Taking in another deep breath, she turned as her cell phone began to chime from inside the house.

Setting her coffee cup on the table, she picked up her phone.

Penny.

"Hey," Taryn said, speaking louder than necessary. She was always happy to hear from her best friend. "What's up?"

"Good morning to you, too," Penny Drake said.

Taryn and Penny had known each other since grade school and had been the best of friends ever since. Where Taryn was short and a little plump, Penny was tall and very slender. Penny's long, dark brown hair hung nearly to her waist, while Taryn's was short and curly. Though opposite in the look's department, their personalities were very similar. Taryn always assumed that was why they had hit it off so well as friends. They could talk about anything together and usually did.

"I was wondering if you'd be free for lunch this afternoon?" Penny asked. "It's been awhile and I thought today would be a good day to catch up."

"Sure," Taryn said, excited at the prospect of spending some time with Penny. "Tom's Kitchen as usual?"

"Of course. I'll see you there at noon, then?"

"Yep, sounds good to me," Taryn said.

"Great," Penny said. "I'll try to get us the booth by the door."

Taryn hated sitting in the back of the diner. She preferred sitting somewhere where she could see everyone who came in and out. It might be the cop training she had, but she didn't like having her back to the room in case someone walked in who wanted to cause trouble. Not that much trouble ever happened in Switcher's Hollow, but still, she preferred the booth by the door.

"Thanks. I appreciate that," she told Penny. "See you at noon."

Hanging up, she quickly got herself ready and headed for the station.

~~~~~

Sitting at her desk, she finished writing out the report on Frank Forrester.

What a shame. He wasn't very well liked around these parts, mostly due to his intolerance of kids, but that was still a horrible way to go. She would have to call Ed Johnson up on Ridge Road to see if he wanted Frank's cows. There were only about twenty of them and Ed's farm was large enough to take them on without him running out of pasture space.

After a quick call to Ed and making arrangements for him to pick up the cows that afternoon, Taryn glanced at the clock.

11:05 a.m.

Only forty five minutes till she met Penny at Tom's Kitchen.

Ron and Troy had gone out this morning to look in on Frank's cows and to feed them. They weren't farmers by any means, but someone had to do it and since things were slow in the office this morning, Taryn figured it wouldn't hurt them to go out and have another look around while they were there.

She wasn't expecting anything to be found since they had thoroughly searched the place the day before, but sometimes, fresh eyes could pick up something that was previously missed.

She was anxious to get the autopsy report from Dr. Middleton, but knew it would still be a day or two, so she settled back in her chair and waited until 11:45 a.m. rolled around. It would only take her a few minutes to get to Tom's, but she was anxious to go and knew the few extra minutes early that she left wouldn't matter much.

"I'm heading over to Tom's to meet up with Penny for lunch," she told Cheryl when she stepped out of her office and headed for the front door. "Wanna join us?"

Cheryl popped her head up from the book she was reading. "Sure," she said. "It beats sitting in here eating soup warmed up in the microwave."

Since it was still several minutes before noon, they decided to walk the four blocks to the diner instead of driving.

As they entered the restaurant, Penny waved at them from the booth nearest the door. "Hey guys," she called.

Tom's was a small diner done in an old time décor. Norman Rockwell prints hung on the wall and an old jukebox stood in one corner. The tables were from the seventies with white and gold speckled tops and red vinyl seats. It was a comfortable place with a lot of charm.

Sliding into the booth next to Penny, Taryn flagged the waitress, Kimmy, over.

After they ordered their sandwiches and sweet iced teas, Taryn looked around the place.

It wasn't full yet, but it would be soon. Tom's Kitchen was the only sit down diner in Switcher's Hollow. There was a McDonald's up the road, but if you wanted anything else, you had to cross the river to find it.

As the three woman began to chat about their week, Taryn noticed that Benji Willis and a couple of his friends had come in and taken a booth across the room from them. They were laughing and carrying on, but no one paid them much attention, including Taryn, until Duke Forsythe walked in.

Taryn knew there was bad blood between them, though she didn't know what about.

She stiffened as she watched Duke walk up to Benji's table.

"What do you think you're doing here, Benji dog," Duke growled at him.

"None of your business, Duke," Benji said. Taryn could tell he was nervous, but hoped he kept his cool. She really didn't want to have to break up a fight.

"I'm making it my business," Duke said, reaching down and grabbing Benji by the front of his shirt and hauling him out of the booth.

Benji hung like a limp rag dog. Taryn knew she better step in now before it got worse.

"Excuse me, girls," she said as she slipped from the booth.

Approaching Duke from behind, she was reminded of just how big he was. His broad shoulders and muscular frame well out did Benji's small, lanky one. He must have been over six feet tall and well over two hundred pounds.

"Duke," Taryn said, as she stepped in front of him. "What's going on here?"

"Just taking out the trash, Sheriff Givens," Duke said, as he lifted Benji farther off the ground and started to walk toward the front door.

"Put him down, Duke," Taryn said, firmly.

"He shouldn't be in here," Duke said, still holding Benji up in the air by the front of his shirt.

"Put him down, Duke, now!" Taryn said, raising her voice. "Don't make me arrest you for assault."

Duke dropped Benji to the floor. He crumpled to his knees, but quickly regained his feet.

"You're gonna pay for messing with me, Duke," Benji spat out, pointing his finger in Duke's chest. "You just wait. One day."

"I'm shaking in my boots, you little coward," Duke said.

"Enough, boys," Taryn said. "Duke, get on out of here. No one wants any trouble here today."

"Me?" Duke said, outraged. "Why me? Make *him* leave."

"He was just sitting here eating his lunch," Taryn said. "You're the one who walked in causing trouble. Now go. This is your last chance."

Duke shook his first at Benji. "This isn't over, you little coward." He turned on his heel and stormed out the door.

Benji straightened out his shirt and looked at Taryn. "Thanks, Sheriff Givens."

"What was that all about, Benji?" Taryn asked, glancing toward the door to make sure Duke had really left.

"Nothing," Benji said. "He's just sore cause he thinks I stole something from him that I didn't."

"Well, whatever is going on between you two, you need to get it squared away. I don't want another scene like that in public."

"Yes, ma'am," Benji said, and slid back into his seat to finish his lunch.

Taryn was just turning to head back to her seat when she saw Vince Cobb sitting at the counter. When had he come in?

As she approached her table, she noticed Vince watching her. Giving him a quick nod, she slid into her seat and let out a deep sigh.

"My job never ends," she told Penny and Cheryl.

"You handled yourself real well over there," said a deep, throaty voice next to them.

All three women looked up to see Vince standing next to their table looking at Taryn.

Vince Cobb was the heartthrob of Switcher's Hollow. At six foot three inches tall, black, wavy hair and muscles galore, every woman in town wanted him, young or old.

"Uh, thanks Vince," Taryn said, her cheeks flushing pink. "Just doing my job."

"Well, Switcher's Hollow is a safer place because of you," Vince said. "Let me buy you ladies lunches."

Before any of them could object, Vince raised his arm in the air and motioned for Kimmy to come to the table.

"Put these lovely ladies lunches on my bill, please," he said.

Kimmy nodded her head and headed back to the kitchen. Taryn noticed that a lot of women had a hard time speaking when Vince was around. His good looks were only surpassed by his good manners.

"Thank you," Taryn said. "We really appreciate it."

"Yes, thank you," Penny said, practically drooling on herself as she looked at him.

"Yeah, thanks," Cheryl said, not making eye contact with him.

"Well, I'll let you ladies get back to your lunch," Vince said. "Taryn, again, thank you for all you do for this community."

He paid his bill and quietly left the diner.

"Oh my goodness, Taryn," Penny said, reaching over and gently slapping Taryn's arm. "He likes you."

"What?" Taryn asked, completely stunned. "He does not."

Cheryl took a sip of her tea. "Yeah, he does," she said quietly.

"You two are nuts," Taryn said. "What in the world would someone like him see in me? I'm short, chubby and at least five years older than him."

"Taryn, you're adorable even with those few extra pounds," Penny said. "Any man would be lucky to have you."

Cheryl nodded her head looking right at Taryn. "She's right, you know."

"Well, if that's true, why didn't Rhobby want me?"

Penny and Cheryl looked at each other, but neither of them answered her.

"See?" Taryn asked. "Besides, I'm not the least bit interested in Vince."

"Why ever not?" Penny asked. "He's downright gorgeous."

"Looks aren't everything," Taryn said.

"How can you not be attracted to him. High school football star, lead runner in track. I mean, yeah, he's such a loser," Cheryl said, sarcastically.

"I heard he joined the military and was in special ops," Penny said.

"Wouldn't surprise me," Cheryl said.

"Guys, can we talk about something else, please?"

"Give us one good reason why you aren't interested in him," Penny said.

"I'm just not," Taryn said. "He isn't my type."

"Honey, he's everyone's type," Penny said.

"Then you go after him," Taryn said.

"I would, but he doesn't show any interest in me at all," Penny said. "It's you he was staring at and drooling over."

"She's right," Cheryl said. "He's got the hots for you, Taryn."

"Oh good grief," Taryn said. "No, he doesn't."

"Why are you being so pigheaded about this?" Penny asked. "You should go out with him."

"No."

"Why not? And don't tell us it's because he isn't interested. We all know he is."

"Because," Taryn stalled.

"Because why?" Penny pushed.

"Because I'm still in love with Rhobby, ok?" Taryn almost shouted.

"Ohhh," Penny said, quietly. "I didn't know."

"Well, you do now," Taryn said, unhappily.

"Even after he cheated on you?" Cheryl asked.

"I guess so," Taryn said. "You can't just turn off feelings like a light switch."

"The best way to get over him would be to go on a date with Vince," Cheryl suggested.

Taryn just rolled her eyes and groaned.

They left the diner and Taryn and Cheryl headed back to the station while Penny headed back to Tucker's Market where she worked as a cashier.

Taryn enjoyed her time with her two friends, but the talk about Vince had made her feel uncomfortable. Sure, he was a very good looking man and his reputation around town as being a well mannered, quick to help anyone type person spoke well of his character, but she just couldn't go there. She just didn't feel any real attraction for him. She knew she was probably the only woman in town who didn't, but she was ok with that. Someday her heart would heal and she would move past her love for Rhobby, but right now, it was still too strong. She hated herself for still feeling that way about him, but she was right, you can't just turn those feelings off overnight. Or even, apparently, after a whole year.

She sat in her office for the rest of the day mulling over the things she needed to do when she got home that evening. She had let the mowing go till her yard was beginning to look like a jungle and it had been several days since she had vacuumed the house.

Just as she was gathering up her things to head home, she heard the front door of the station burst open and a loud ruckus ensue.

Rushing out to see what was going on, she saw Gerti Willis standing over Cheryl's desk with her beefy finger pointed in her face.

"Something better be done," Gerti roared.

"What's going on out here," Taryn demanded. "Gerti, what happened?"

Gerti Willis was a large woman. Well over three hundred pounds, her greasy, gray hair and dirty hands seemed to quiver as she glared at Taryn.

"I'll tell you what happened," she spat at Taryn. "That horrible fellow, Duke Forsythe, beat up my Benji this afternoon."

Taryn groaned inwardly. "Please, calm down and tell me what happened, Gerti."

"We was sitting out on our front porch, Benji and me, and here comes Duke up the drive. He jumps outta his truck and attacked Benji. Right there on our own front porch."

"Is Benji ok?" Cheryl asked before Taryn had a chance to.

"He's got himself a black eye and a busted lip, but he'll live. But something needs to be done. You need to arrest Duke or something," Gerti demanded.

"I'll go talk to Duke and see if I can't figure this out," Taryn said, calmly. "But for now, Gerti, you need to go home and tend to Benji."

"You'd better do something about Duke, Sheriff, or I will," Gerti threatened as she turned and stormed out the door.

"Well, Cheryl," Taryn said. "Has today been less boring for you? You wanted more excitement around here, so there you go."

Cheryl laughed and grabbed up her things to leave. "It sure makes things more interesting around here when something like this goes on."

"Tell you what," Taryn said. "How about you go talk to Duke?"

"No way," Cheryl said. "That's your job. I'm just the receptionist."

~~~~~

Where were Ron and Troy when she needed them. Probably still out at the farm helping Ed with the cows. She probably should have called them to join her or maybe even do this without her, but no sense in worrying about that now. She was already here.

Pulling up to Duke's place, Taryn felt her skin crawl. How could anyone live like this.

The single wide trailer was a putrid shade of cream and green mixed. Grass grew up so high it reached the bottom of the window frames. Trash was piled up all over the yard and flies swarmed the air as she stepped out of her SUV. Several dogs were tied on four foot chains attached to rotting wooden dog houses all around the house and the horrid smell of animal feces assaulted her senses as she made her way to the front door.

Kicking beer bottles and old chips bags out of her way, she knocked on the sticky, dirty door.

The door flew open and Duke stood there looking down at her with malice and hatred on his face.

"What do you want?" he asked.

"I'm here to talk about Benji," Taryn said, trying to keep her cool. She didn't want him to see how scared she was that he might do something to hurt her. She rested her right hand on the butt of her gun.

"What about him?"

"I understand you got into a scuffle this afternoon."

"He had it coming," Duke said.

"What's going on between the two of you?" Taryn asked. "What's the fighting all about?"

"He stole something from me."

"What did he steal, Duke?"

"He stole beer out of my car while it was parked at Tucker's Market."

Taryn just shook her head. "No more fighting. No more going over to his house and attacking him. No more going into public places and starting a ruckus, you hear me? Next time, I will bring you in for assault. Benji's mother showed up at the station a little while ago and demanded I arrest you. If this happens again, rest assured, I will."

"Do whatever you have to do, Sheriff, but if Benji comes anywhere near me or my stuff again, I'll kill him."

Taryn was in a horrible mood by the time she got home. What a day!

Peeling off her uniform and slipping into her pajamas, she flopped down on the couch. The grass and vacuuming would just have to wait till tomorrow.

Chapter 5

Tonight. Tonight I am going after that scumbag. Tonight he will pay. I will not rush this one. I want to watch every agonizing second as I make him suffer.

Feeling myself change tonight wasn't as bad as the first time. It must get easier each time I do it. It was quicker, too. Good.

I stand in my bathroom and look in the mirror at my red, glowing eyes and curved fangs. My huge muscular body and my long, sharp claws that are perfect for ripping flesh from bone. I am the perfect monster. I will have to remind myself to go thank the old crone in the woods for this gift. Without her, none of this would be possible.

I quietly slip from my house and dash off into the woods that surround my place.

There's no moon out tonight. It's dark, but I don't have to worry about that. I can see perfectly in the dark now, so I'm not worried. The less light there is, the less likely I could be seen.

I love living in such a rural town. So many woods and back roads around here that I don't have to worry about anyone seeing me as I creep around out here. I can come and go and never have to worry about being seen.

Perfect.

I make my way through the heavily wooded area until I come out behind his house. It isn't too far from my place, so it didn't take me long to get here.

The dogs that he has tied up all over the place haven't picked up my scent yet. It won't be long. I can see the lights shining out from the windows of that pig sty he calls a home.

I can hear the dogs start to whimper. They know I'm here now. No barking. Just whimpering. Good. They won't alert Duke to my presence until it's too late.

He will never know who killed him or why, but that's ok. I'll have my revenge nonetheless.

He probably doesn't remember the torment and torture he put me through in school. Particularly that day in gym class in high school. It's humiliating to have your shorts pulled down around your ankles while you're climbing that stupid rope that's attached to the ceiling. And on co-ed day, too. I still burn with rage at the embarrassment. All the girls started laughing and pointing at me. All the guys laughed, too. Ohhh, how I wanted to kill him that day. Ohhh, how I wanted to hurt him so bad. Well, no worries. Tonight is my night for revenge.

Ready or not, Duke, here I come.

There must be about four or five dogs tied up around his place, but not one of them barks. They all cower and whimper in their so-

called dog boxes. What kind of a person treats his dogs this way?

Creeping up to the first dog box, I yank the chain holding the dog and break it loose from the box. The poor creature has wet himself. It doesn't understand that I'm not here to hurt him. I release his chain, but he just crawls into his box and hides. Poor thing.

I make my way to each dog and release them. None of them run away. They all cower in their boxes. Another reason to hurt Duke. No animal should ever have to live this way. They're scared out of their skin and it's not because of me. They're expecting to get hurt. Duke must abuse them regularly. No worries. He won't hurt them again after tonight.

I sneak up to the trailer and as I walk around toward the front, I drag my claws along the side, digging deep grooves into the vinyl siding. The screeching noise, like nails on a chalkboard, causes the dogs to begin to howl and whine.

I hear the front door open and Duke's heavy footfalls step outside onto the front porch.

Not yet. I'm not done terrorizing him yet. I want him good and scared.

I step back into the shadows so he can't see me.

"Whose out there?" Duke yells. "Benji, is that you, you little jerk?"

I laugh to myself and I grab up a rock from the ground and hurl it as hard as I can at one of his windows. My aim is true and the glass shatters as the rock sails through into the house.

"Whose there?" Duke shouts out into the darkness. "I'm gonna get you, you stupid little coward."

He must have run back inside, because I hear him stomp across the porch and then the door slams.

Good. He's scared.

I make my way to the other end of the trailer and peer around the corner so I can see the front porch. I'm in the shadows. He cannot see me here.

As he steps out onto the porch, I watch as he looks around. The idiot thinks he can see in the dark? Where's your flashlight, Duke?

He steps off the porch and heads around to where the dogs are. I hear him scolding them for not barking.

I stalk off around the end of the trailer and see him standing in front of one of the dog boxes.

Now…

~~~~~

Duke stands looking down at his whimpering, cowering dog.

"You stupid animal," he scolded it. "What good are you if you don't even bark?"

He swung his leg back as if he was going to kick the dog when a twig snapped off to his left, causing him to whip his head around in that direction.

"Whose there?" he shouted. "I know someone's there. I got my gun and I will shoot you."

A low rumble drifted across the night air toward him. The hair on the back of Duke's neck stood up and his heart skipped a beat. A shred of fear crawled up his spine as his palms suddenly became sweaty.

Lifting his rifle, he fired it in the direction the growl had come from.

The loud rapport of the gun echoed off the surrounding hills, reverberating back to him several times.

Listening intently for any more growls, he slowly lowered the gun to his side.

"I told you I'd shoot you," he bellowed. "Come around again and I'll put another bullet in you."

A loud, rumbling growl came from the end of the trailer where the woods were so thick it was impossible to see into them.

Duke's blood ran cold at the sound. He squinted his eyes, but it was too dark to see who, or what, might be down there. It wasn't like any animal sound he had ever heard before. It definitely wasn't a bear or a bobcat.

What was it, then? A wolf? It sounded way too big to be a wolf.

A deep, unearthly howl pierced the night air. It was so deep it rumbled and vibrated the ground beneath his feet.

The dogs quivered and curled up tighter in their boxes, not daring to make a sound.

Chills raced up Duke's spine and he trembled as he looked down in disgust at the urine running down his leg.

He glanced down at the dog who was laying at his feet with its tail tucked between its legs. The dog had vacated its bowels on Duke's foot. He couldn't blame the dog. Whatever had made that howling sound had unnerved him as well. It was close. Too close.

Slowly backing away from the dog, he turned and attempted to make a dash for the house, but as he took the first step, a sharp, searing pain exploded down his back. He could hear a weird ripping sound and realized in utter terror that it was his skin being torn away from his body.

Shrieking in pain, Duke fell to the ground. Dust flew up his nostrils and into his mouth. Blinking several times to clear the dirt out of his eyes, he dug his fingers into the earth and tried to crawl away from the animal that hovered over top of him.

He turned his head to look back at it as a large, hairy hand swung through the air and crashed into the side of his head. He felt its claws dig deep into the skin of his face, ripping it back, exposing the bone. Blood ran thick between his bared teeth, choking him.

His heart pounded so hard he could hear it in his ears. Barely able to breathe, his head began to swim in an overwhelming wave of dizziness.

Frantically, he began dragging himself along the ground toward his trailer, but he only made it a couple of feet when the animal stomp down hard on his lower back.

Suddenly, a ripping noise was heard and the worse pain he had ever felt in his life tore through his body. He could feel his whole left side being laid open by the massive claws of the monster.

He knew he was going to die. He knew this was the end. He squeezed his eyes shut and prayed for it to be over soon.

He lay there in excruciating pain, barely able to breathe because of the intensity of it, waiting for the final blow, but nothing happened.

He mustered every ounce of strength he had left and slowly rolled over onto his back. As he blinked away the blood and dirt that now caked his eyes, he stared up at the most terrifying sight he had ever seen.

A huge, monstrous beast stood at his feet. Well over six feet tall, it was broad and muscular, with pure hatred reflecting in its eyes. Curling back its lips, it snarled at him. Blood and tissue clung to it's hands and blood dripped from its jaws.

"Please," Duke begged, barely about to speak with all the blood in his mouth. "Please, don't kill me."

The beast stared at him for several long moments, then suddenly it lunged forward, landing on Duke's abdomen, knocking the breath out of him.

Thrusting its head down, it clamped its jaws around Duke's face and slammed its jaws closed, shattering the bones in Duke's face. With a jerk of its head, it ripped off the skin in one fluid motion. Blood and broken bone fell to the ground around Duke's head.

The monster then reared back and pointing its head toward the sky, howled a long, low, deep howl that shattered the quiet, stillness of the night.

~~~~~

Ahhh, revenge is so sweet.

Look at him now. Not so tough after all, is he?

I can still taste the hot, sticky, metallic flavor of his blood in my mouth.

Looking down at my hands, I see his flesh and blood still clinging to my claws and fur.

No matter. I'll clean it off later.

I shake off as much as I can and look around.

No one is close by. No one would have heard anything. Except maybe my howl.

Who cares. They'll just think it is a stray dog or something.

Looking down at my handiwork one last time, I smile to myself.

Turning, I lope off into the woods in the same direction I came in.

Back in my bathroom, I change back into my human form as I stare at myself in the full length mirror behind the door.

I'm covered in blood and I can still feel bits of flesh stuck between my teeth.

After a quick flossing and brushing, my teeth are Duke free once more.

Standing under the shower, I lean my head back and let the water pour down over my hot, tired body.

Satisfaction. That's what I feel. No regret. Only satisfaction.

Duke Forsythe won't be bothering anyone ever again.

Chapter 6

Rolling out of bed, Taryn looked over at the clock.

9:00 a.m.

"Oh, I love Saturdays," she said, aloud to herself.

Dressing in old, ripped up shorts and a tank top, Taryn gulped down her third cup of coffee and headed outside to get started on the grass. She had put it off for so long, it was beginning to look as bad as Duke's.

Duke. That man was just plain trouble. Taryn didn't understand what made a person so disagreeable. It seemed like he didn't get along with anyone.

Thinking of Duke reminded Taryn that she probably needed to stop in later today and check on Benji.

Benji was a good guy. He just frequently made the wrong choices when it came to making decisions. He was generally harmless and didn't cause anyone much trouble, but his mother sure could. She would defend Benji to the death, no matter what he did.

After yanking on the cord several times, the lawnmower finally purred to life.

Taryn was thankful that even though she owned three acres, most of that was wooded. It only took her thirty minutes to mow the yard and stuff the mower back into the garage.

Wiping sweat from her forehead she started toward the house when she saw Rhobby pull up.

"Great," she mumbled to herself.

She stood on the porch and waited for him.

Stepping into the house, she offered him a bottle of water.

"So, what brings you here today?" she asked him, as she swigged down half of the bottle of water she was holding.

"I just wanted to come check up on you," Rhobby said. "I was in the area, so..."

Taryn just stared at him. There was no where to be out here unless you lived here or were visiting someone.

"Ok, fine," he said. "I just stopped by cause I miss you and wanted to see you."

"Rhobby, please don't do this," Taryn said, feeling sad all of a sudden.

"What? Am I not allowed to miss you?"

"No, actually, you're not," Taryn said. "You left me, remember? You can't just show up one day and tell me you miss me. In fact, it would be best if you quit showing up at all. You're only making this harder on both of us."

"Taryn," Rhobby said. "Why can't you just forgive me? How many times do I have to say I'm sorry?"

"Until it stops hurting. Until I stop feeling anger and hurt by what you did."

"And just how long is that going to take?" Rhobby asked.

"A lifetime," Taryn said. "You hurt me in the worse way you could. You broke my trust and my heart."

"I want to make it up to you, Taryn."

"Until the next time Norma Sue calls? Or until someone else comes along?" Taryn asked, feeling tears well up behind her eyes. "I just can't trust that you will be faithful. I can't trust that you will stick around this time."

"I will, I promise," Rhobby said, reaching out and placing his hands on both her shoulders.

Taryn shrugged out of his reach and stepped away from him. "Don't," she said. "You have no right to touch me anymore."

Rhobby was just about to argue with her when a car pulled into her driveway, flowed by a cloud of dust.

"Who is that?" Rhobby asked.

Taryn moved past him and opened the screen door and stepped out onto the porch.

The small, green sports car emerged into view as the dust settled.

"It's Troy," Taryn said, as she stepped off the porch and made her way over to Troy's car, followed by Rhobby.

"Taryn," Troy said, looking apologetic. "Didn't mean to interrupt your Saturday, but we have a problem."

"What is it?" Taryn asked, glad for the interruption.

"Gerti," Troy said.

"Oh great," Taryn sighed, rolling her eyes. "What did she do now?"

Troy never got out of his car. Instead, he leaned out the window and shook his head. "You're not going to want to hear this, but she didn't think you would take care of Duke Forsythe to her satisfaction, so she went over there this morning to give him a 'what for'."

"And?" Taryn asked, when he didn't finish.

"We have another dead body, Taryn," he said. "Another animal attack."

"Animal attack?" Rhobby asked.

"Rhobby, go home," Taryn said. "We'll talk later."

Rhobby didn't budge. "I want to hear about this animal attack."

"It's police business," Taryn said, sternly. "Go home. I'll talk to you later."

Rhobby shot her an angry look and stormed off to his truck. He spun gravel and squealed tires as he tore off down her driveway.

Once he had pulled out onto the road and left, Taryn turned back to Troy. "Is Ron handling it?"

"He's the one who got the call from Gerti," Troy said. "She said she tried to call you, but got no answer."

"I was mowing. And it's Saturday. I was hoping for a quiet, peaceful day, but it hasn't turned out that way."

"Ron says he thinks you need to come and check it out."

"Why? Can't the two of you handle it?"

"Taryn," Troy said. "It's bad. Worse than the last one."

Taryn dropped her head in defeat. "Ok, fine. Let me change clothes and I'll be right out."

Slipping into her uniform and brushing her curls into a small pony tail on the back of her head, Taryn stepped outside into a beautiful, sunny afternoon that she wasn't going to get to enjoy.

The drive to Duke's didn't take long.

Pulling up into the driveway, Taryn saw Ron's car and Gerti's beat up old station wagon sitting next to it.

Following the voices to the back of the house, Taryn's heart shuddered to a stop at the sight that unfolded before her.

A body, ripped and torn to pieces lay just feet away from one of the dog boxes where a dog sat shaking and whining, scared of all the chaos going on around it.

Blood soaked the earth around the body and flies and knats swarmed over the corpse in thick clouds. The iron smell of blood mingled with the heavy smell of dog feces and dirt. The heat from the sun only making the stench that much worse.

Stifling a gag, Taryn stepped over to where Gerti was sitting on an old metal chair pushed up against the side of the trailer.

Gerti was sputtering and gulping in air, as Ron was trying to console her.

Ron looked up at Taryn, relief flooding his face.

"Glad you made it," he told her.

"Like I had a choice," Taryn mumbled. "What happened?"

Gerti looked up at her with red rimmed eyes and chunks of food stuck to her chin and smeared down the front of her dress. She must have vomited when she found the body. The sickening smell of bile and stomach acid turned Taryn's stomach.

"I found him," Gerti said, choking back a sob. "I was coming over to give him a piece of my mind and that's how I found him."

She pointed over to the body.

"Did you touch anything?" Taryn asked her.

Gerti looked at her like she was mad. "No, of course not," she said. "When I found him, I tried calling you, but when you didn't answer, I called Ron. I never touched anything."

"Did you see or hear anything when you got here?" Ron asked.

"No, nothing," Gerti said. "His dogs didn't even bark at me."

Taryn looked at the dogs and noticed that all their chains had been ripped from the boxes and left dragging on the ground. The dogs had stayed put, though.

Looking up at Ron, Taryn asked, "Did you call Dr. Middleton?"

"Yeah," Ron nodded. "He's on his way."

Troy had been standing next to the body, looking at it. Finally, he stepped away and rubbed his hand across his mouth, as if to keep himself from throwing up.

"What kind of animal could do that?" he asked, walking over to Ron and Taryn.

"I don't know," Taryn said. She was afraid to go exam the body. From this distance, she could see the carnage and knew that up close, it was probably much worse.

Ron helped Gerti to her station wagon and told her they would be by later to get her statement.

As he came back around the trailer, he was followed by Dr. Middleton.

"Good night, Taryn," Dr. Middleton said. "What is going on around here?"

He stepped gingerly over to the body and began examining it.

"What can you tell us, Dr. Middleton?" Taryn asked. "Same animal that killed Frank?"

Dr. Middleton examined the body for several minutes before answering Taryn.

"I've never seen anything like it, to be honest," he said. "The wounds are so severe."

Taryn finally walked over and looked at the body.

The face was gone, ripped completely off. Dried blood and bone was all that was left.

Taryn gasped and stepped back.

"I think it's worse on the back," Dr. Middleton said. He motioned for Ron to help him and they gently flipped the body over.

Dr. Middleton was right. The skin on the back was shredded into ribbons and the left side of the body was sliced open, spilling the internal organs out on the ground.

Taryn couldn't help herself. She walked several feet away and retched.

Troy walked over to her and handed her a tissue that he pulled from his pocket.

"Troy," Taryn gasped for breath. "What did that? What animal in these parts could do that?"

"I don't know, Taryn," he said. "I just don't know."

"Taryn," Dr. Middleton called. "Come over here."

Taryn took several deep breaths of fresh air, squared her shoulders, then walked back over to the body.

"What can you tell us, Dr.?" she asked, trying to hold her breath from the smell.

"Time of death was between 10 and 11 p.m. would be my guess."

"Do you know what could have done this? What kind of animal?" Troy asked.

"You know I will have to run test to be sure, but I'm guessing this was some kind of canine. Look at the bite marks around the face...er...head," he said. "Those are consistent with a dog bite. However, it must have been one massive dog to be able to do that."

"A wolf, maybe?" Taryn asked.

All three men turned to look at her.

"Normally, I would say no, since there aren't usually wolves in this area. However, given the size of the animal that did this, I'm starting to believe it's possible," Dr. Middleton said.

"Can you tell us anything else at this point?" Ron asked.

"No, I need to do a thorough exam first before I commit to any guesses."

"Have you gotten any results from Frank's autopsy yet?" Taryn asked.

"I'm waiting for the lab results to get back to me, but the wounds on Frank were consistent with an animal attack for sure."

"What kind of animal attack?" Troy asked.

Dr. Middleton just stared at him.

"I know, I know," Troy said. "We have to wait for the results."

"I am going to put a rush order to the lab," Dr. Middleton said. "We now have two animal attacks only a couple of days apart."

"I think it may be a good time to put out a notice to the community that we have a possible wild animal running around the area and they need to be on the lookout for any strange sightings. And to stay indoors at night as much as possible till this thing is caught and killed," Ron suggested.

"Good idea," Taryn said. "Ron, I'll leave you in charge of that. Troy, I want you to go get a statement from Gerti."

"You got it, Boss," Ron said.

"Let's do our check of the area before we head out," Taryn said. "We'll leave Dr. Middleton to deal with the body."

After Dr. Middleton gathered up the body and left, Taryn, Ron and Troy began the tedious job of scouring the area for any clues.

As Ron and Troy checked around the trailer, Taryn walked over to the dogs. They were still huddled in their boxes and wouldn't come out.

"Poor things," Taryn cooed to them. "Don't worry, we'll find you all good homes."

She had put in a call to the local animal rescue and they were going to send someone out to gather up all the dogs and take them to the shelter. Taryn sincerely hoped they would find them all loving homes. People in this area loved dogs, so she felt sure they wouldn't have any trouble placing them with good families.

Stepping around one of the boxes, something on the ground caught Taryn's eye.

A footprint.

A huge footprint.

Leaning down for a better look, she noticed it was the distinct paw print of a dog. Only this one was much larger than any dog print she had ever seen.

"Guys!" Taryn called to Ron and Troy. "Come look at this."

Ron reached her first and looked at the print, let out a long, low whistle. "That is one huge dog."

Troy came over and Ron pointed out the print to him.

"You gotta be kidding me," Troy said. "That can't be a dog print. It's way too big. Is it a wolf print?"

"If it is," Taryn said. "It's the biggest wolf print I've ever seen."

"How many wolf prints have you seen?" Ron asked, sarcastically.

"Shut up," Taryn said, bumping him with her elbow. "You know what I mean. Look at the size of that. Do you believe a wolf could be that big?"

"A Dire Wolf would be," Troy said.

Taryn and Ron looked at him questioningly.

"A what?" Ron asked.

"A Dire Wolf," Troy said. "They're extinct now, but they were once a huge wolf species that roamed North America around ten thousand plus years ago."

Taryn and Ron just stared dumbly at him.

"And how is that relevant now?" Ron asked him.

"Well, it isn't," Troy said. "But what else could make a print that big?"

"Ok, fellas, Taryn said. "Aside from it being a long extinct breed of wolf, is there any other kind of dog that could make a print this large?"

"No known breeds that I know of," Ron said.

Troy shuffled his feet drawing the attention of Taryn. "Do you have a suggestion, Troy, or dare I ask?"

Troy looked from Taryn to Ron and back to Taryn again. "It's nothing."

"Troy…," Taryn said, a warning in her voice.

"Ok, fine," Troy said. "But you asked."

"What?" Ron said. "What are you thinking?"

"It could be a werewolf," Troy said, almost under his breath.

"A werewolf…," Taryn said, sarcastically. "Really? That's the best you could come up with?"

"Werewolf lore goes back thousands of years," said Troy. "Legends and myths have been known to have some basis in reality."

"Oh do tell," Ron said.

"Don't get him started, Ron," Taryn said. "Go back to the station and get some plaster and we'll make a mold of this. Maybe someone around here will know what to make of it."

Ron volunteered to make the trip to the station to get the plaster, while Taryn and Troy continued to look for more prints.

Finding none, they sat in the car and waited for Ron to return.

When Ron returned, the man from the animal shelter pulled in behind him.

Taryn rushed over and greeted the man as he got out of the truck.

"Sir, could you possibly look at a print we found and tell us whether or not it could be from a dog?"

"Sure," the man said. "Let me get the dogs loaded up first and I'll take a look."

Taryn, Ron and Troy helped the man, who told them his name was Randy, load the five dogs into crates and place them in the back of the truck.

After the dogs were safely in place, Taryn led Randy around to the back of the house and over to where the print was.

Randy let out a whistle just like Ron had and shook his head. "I've never seen a dog big enough to leave that size of a print."

"Could there be a dog big enough to leave one that big?" Taryn asked.

"Not that I've ever heard of," Randy said.

Taryn thanked him and walked him back around to his truck.

Ron was mixing up the plaster when Taryn walked over to him. "Let's hurry up and get this thing cast. I'm starting to get the willies."

"I agree," said Ron.

After pouring the plaster in the print and waiting for it to set up, Taryn sat in Troy's car with him and listened while he gave her the history of the werewolf legend.

"So," Taryn said, trying not to sound bored. "Is there any way to kill a werewolf?"

"Silver," Troy said. "You have to shoot it with a silver bullet."

"Of course," said Taryn. "I'm sure those are easy to find." She was just trying to make conversation. It was better than sitting there twiddling her thumbs waiting for the plaster to dry.

Ron had been smart, he had decided to take a walk down the road to get away from the smell of death for a few minutes, leaving her to listen to Troy's stories.

"It's not hard to find some if you know where to go," Troy said.

"Troy," Taryn said, letting out a long breath. "Let's go check the cast. Maybe it's dried by now."

The plaster had set up quicker than Taryn thought it would. As she gently wriggled and pried the cast up off the ground, she was amazed at the detail it captured. It showed the pads, claws and even dermal ridges.

"Let's get this back to the office for safe keeping till we can show it to a wildlife expert," Taryn said, carefully plucking small strands of grass from the plaster, then placing the cast in an old towel Troy had in the back of his car.

After stashing the plaster cast in her desk drawer, Taryn sent Troy off to talk to Gerti and Ron was tasked with putting out a notice to the townsfolk to watch out for any suspicious animals they may come across.

By the time Taryn got home, it was starting to get dark.

"So much for a quiet, relaxing day at home," she grumbled to herself as she stepped into the shower.

It felt good to stand under the hot water and let it wash the dust and grime from her body, as well as remove the stench of death that seemed to cling to her hair and skin.

Throwing her uniform into the washer, she brushed her teeth and crawled into bed.

As she lay in bed that night, her mind kept going over the details of the day. What kind of animal would do that? And what about that paw print?

She had looked up the number for a wildlife expert that she knew of over in the next county. He was supposedly one of the best in the area. Maybe he would be able to shed some light on the situation.

But that would have to wait till Monday. Tomorrow, she was going to hide so no one could find her. All she wanted was one day to herself. Just one day. And by golly, she was going to get it.

As she drifted off to sleep that night, her mind conjured up images of shape-shifters and werewolves.

Little did she know, that she would soon come face to face with one.

Chapter 7

Sunday had come and gone too quickly in Taryn's opinion. She had turned off her cell phone, locked the front door, pulled the curtains closed and spent the day watching old movies and eating popcorn.

Now it was Monday morning and as she sat looking out her front window drinking her usual cup of coffee, she wondered what the day was going to hold.

She still hadn't turned her phone on and realized with a bit of trepidation, that she probably should.

As soon as she turned it on, it immediately began pinging, alerting her that she had several messages.

"Ugh," she grumbled to herself. "I should have left it off."

Clicking on the message icon, she noticed that every message was from Rhobby.

Ignoring them, she laid the phone down on the table and went to her room to get dressed.

~~~~~

When Taryn walked into the station, Cheryl was on the phone.

As she started to walk past, Cheryl held her finger up, indicating for Taryn to wait.

"Ok," Cheryl said into the receiver. "I'll have her call you as soon as she comes in."

Hanging up, she handed Taryn a slip of paper with a number written on it.

"Don Swagger called," she said. "Said he would be here around noon."

Don Swagger was the wildlife expert that Taryn had called on Saturday.

"Good," Taryn said. "Do I need to call him back?"

"Yeah. He wanted to make sure you'd be here."

"Thanks, Cheryl."

"That's my job," Cheryl said.

Ron and Troy walked in just as Taryn sat down at the desk in her office.

"Boys," Taryn called to them. "Come on back here for a minute, will you?"

Ron was the first one through her door, followed closely by Troy.

"What's up, Boss?" Ron asked.

"Did you post a bulletin to the townsfolk about keeping an eye out for any strange animals?"

"Yes," Ron said. "I got it turned in to the radio station early this morning and it will run in this afternoon's paper. I also put up fliers at Tucker's and Tom's."

"Great," Taryn said. "I appreciate it. Troy, did you get a statement from Gerti?"

"Yes, I did," Troy said. "She was still rather shook up about the whole thing. Thought we were going to blame Benji."

"Why would we blame Benji?" Taryn asked. "Is he turning into a wild animal at night and killing people?"

She snickered at her own joke, but the two men just stared at her without laughing.

"Oh, come on," Taryn said. "That was a joke."

Troy leaned his hip on her desk and said, "If we're dealing with the supernatural, then maybe he is."

Taryn looked at Troy and realized he wasn't joking. She looked at Ron, who only scrunched up his lips and lifted his eyebrows.

"Oh, please tell me you're not falling for any of Troy's wild ideas," she said, looking at Ron incredulously.

"Well, there's a lot of stuff that just isn't making sense," Ron said. "That's all I'm saying. Something weird sure is going on, though."

"It's not as far fetched as it seems," Troy said, with a slight pout on his face. "Many cultures out there believe in shape shifting and werewolves, among a slew of other things. Why is it so hard to believe that some of it could be based in reality?"

"I'll admit," Taryn said. "The killings seem too gruesome for a regular dog or wolf to commit, and the paw print we cast is rather large, but a werewolf? What are we? Twelve?"

"Well, whatever, or whoever, is doing this needs to be stopped," Ron said.

"It's not a 'whoever'," Taryn said. "Dr. Middleton confirmed it was an animal attack."

"Shouldn't we be hearing from him today or tomorrow?" Troy asked.

"I hope so," Taryn said. "I'd like some answers."

"So, what's on the books for today, Boss?" Ron asked.

"Nothing so far," Taryn asked. "If you wanted to, you and Troy could run down to Pandy's and get some donuts."

Taryn plastered a huge smile on her face and lifted her eyebrows, wriggling them at the men.

"Let me guess," Ron said. "Creme puffs?"

"You know me so well, it's scary," Taryn teased. "And make sure you get enough for you guys and Cheryl, too."

Handing them some money, Taryn watched them walk out of the office.

She felt blessed to work with such great people. She may not always agree with them or their ideas, but she wouldn't trade a single one of them for anything. It was important to have people you trusted and who were dependable and the three people she had working for her were exactly that.

Not wanting to be eating her lunch when Don Swagger came in, she ate the sandwich and chips she had brought from home at around eleven, giving herself plenty of time to finish before he arrived.

He was punctual. He arrived right at noon.

Taryn heard the front door open and went out to meet him.

Don Swagger was an attractive man for being almost sixty. At just over six feet tall, his lean body and graying hair offered him an air of sophistication.

He was wearing a pair of jeans and a button up shirt. Not what Taryn expected. Somehow she thought he'd be wearing khakis and hiking boots.

"Good afternoon," Taryn greeted him. "You must be Don."

"It's good to meet you," Don said, in a smooth, deep voice. "I understand you have an animal problem."

Taryn was impressed that he cut right to the chase. No small talk needed. She knew immediately that she was going to like him.

"Well, it appears so," Taryn said. "Come on back to my office and let me show you a plaster cast of a paw print we got from the site of one of the victims."

He followed her back to her office and took a seat across the desk from her.

She pulled the casting out from her desk and opened up the towel it was still wrapped in and handed it to him.

He took the cast and turned it over and over in his hand. His brow furrowed the longer he looked at it.

"You said you found this near one of the bodies?" he asked her, scrutinizing the cast at length.

"Yes, the last one. It was just a couple of feet from where the body was laying."

"Interesting."

"What?"

"This is not a dog print," Don said. "It more resembles a wolf, but it's much too large for any known wolf breed. Let alone the fact that we don't have wolves in West Virginia."

"So, what is it then?" Taryn asked, coming around the desk to stand over his shoulder to look down at the casting.

"Honestly? I'd say it's some kind of a wolf, but that's not possible, unless a Dire Wolf has come back into existence."

"Troy mentioned a Dire Wolf the other day, too," Taryn said. "Is it possible they aren't extinct and we have one roaming around the area?"

Don laughed. "No, my dear," he said. "The Dire Wolf died off thousands of years ago. Unless someone cloned one and set it loose, this is not a Dire Wolf."

"Then we have a large, over sized wolf?"

"That's the problem," Don said. "The closest thing this resembles is a wolf, but it is *not* a wolf."

"How do you know for sure?" Taryn asked.

"A wolf's footprint is more rectangular, whereas a dog's are more rounded," explained Don. "This print almost looks like a combination of a human footprint and a wolf footprint. Odd."

"Sooo," Taryn said. "You're telling me that we have a half human, half wolf running around?"

"No, I'm not suggesting any such thing. That would be ludicrous," Don said. "I'm suggesting maybe the print got altered or misshapen a bit before it was cast."

"I assure you, it didn't. That is exactly what it looked like when we found it," Taryn said, pointing to the casting.

Don furrowed his brow again. "Can you take me to the kill sights?"

"Both of them?" Taryn asked, perplexed.

"Yes, please."

"Sure, let's go," Taryn said.

They arrived at Frank's place to find it empty and deserted, as Taryn expected. What she didn't expect was the eerie, creepy feeling the place now had. No sounds were heard. No rustling of tree branches. No mooing cows. Nothing. Just the smell of old hay, cow dung and weathered wood.

Walking up to the pasture, Taryn stood outside the gate while Don walked around the area where Frank had been killed.

Taryn watched as Don knelt over the ground where blood could still be seen soaked into the earth.

He then walked several feet out from where the body was found, being careful not to step in any cow paddies and scanned the ground in all directions.

Finally, he walked down to the barn and surveyed the ground there, as well.

"Taryn," he called. "Come here, please."

Taryn made her way over to him, watching the ground as she went. She didn't want to step in any blood or bodily remains that might have been left behind. The thought grossed her out, so she shoved it from her mind till she reached the spot where he stood.

"What did you find?" she asked.

"Look here," he said, pointing to the ground between his legs. He had straddled the spot to keep her from stepping on it.

Taryn leaned down and gasped. Another huge paw impression was embedded in the mud at his feet.

"Is it just like the other one?" she asked.

"It certainly appears so," Don said.

"Did you find anymore?"

"No, just this one, but I'd say the same animal that left this print also left the one you got the casting of."

Don stood and scanned the area behind the barn. The woods were deep with thick overgrowth. It would be easy for an animal to hide there until it was ready to attack.

"Any idea yet what it could be?" Taryn asked.

"Let's go check out the other location," Don said. "I don't want to make any assumptions just yet."

The got back in the car and headed to Duke Forsythe's house.

As soon as they got out of the car, Benji Willis came from around the back of the house.

Upon seeing Taryn and Don, he paused mid-step, then turned and started to run off.

"Benji," Taryn called out to him. "Stop!"

Benji stopped and slowly turned back to Taryn.

"What are you doing here?" Taryn asked him.

"Nothing. I was just…," Benji said.

"Just what?" Taryn demanded.

Benji began wringing his hands and hung his head.

"Benji?"

"Sheriff, I wasn't doing anything wrong. I just wanted to see where Duke died, is all."

"Why would you want to see that?" Taryn asked. "Do you know something? Is there something you need to tell me?"

"No, ma'am," Benji said, looking scared. "I just come to pay my respects."

"Where he was killed? Usually people pay their respects at the funeral," Taryn said.

"I feel real bad, Sheriff," Benji said, his voice shaky. "I never wanted him dead."

"What do you feel bad about, Benji?"

"He was right. I stole the beer out of his car while he was in the store. I did it to get even with him for always picking on me, but I never wanted him to die."

"Benji, do you know something about his death? Did you see something? Hear something?" Taryn asked.

"No, honest," Benji said, still looking nervous. "I know my mama was spitting mad, but she ain't capable of this either, if that's what you're thinking."

"No one is accusing you or your mama of killing Duke," Taryn told him.

"Then why are you upset that I'm here?"

"I'm not upset. I just think it's a bit weird that you are, though."

"Am I in trouble?" Benji asked.

"No," Taryn said. "You're not in trouble. But if you're going to roam around in the woods or anywhere out away from things, please be careful. I don't want to see you get hurt."

"What's going to hurt me out here?" Benji asked, spreading his arms out to encompass the area. "I have more to fear in town then I ever would out here."

Taryn knew Benji was right. A lot of folks in town gave him a hard time and she knew that was why he spent so much time out in the woods alone. It was the only place he felt truly safe. But now, with a wild animal running around, Taryn wasn't so sure he was safe out there anymore, either.

"Benji, you know we have a wild animal running around killing people, right?" she asked him. Maybe he hadn't heard the news.

"I heard an animal killed Frank and Duke, yeah," Benji said. "A wild dog or something. But I roam all over these woods and I ain't seen anything like that."

"Just be careful, alright?"

"I will, Sheriff," Benji said. "Can I go now?"

"Sure," Taryn said. "Tell your mama 'hello' for me."

Benji took off at a dead run down the driveway and out of sight.

"Strange young man," Don said.

"Benji? He's alright. He just gets a raw deal sometimes. People don't like him much. They think he's a no good slacker and don't have much use for him, but he's harmless."

"Are you sure?"

"Yeah, why?"

"He just seemed edgy to me, like he was hiding something," Don said.

"He always acts that way," Taryn said, starting for the backyard. "I think he's so used to always *being* in trouble, that he naturally acts defensively."

They scoured the backyard, but didn't find any more prints. Taryn showed him where they had found the one they had cast and Don seemed uneasy and in a hurry to leave.

"Are you ok?" Taryn asked him as they headed back to the car.

"I got a real creepy feeling back there," Don said. "I've worked with wildlife for thirty five years and I've never felt like that at a kill sight before. It's like an evil residue was left behind. I really can't explain it. I'm just glad to be leaving here."

Taryn looked over her shoulder toward the backyard. She had to admit, she felt rather creeped out back there, too.

As they drove back to the station, Taryn glanced over and saw Don examining the plaster cast again.

"So?" she asked. "What do you think?"

"Taryn," he said, with a serious tone in his voice. "I don't know what you have here, but it's not normal."

"What do you mean?"

"I've examined this cast over and over and I can't honestly tell you what it's from. I know every single foot print, blade of hair, howls, screeches, calls, hoots, you name it, but I am totally stumped on this one. It's nothing I've ever seen before."

"Are you absolutely certain it's not some kind of dog or wolf?"

"It is definitely not a dog or any known wolf breed. I'm telling you, it looks like a human/ wolf mix. That's the best I can do."

Taryn looked over at him with her mouth gaping open. "You're the expert. If you don't know what it is, then what I am supposed to do?"

"Maybe you need to look into alternative answers."

"Like a werewolf? Seriously?"

"I'm at a loss here."

"There has to be a more rational explanation."

"If you have one, I'm all ears," Don said.

Pulling into the station, Taryn got out of the car and walked Don over to his vehicle.

"I really appreciate you taking the time to come check this out for us," she told him.

"I'm just sorry I couldn't figure it out for you," Don said.

"Me, too," Taryn said.

She watched him pull away and headed inside.

Cheryl laid down the magazine she was reading and looked at Taryn expectantly. "Well?"

"He has no idea what it is," Taryn said, feeling a slight headache building behind her eyes.

"How can he not know?"

"Beats me," Taryn said. "He said he's never seen a print like that before."

"What are you going to do?" Cheryl asked.

"I have no idea," Taryn said. "I don't know what to do at this point. We've warned everyone of a possible wild animal around these parts. Let's just hope folks take it seriously and stay indoors at night."

"Fat chance," Cheryl said. "Cookouts, barbecues, camping. It's summer. No one is going to stay indoors."

"That's what I'm afraid of," Taryn said.

~~~~~

Rhobby was outside Taryn's house when she pulled into the drive.

He stood leaning against his truck with his arms folded over his chest and a very unhappy look on his face.

Taryn inwardly groaned as she got out of her vehicle and walked over to where he stood.

"I left you tons of messages," he said. "You totally ignored me."

"I know. I'm sorry. I just needed a day to myself."

"What about today? You couldn't even be bothered with them today?"

"I forgot about them," Taryn confessed. "Things have been very hectic the last few days. I'm sorry."

"Did you even look at them. Or read them?"

"No, I didn't. I'm sorry."

Rhobby pushed himself away from the truck, shaking his head as he paced. "I was worried when I didn't hear back from you, you know."

"What right do you have to demand I respond every time you call or text?" Taryn demanded, feeling anger welling up inside of her. "You gave up that right when you walked out on me to go running off with Norma Sue."

Taryn knew she was letting her anger get the better of her, but it had been a long day and she was feeling a bit stressed. She had so much on her mind right now that the last thing she wanted to do was fight with Rhobby.

"I'm not allowed to care about you?" Rhobby demanded, his voice rising in anger, as well. "Well, tough luck Taryn, because I do still care."

"Rhobby, I don't have the energy to fight with you right now. There is a lot going on at work right now and I just don't need anything else on my plate to deal with."

"Do you even want to know why I tried to get a hold of you?"

"Not really," Taryn said. "But I know you're going to tell me anyway."

"I wanted to know if you would like to spend an afternoon with me. On a date. You know, maybe start over from the beginning."

Taryn jaw dropped open as she stared at him completely dumbfounded. "You're serious?"

"Yes, I am."

Shaking her head, she turned and headed off toward her house without another word.

"Taryn," Rhobby called after her. "Come on. Give me another chance. Please."

Taryn kept walking toward the house. Frustration was building and she didn't want to say something she might regret.

Shaking her head, she waved at him over her shoulder and stepped up onto her porch.

Unlocking the door, she stepped inside and shut the door behind her, never turning to look at Rhobby again, though he continued to call after her, pleading with her.

Leaning her back against the door, she heard his truck start up and drive away.

How could he ask her to just start over? What made him think she could just forget what he had done? Norma Sue was everything she was not. Tall, blonde, beautiful. And ten years younger. How could she compete with that? She would never be able to trust him again. He had been her high school sweetheart. They had been together since they were fifteen years old. He had been everything to her. But she hadn't been everything to him.

Wiping a tear off her cheek, she stripped off her uniform and slipped into a pair of shorts and a tank top.

After throwing a couple of hot dogs into a pan of boiling water, she prepared her buns and grabbed a bottle of water out of the refrigerator.

Once the hot dogs were plump and cooked through, she dropped one into each bun and grabbed up her plate and headed for the front porch.

Pulling up a lawn chair, she situated herself so she was facing the driveway, the front door to her back.

As she sat there eating her hot dogs, she heard the crickets begin their nightly serenade and watched as lightning bugs flickered their tiny lights out across the yard.

A soft breeze blew across her bare skin. The sweet smell of grass and wildflowers floated on the air all around her.

Taryn leaned her head back and closed her eyes.

Taking a few deep breaths, she slowly let them out.

Relaxing her shoulders, she slowly opened her eyes.

It was peaceful out here on her three acres. The road she lived on wasn't traveled a lot, so she felt isolated, even lonely at times, but she loved it anyway.

She finished her hot dogs and set the plate down on the floor next to her chair. As she sat back up, a slight movement in the woods next to the house caught her attention.

Squinting to see more clearly into the thick cluster of trees, she didn't see anything, but suddenly, the hairs on the back of her arms stood up and an eerie, creepy feeling inched up her spine.

"Hello?" she called out.

No response.

"Is someone there?"

She inched forward on her seat and scanned the wood line again.

She couldn't see anyone, but her gut told her someone was there. Watching her.

"I know you're there," she called out.

A shift in some branches several feet back in the trees warned her that she was not alone.

Getting quickly to her feet, she shoved the chair back out of the way and walked to the edge of the porch and stared off into the woods.

"I see you," she yelled. "Get out of here before I get my gun."

She didn't want to show the fear she felt. Something didn't seem right about this. The hair at the nape of her neck was on end and her heartbeat had doubled in pace. A cold sweat broke out on her skin and suddenly, her knees felt weak. An uneasy feeling came over her. She felt like prey.

Grabbing her plate up, she hurried to the door and slipped inside, shutting the door firmly behind her and sliding the lock into place.

She pulled the curtains back an inch from the window and peeked out the crack toward the woods and watched.

Nothing moved.

"Get a grip, Taryn," she scolded herself. "You're letting all this wolf stuff play with your mind."

Letting the curtain fall back into place, she rechecked the lock on the front door and for safety's sake, went through the house and checked all the windows and the back door to be sure all was secure.

Satisfied that she was safe, she hopped in the shower and stood under the hot stream for several minutes until she felt more relaxed.

It was only nine o'clock when she stepped out of the shower, but she was ready for bed. She crawled under the covers and picked up the book she had started a month ago and tried to read, but her mind just went in circles about what Don had told her today. None of it made sense. A half human, half wolf footprint? It just wasn't possible.

Finally, closing her eyes, she drifted off into a fitfull sleep.

~~~~~

I'm feeling a bit antsy tonight. I need to get out.

Not to kill.

Not tonight.

I need to see her.

Being in my human form, it will take me longer to get to her house, than if I was in my wolf form. I have to travel at a much slower pace or the branches and bushes will rip and tear at my skin. I can't allow that. I can't let anyone know I was out taking a stroll through the woods. Even though I spend a lot of time out here, I am always careful to cover my skin. I don't want cuts and scrapes giving away my nightly prowlings.

The sun is starting to sink, so it's the perfect time to be out. I hear the crickets begin their chirping.

Good.

With nightfall so eminent, I will be masked by the darkness of the woods. She won't be able to see me hiding in plain sight.

I reach her house just as the sun drops down over the horizon. I eagerly make my way to a vantage point that I can see the front of her house.

What luck! She's sitting outside on her front porch.

I can, undetected, watch her from here. Her soft, curly brown hair. Her short, little body sitting there so perfectly in her chair.

She is perfect. Simply perfect.

Oops, I wasn't paying attention to what I was doing. I was too wrapped up in watching her. I shifted my position and I think she saw me.

I freeze. I don't move a muscle.

She calls out toward where I am standing and asks if anyone is here.

I am, but you aren't suppose to know that. You aren't supposed to see me.

I step back a couple of steps to make sure she doesn't spot me among the trees.

Crap. She called out to me telling me she sees me. Does she? Can she really see me through the shadows and trees? I don't think she can. I think she's bluffing.

She threatens to get her gun. I must leave now. I don't want to risk getting shot.

I slowly melt back into the trees, careful not to move too quickly or step on any fallen branches.

When I am far enough back, I turn and head for home.

I wanted to watch her for a longer period of time.

Not tonight, though.
I'm still feeling antsy.
I need to kill again.
Not tonight.
But soon. Very soon.

Chapter 8

The loud buzzing of the alarm clock caused Taryn to nearly jump out of her skin.

Dark dreams and terrifying images of large wolves had plagued her through the night.

Hitting the snooze button, she lay in the half light of the early morning and let her mind run over everything that had happened over the last few days.

Something was killing people. But what? Would there be any more killings? She sure hoped not. What was her next step in discovering what kind of animal it was? If Don was unable to identify the animal by the plaster cast, then what was her next move?

Then, there was Rhobby. Her heart still ached for him every time she saw him, but she just couldn't go down that road again. She was just too scared it would lead to more heartache. Every time he showed up outside her door, it was harder and harder to tell him no. He seemed so genuine.

Rolling over onto her stomach, she began beating her fists over and over again into her pillow.

Once her frustration was alleviated, at least for the moment, she rolled out of bed and got dressed.

As she pulled up to the station, Ron and Troy were standing outside the door talking.

"What's up boys?" she asked as she approached them.

"Gerti was here a few minutes ago," Troy said.

"What did she want?" Taryn asked.

"She's demanding we find the animal responsible for the killings," Ron said, rolling his eyes.

"What does she think we're doing?" Taryn asked. "Sitting around twiddling our thumbs?"

"Apparently," Troy said.

"She's all concerned because she said Benji spends so much time in the woods that she's afraid he'll be eaten," Ron added.

Taryn just shook her head. "That boy's got more knowledge of these woods than anyone else around here. He knows how to be safer out there than the rest of us combined."

"Tell that to his mama," Troy said.

When they stepped inside, Cheryl hung up the phone. "Taryn, that was Dr. Middleton. He said for you to call him as soon as you got it. He has the results from the autopsy."

"Awesome," Taryn said. "Boys, stick around. I want you to hear this, too."

Taryn went back to her office, followed by Ron and Troy.

Flipping through her rolodex, she punched Dr. Middleton's number into her phone and waited for him to pick up.

"Hello?" Dr. Middleton's voice came on the line.

Taryn put him on speakerphone so Ron and Troy could hear the results as well. "Dr. Middleton, it's Sheriff Givens. I got your message. What can you tell me?"

"I'm not sure how to tell you this, but I got the lab results back on the saliva we retrieved off both bodies."

"And?" Taryn asked, impatiently.

"It came back as human...and wolf," Dr. Middleton said, reluctantly.

"Excuse me?" Taryn asked. "That doesn't make sense. Was the sample contaminated?"

"I've been doing this job for more years than you've been alive. I have never contaminated a sample yet. It was a pure sample."

"I'm sorry, Dr. Middleton. I didn't mean to imply that you didn't know how to do your job. It's just that the results are a bit confusing."

"Tell me about it," Dr. Middleton said. "And that's not all. The autopsy revealed that the bite marks are consistent with an animal attack, just like I suspected. But what kind of an animal is a mystery. The bite marks are identical to a wolf's bite, only much larger. No known wolf breed could have made those bite marks. The claw marks are not those of a wolf, though. They're more consistent with a long bladed knife."

Taryn looked up at Ron and Troy trying to gauge their reactions.

Ron's brows were furrowed in question, but Troy's face had a look of smugness to it.

"So what's your conclusion, Dr. Middleton?" Taryn asked, almost afraid of the answer.

"To be honest," said Dr. Middleton. "I'm ruling it an animal *and* human attack."

"You mean you think it's a human and his pet wolf that are killing people?" Taryn asked.

"I don't know what other explanation to give," Dr. Middleton said on a long sigh. "We've definitely got wolf DNA, but also human DNA. The only logical explanation is that it's a man and his wolf doing double duty on the killings."

"Or it's a human who is also a wolf," chimed in Troy.

"Excuse me?" Dr. Middleton said. "Are you telling me you think it's a werewolf?"

"It makes sense," Troy said.

"Please don't pay any attention to him, Dr. Middleton," Taryn said. "Thank you for getting back with me so quickly with the results. I really appreciate it."

"Good luck, Taryn," Dr. Middleton said. "You're gonna need it."

Hanging up the phone, she glared at Troy. "Really? You had to say that to him?"

"Hey, look at the facts," Troy said, defensively. "A print that is part human, part wolf. Saliva that is part human, part wolf. An attack that is part human, part wolf. Do you have a better explanation?"

Taryn rubbed the bridge of her nose between her thumb and forefinger. "No," she said, quietly. "No, I don't, but I just can't buy into the belief that there's a werewolf stalking our little town."

"Well, when you come up with a better explanation, I'm willing to listen," Troy said.

"Don't you two have streets to patrol?" Taryn asked, not unkindly. A headache was beginning to throb just behind her eyes and she needed a few minutes to herself to digest the news from Dr. Middleton.

"On it, Boss," Ron said, as he tugged on Troy's arm. They walked out of her office, closing the door behind them.

Taryn laid her head down on the desk and closed her eyes.

A knock at her door brought Taryn's head up with a jerk.

"Come in," she said to whoever was on the other side of the door.

"It's noon, Taryn," Cheryl said, poking her head around the door.

"What?" Taryn asked, grabbing her phone and checking the time. "Ugh, I must have dozed off."

"You must have," Cheryl said. "You gonna stay here for lunch or go to Tom's?"

Taryn sat back in her chair and ran her fingers through her hair and rubbed her eyes. It didn't surprise her that she had fallen asleep. She had tossed and turned all night and woke up feeling rather groggy.

"I didn't bring a lunch today, so I guess Tom's it is," she said. "You coming, too?"

"Not today. I brought my lunch and I was going to use the hour to call a friend of mine that I haven't talked to in awhile."

"Ok," Taryn said. "I guess I'd better get going then. The lunch crowd will probably already be there and I'll be lucky to get a seat."

After a quick trip to the bathroom to freshen up and fix her hair, Taryn walked the four blocks to Tom's.

When she pulled the door open, she realized with some dismay that she had been right. The lunch crowd had swarmed in and there were no seats to be had.

Just as she was turning to leave, she heard her name being called.

Turning to see who it was, she saw Vince Cobb sitting at a booth in the corner all by himself.

Walking over to his table, she smiled down at him. "Good afternoon, Vince," she said. "How're you doing?"

"Would you like to share my booth?" he said, indicating the seat opposite himself.

Taryn figured *why not* and slid into the booth across from him. "Thank you," she said. "I thought I'd have to run through the drive-thru at McDonald's."

"Well, I did you a favor then," Vince said, flagging the waitress over.

Taryn ordered a BLT and some chips.

While she waited for her order to arrive, she sipped on the iced tea that Kimmy, knowing what she would order, brought over to her.

"No offense intended, but you look a little rough around the edges. Tough day?" Vince asked her.

"You could say that," Taryn said, not taking offense to his comment. She knew she looked rough and tired, because she was.

"Wanna talk about it?"

"It's been a long few days."

"I heard about the animal attacks. Have you found the animal responsible yet?" Vince asked.

"No, unfortunately," Taryn said.

Kimmy choose that moment to bring Taryn's food over. Taryn realized she was far more hungry than she had thought and she snatched up the sandwich and took a big bite.

"Talk around town is that they were pretty horrific attacks. Are you able to talk about it?" Vince asked.

"Let me guess. Gerti has been doing some talking?"

"How'd you guess?" Vince laughed. "She was in here a little earlier telling everyone she was the one who found Duke. Is that true?"

"Yes."

"Oh wow," Vince said, shaking his head. "I bet that messed her up a bit."

"You could say that again," Taryn said. "She was a mess by the time we got there."

Vince reached over and covered her hand with his. "I'm sorry you're having to deal with all this. I know it must be difficult."

Taryn looked down at his hand covering hers and slowly pulled it away. "Vince," she said, quietly. "I'm sorry, but I'm not looking for a romantic connection right now."

"Oh, no, Taryn," Vince said, stumbling over his words. "That wasn't meant as one. I'm sorry if it came across that way. I was just offering emotional support."

"It's just…," Taryn started. "I'm not really over Rhobby yet and..."

"Taryn," Vince said, cutting her off. "I'm sorry, but I was not hitting on you. You're a real nice lady and all, but I'm just not interested in you that way. In fact, I'm not interested in dating anyone right now. Since Steph left, I've kinda sworn off women for awhile."

Embarrassed that she misread the circumstances, she felt heat creep up her cheeks. "Vince, I am so sorry," she said. "The other day when Penny, Cheryl and I were having lunch, they swore up and down that you were flirting with me. I took it to heart and thought your motives were of the romantic nature. I feel like a fool."

"No need to be embarrassed. My interest in you is purely one of respect. I really admire the job you do and how well you do it. I apologize if I gave you or your friends the wrong idea."

Taryn knew her face was still red, but she reached over and squeezed Vince's hand. "Still friends?"

"Of course," Vince said, squeezing her hand back. "I wouldn't want it any other way."

Feeling relieved, Taryn finished her lunch and when she was done, Vince walked her back to the station.

As they walked, the conversation turned back to the animal attacks.

"So what do you think is responsible for the attacks?" he asked her.

"Honestly, I don't know," Taryn said. "The medical examiner seems to think it's a man and his pet wolf working together."

"Really? How did he come up with that conclusion?"

"Apparently, both human and wolf DNA were found on the victims," Taryn said.

"So we need to be keeping an eye out for a man with a pet wolf?" Vince asked, jokingly.

"Seems like it," Taryn said. "Vince, do you spend any time in the woods around here? You know, hunting, hiking or anything like that?"

"I'm not much of a woodsy kind of person. I prefer the gym or the track if I want to exercise. Why?"

"I was just thinking that if you were, then maybe you might have seen or heard something that could help us out with this case."

"I wish I could, but woods and me don't mix," Vince said. He stopped in his tracks and turned to face her, flexing his muscles. "I wouldn't want to mess up all this sexiness by getting cuts and scratches all over me."

Taryn burst out laughing. "I suppose you're right."

They reached the station and Vince opened the door for her and ushered her inside. "I hope you find your bad guy," he said, as she stepped inside.

"Me too," Taryn said. "Thanks for letting me join you for lunch. And thanks for forgiving me for jumping to conclusions about your intentions toward me. That was embarrassing, but you didn't make me feel stupid about it."

"Hey, what are friends for, right?" He gave her a quick hug, then turned and headed off down the street.

Taryn closed the door and turned to see Cheryl staring at her with a knowing look on her face.

"It's not what you think," Taryn said, laughing. "Turns out, he's not interested in me in that way at all."

"He told you that?" Cheryl asked, incredulously.

"We had a discussion at lunch," Taryn told her. "We cleared the air."

"Do tell," Cheryl said, scooting to the edge of her seat, excitement etched on her face.

"Nevermind," Taryn said. "Let's just drop it. Suffice it to say, he's not interested in me romantically, but he does admire me for my job skills."

"You know I'm going to want to hear the whole story," Cheryl said. "And if he's not interested in you, maybe I have a shot with him."

"Good luck with that," Taryn said. "I'll leave that between the two of you."

Cheryl laughed and Taryn headed back to her office to finish up some paperwork.

Chapter 9

The blood lust is getting too strong. I must kill. I must kill tonight.

And I know who is next. My rage still burns thinking of the injustice.

How dare she. How dare Ginny Lee Maloney walk around town acting all high and mighty. Does she ever think of what she did? Does she ever feel guilt?

Probably not.

People like her never do.

She'll pay, though. Oh, how she'll pay.

Anger rages through me as I remember that awful day.

I had walked into Barrett's Drug Store down on Main Street. I was minding my own business just looking for some foot powder when I saw Ginny Lee walk in.

She was beautiful. Long, blond hair. A shape like Barbie with full, pink lips and big blue eyes. Every guy in town wanted her and every girl wanted to be her.

I watched as she casually strolled through the store. She seemed like she was up to something, so I kept a stealthy eye on her.

Sure enough, after walking past a figurine display several times, I saw her pick up a small, glass statue of a wolf and drop it into her purse.

She turned and saw me watching her. Tossing her hair over her shoulder, she looked smugly at me, then started toward the front door.

I stepped in front of her and blocked her from leaving the store and told her I saw her trying to shoplift the little wolf figurine. She glared at me and said, "What are you going to do about it? Leave me alone and get out of my way." Then, she shoved me. Hard.

I stumbled back against the counter, knocking a display of greeting cards off onto the floor. The ruckus caused Mr. Barrett to come from the back of the store where he was stocking shelves to see what was going on.

Ginny Lee pulled the wolf figurine out of her pocket before he got to us and held it up. "This thief was trying to steal this," she told him.

Mr. Barrett came rushing over and grabbed the statue. "I'm calling the cops. You think you can come in here and steal from me?" he demanded.

I tried to explain what really happened, but Ginny Lee gave Mr. Barrett one of her little pouts and he melted like butter in her hands.

I knew he would believe her over me, so I offered to pay for the statue. That calmed Mr. Barrett down, but he told me never to come back into his store again.

That statue cost me $79. And Ginny Lee had laughed at me as I pulled out my credit card.

I watched as she leaned over and gave Mr. Barrett a peck on his cheek and told him she didn't understand how anyone could steal from such a sweet, old man.

I was burning inside. It was so unfair.

I still have the statue. I put it on a shelf above my bed so whenever I looked at it, I wouldn't forget what she did.

Time for payback.

The irony of the situation did not go unnoticed. All of this started with a wolf. A wolf statue. And it would all end with a wolf. A werewolf.

I stand in front of the full length mirror in my bathroom.

As I change into my wolf form, I realize just how easy the transformation is becoming. The pain isn't as severe. The time it takes is only moments instead of minutes. Somehow, I even appear fiercer looking.

I like it. A lot.

Sneaking quietly out into the darkness, I drop down to all fours. Ginny Lee's place is a couple of miles away. I'll get there quicker moving on all my legs, instead of just two.

I'm going to enjoy ripping her limb from limb. I'm going to savor every minute of it.

I negotiate my way through the thick trees and overgrowth along the dirt road that leads to her house.

Thankfully, she lives out in the middle of nowhere. The only thing surrounding her house is cornfields and woods for miles.

No need to hide in the woods out here. No one ever travels this road, especially at night.

The rough, bumpy road has so many potholes and ruts that most people don't want to drive their cars over it. It would almost take a four wheel drive to get back here.

Loping along the road, the moon catches my eye. It's a huge silver sliver in the sky. It's not a full moon yet, but it's misty glow casts enough light over the field and road to illuminate my way.

The evening is chilly and the air cools my face as I trot along.

I stop short.

I see something.

A car. Just up ahead. The lights are off, but the motor is running.

I smell human scent coming from the open windows. One male. One female.

I hunker down close to the ground and inch my way closer to the vehicle. I step slowly and carefully so I don't crunch the gravel too loudly under my massive paws.

As I near the vehicle, I can hear sucking, slurping noises. Moans and groans follow.

Someone is parked out on this lonely road making out.

Two for one tonight. I lick my lips in anticipation. I hadn't counted on this, but what luck!

The beat up, old truck begins to bounce around.

I stand up on my hind legs and peer into the driver's window.

Oh, what luck!

Looks like I won't have to go any farther to find my prey tonight.

Ginny Lee is flat on her back with Dillon Wyatt sprawled out on top of her.

I raise up to my full height, just as Ginny Lee spots me over Dillon's shoulder.

~~~~~

The old pickup truck wasn't exactly where Ginny Lee had pictured her romantic evening with Dillon Wyatt.

She understood why they hadn't gone back to his place, though. He still lived with his parents.

At thirty years old, Ginny Lee thought that was pretty pathetic, but whatever. She was just glad to have finally hooked up with him.

She'd been trying to for years, but he had been in a relationship with Sandra Martin and until they had broke up a month ago, he hadn't been interested.

Every man was interested in her.

She recognized the fact that she didn't love Dillon. She just needed to know that he wanted her like every other man did. He was proving it tonight. Another conquest conquered.

She had suggested they go back to her place, but for some reason, Dillon thought it would be more fun 'doing it' in his pickup.

Whatever. She would never understand men.

The sound of gravel crunching under foot somewhere out in the darkness caught her attention.

"Dillon, I thought I heard someone out there," Ginny Lee said, pushing him on the shoulder to stop him from kissing her neck.

"There's no one out there, Ginny Lee," he said, impatiently. "No one hardly ever travels this road. Especially at night. Relax, would you?"

He leaned in and began to kiss her neck again. Getting more into it as he went.

He wrapped his arms around her and lowered her onto her back across the front seat. Spreading her legs, he positioned himself on top of her and leaned down to press his lips to her mouth.

Gravel crunched again. Only this time it was closer.

Jerking her head away from him, she froze. "I'm telling you, someone's out there," she whispered. "I hear gravel crunching."

"It's probably just a deer," Dillon said, blowing off her concerns.

"I'm serious," Ginny Lee said, feeling irritated that he didn't believe her. "Please, just take a look to make sure."

Dillon looked down at her and rolled his eyes. He was just about to get up when Ginny Lee looked over his shoulder and let out a scream that pierced his ears and shattered the night.

Ginny Lee stared helplessly at Dillon as a look of horror crossed his face. He was violently jerked backward off of her. His body seemed to fold in half as he was pulled through the window in one quick movement.

Ginny Lee screamed at the top of her lungs. Through the open window of the truck, she saw a huge, hairy monster with red, piercing eyes staring back at her. Dillon hung limply in it's arms.

She watched in horror as the monster dipped it's head and sunk it's teeth deep into Dillon's throat. Blood squirted out in all directions and a grotesque gurgling noise erupted from Dillon's mouth.

Not waiting around to see what the monster did next, Ginny Lee threw open the passenger side door and dropped to the ground on the other side of the truck.

Without looking back, she tore off down the road as fast as her legs would carry her.

She had kicked off her shoes when she and Dillon had started making out, so now she was barefoot.

The rocks under her feet dug into the tender flesh of her soles, but she didn't feel it.

Terror pumped through her veins and a sheer, blinding need to get away from the area was all her brain could register.

Somewhere behind her she heard the most chilling noise she had ever heard in her life. A low, deep, gut wrenching howl split the air.

Her blood ran cold at the sound and fear, unlike anything she had ever experienced before, filled her. Tears blinded her eyes as she ran.

The road wound around through the woods and eventually turned and dropped down toward the cemetery.

Hazy moonlight lit the road just enough for Ginny Lee to see the wrought iron gate that closed off the entrance to the cemetery at night.

Her mind raced as she tried to think what to do to get away from the beast she knew was closing ground behind her, chasing her down, intent on killing her.

Slipping between the brick pillar and the wrought iron fence that marked the entrance to the cemetery, she dashed between headstones looking for one tall enough to hide behind.

In the middle of one of the rows, she saw a tall, wide gravestone that was broad at the base.

Rushing over to it, she ducked down behind it and knelt on the ground.

From this location, she watched the entrance, waiting to see if the monster came in.

Since this was a cemetery, was it sacred ground? Could something evil come in here? Would that thing be able to step foot in this place?

She heard gravel crunching and stones skittering across the road as the beast approached the cemetery. It wasn't trying to be sneaky. It wasn't trying to be quiet. It knew that she knew it was coming.

The silvery shadows of the tombstones cast by the moon caused a feeling of eerie foreboding to crawl over Ginny Lee's skin.

She noticed with increasing fear that the crickets had stopped chirping and the night had become deathly quiet. So quiet, she could hear her heartbeat beating in her ears. Loud, like drums.

A dark shadow crossed over the gate.

Ginny Lee froze and sucked in her breath, afraid that even breathing would draw the creature to her.

She knew it was a werewolf. How was that possible? They were the stuff of myths and legend. Not real animals. But this was definitely a living, breathing werewolf.

Nausea washed over her and she watched the beast stop and lift its head toward the sky. She saw it sniffing the air, then let out a howl that sent shivers racing through her.

Pressing herself closer to the gravestone, she peeked out around the side and quickly clamped her hand over her mouth.

It was staring right at the gravestone she was hiding behind, sniffing the air.

It knew she was here. She could run, but she knew she couldn't out run it even if she tried.

Ducking back behind the gravestone, she felt hot tears streaming down her face. She didn't want to die. She didn't want her life to end this way.

She sunk closer to the ground and saying a quick prayer, surrendered herself to her fate.

She felt the werewolf's hot breath brush across her face as she turned and look up at the most terrifying sight imaginable.

~~~~~

I didn't get any satisfaction from killing Dillon. He wasn't even a target, but he was in the way.

What a shame. I always liked him.

I finished him off quickly. No need in making him suffer. He had never done anything to me.

Ginny Lee's scream excited me. She was terrified.

Good.

My heart quickened with exhilaration at the thought of the terror she was feeling. Now she would know what I felt like that day at Barrett's.

I see her run away. I hear her feet pounding on the gravel as she runs for her life.

Ahhh, a chase. I had not anticipated this, but what fun!

I'll give her a good head start. Let her think she has a chance.

She can't outrun me. She can't hide from me. I can smell her from a mile away.

I know where she's going. The cemetery. It's the only place on the road for miles.

I give her several minutes before I take off after her. I don't want her to get too comfortable thinking she has gotten away from me.

I can hear her heart pounding even from here. It calls to me. Beckons me.

Yep. Just what I suspected. She has gone into the cemetery.

I easily jump the gate. It takes little effort.

Stopping to sniff the air, her scent tells me which direction she went in.

I smell her tears. The salty scent thrills me.

I want her good and scared. I want her to beg for her life, like I begged my innocence.

Across the gray, shadowy grounds, I see her blond head poking out around a gravestone.

There you are.

I waste no time making my way through the maze of headstones to stand next to the one she is cowering behind.

I let out a long, slow breath and watch with gut deep satisfaction at the horror on her face as she turns to look at me.

With a quick swing of my arm, I grabbed her and yank her out from behind the stone.

She screams.

Ohhhh, yes. I love the sound.

I watch her laying at my feet for a moment, shaking and crying. She doesn't beg for her life, yet, but she will.

I lift my leg and stomp it down on her stomach. I feel the rush of air leave her lungs with a hard grunt.

Still, she doesn't beg. She just continues to stare up at me.

Digging my claws into her left shoulder, I yank, ripping her whole arm off. Blood pours out of the open, gaping wound.

She screams, but still doesn't beg.

Digging my claws into the other arm, I rip it from its socket, as well.

Tears cover her face and she is panting and sucking in gulps of air.

Leaning down, drool from my mouth drips onto her chest, her face.

"Please," she croaks out. "Do it quick."

There…finally, she begged.

Hatred and anger well up inside me so thick and hot, I lose control.

Swinging both arms, claws extended, I shred her body.

Clamping my teeth down on her flesh, I rip and tear.

Soon, she is almost unrecognizable. I have torn her body to pieces. I am covered in her blood.

I watch as the light goes out of her eyes and I feel such a deep satisfaction that I throw back my head and howl.

I howl so long and so deep that I feel all the tension and pent up anger leave my body.

I looked back down at my work.

She is beautiful no more.

~~~~~

Lester Flynn sat on his bedroom floor with his legs drawn up to his chest and a blanket pulled tightly around him.

He heard the screams. He heard the howls.

As soon as the noises started, he had rushed through his house, locking the doors and turning off all the lights.

He knew what he was hearing was unnatural, evil. He wanted no part of it.

He sat for the rest of the night huddled on the floor next to his bed, afraid to move.

He remained tucked under his blanket until the sun peeked through the edge of his curtains, announcing the dawn of a new day.

The nightmare, at least for the night, was over.

Chapter 10

Taryn could hear her phone ringing from the other room. Rolling over, she looked at the clock.

6:05 a.m.

Who would be calling her this early in the morning? No one called this time of the morning unless it was bad news.

Stumbling out of bed, she rushed down the hallway and grabbed up her phone off the counter in the kitchen, where she had it charging.

"Hello?" she asked, her voice gravelly from sleep.

"Sheriff, this is Lester Flynn," came the voice on the other end. "You better get over here quick."

"What's going on, Lester?"

"Just get over here."

"On my way," Taryn said with a sigh as she hung up the phone.

Dressing quickly, she flew out the door without the benefits of her morning cup of coffee.

Lester lived at the beginning of the road that Ginny Lee lived on. His house sat across the road from an old, stone church that was built in the early 1800s. Up the dirt road beyond the church sat the cemetery. Ginny Lee's house was several miles beyond that. Those were the only places that still existed along that road. All the other homesteads had been torn down long ago.

The sun was just barely rising over the horizon as she pulled into Lester's driveway. He was waiting for her on the front porch.

"What's going on?" Taryn asked, as she stepped out of her vehicle and walked up onto his porch.

Lester was obviously agitated about something. He was dressed, but his clothes were rumpled and his hair had not been combed.

"Something happened here last night," he told her.

"What happened?" Taryn asked, confused. Looking around, nothing seemed out of the ordinary.

"I heard screams and howls last night," Lester said with a full body shiver. "Someone was killed."

"How do you know someone was killed?" Taryn asked, feeling a prickling sensation crawl up her skin.

"You should have heard those screams, those howls. It was horrible."

"Where did the sounds come from?"

Lester turned his head and pointed up the hill toward the cemetery.

Taryn followed the direction his finger was pointing and swallowed hard. Not the cemetery. The place was creepy enough as it was. It didn't need a macabre killing to make it any worse.

She called Ron and Troy. She knew if there was another killing, she didn't want to deal with it alone. Especially up in the cemetery.

While she waited, she continued to question Lester.

"What exactly did you hear?" she asked him.

"Screams," he said. "Blood curdling screams. And howls that would make the hair on the back of your neck stand up."

"Why didn't you call me last night when all this was going on?"

"I didn't figure there was anything you could have done. Not at that point."

"I could have come out and checked it out," Taryn said.

"No, Sheriff," Lester said, shaking his head. "By the time I heard it, it was already too late. There's nothing you could have done, except get yourself killed if you had shown up."

Taryn was really regretting not having her caffeine fix. A dull headache was beginning to throb in the back of her head.

"Where were you when all this was going on?" Taryn asked.

"In my house. I wasn't about to come outside. I locked my doors and closed all the windows."

Taryn nodded and patted his arm. "I understand."

Ron and Troy pulled up about twenty minutes later.

Taryn wanted to hug Ron when he handed her a cup of coffee from Pandy's Pasteries.

Taking a long swallow, she closed her eyes and let the hot brew slide down her throat.

"We need to check out the cemetery, boys," Taryn said. "Lester believes there was another attack last night."

"In the cemetery?" Ron asked. "This should be fun." His sarcasm was not lost on Taryn.

"That's why I called you out," she told him. "I didn't want to go up there alone.

"Why does he think there was another attack last night? And how does he know it was in the cemetery," Troy asked.

"I might be old, young man," Lester said. "But I can still hear. I heard noises last night that would curl your toes coming from up there." He pointed toward the cemetery. "That's how I know."

"Let's get up there and check it out," Taryn said. She didn't want Lester getting his britches in a bunch about Troy's comment, so she hastily gulped down the last of her coffee and got ready to leave.

"Just a minute," Lester said. "I'll need to go unlock the gate."

Lester rode up to the cemetery with Taryn.

After unlocking the gate, he turned and headed back down the road.

"Do you want a ride back down, Lester?" Taryn asked.

"No, thanks," Lester said. "It's not that far back down."

Taryn stood at the opened gate and gazed around the cemetery. It was old. One of the earliest graves dated back to the early 1800s. It was originally located here for the church at the bottom of the hill, but was still being used today. New graves could easily be distinguished from the old ones by the shiny new markers.

Even though it wasn't a very large cemetery, it had a creep factor that gave Taryn the willies.

Surrounded by deep woods on all sides, except where the road came in, a palpable gloom seemed to hang over the whole area, even when the sun was shining.

A low, wrought iron fence surrounded the cemetery on all sides. Thick vegetation grew over it and almost completely obscured it from sight.

Old, stone grave markers dotted the landscape. A lot of them were broken or crumbling. Some were almost completely covered in moss. Most of them were so worn the inscriptions were no longer visible. The newer section was off to the right and downhill a little ways.

Ron and Troy had pulled up next to her and got out.

Coming to stand next to her, none of them made a move to enter the grounds.

After several, long, uncomfortable moments, Taryn finally took a step forward.

"Come on, boys," she said over her shoulder. "May as well get this over with."

As soon as they entered the cemetery, an eerie, creepy feeling settled over them.

Making their way back through the rows of headstones, Ron suddenly stopped and pointed.

"There," he said, pointing to a tall headstone just up ahead.

Even from this distance, Taryn could make out the lifeless form of a body laying at the foot of the grave. Blood was splattered across the headstone and the sickening smell of death filled the air.

"Oh no," Taryn said, groaning. "I was hoping Lester was wrong."

Walking up to the body, Taryn quickly turned away and retched.

So did Troy.

Ron knelt down and examined the body as best he could.

"Call Dr. Middleton, Taryn," he said. "Looks like another animal attack all right."

Taryn considered herself a tough woman, but when she had walked up to the body, she had not been prepared for the carnage she was about to see.

Both arms had been ripped from the body. Deep slash marks had completely shredded the skin on the face and chest making it hard to determine whether the victim was male or female. Skin was ripped off in different places and blood covered the whole area. It was a massacre. The worst Taryn had ever seen.

Not able to stay with the body, Taryn leaned against the hood of her car and waited for Dr. Middleton to examine the body and the EMTs to remove the remains.

Ron walked over and laid his hand on her shoulder. "This is the worst one yet. It took some work, but we think we've finally identified the body. It's Ginny Lee Maloney."

"Benji"s old girlfriend?" Taryn asked.

"Yeah," Troy said. "She's torn to shreds. Never seen anything like it before."

Taryn noticed that Troy was still looking a little green in the face. She understood that completely. She was glad she hadn't eaten anything that morning before leaving the house. If she had, it would have been all over the ground next to the body.

Once the body was loaded into the ambulance, Dr. Middleton came over to where Taryn was still leaning against her car.

"It's another animal attack," he said. "Much worse than the first two, though. Seems this animal is getting angrier or more blood thirsty."

Taryn was about to respond when her cell phone rang.

"Hello?" she said, when she answered the phone.

"Sheriff, I got a call from Della Wyatt, Dillon's mom," Cheryl said. "He never came home last night."

Taryn dropped her head and rubbed the bridge of her nose. "Does she know where he went last night?"

"He was supposed to be with Ginny Lee Maloney."

Taryn's blood ran cold. "Thanks, Cheryl."

Ron and Troy were staring at her, waiting for her to tell them what was going on.

"I don't think we're done here," she told them, addressing Dr. Middleton, as well. "Della Wyatt called in to the station this morning to report that Dillon never came home last night."

"Her place is only a few miles from here," Ron said.

"Let's go up that way and see if we can find him," Taryn said.

Troy was looking at her with an odd look on his face.

"What?" Taryn asked him.

"He's upping his game," he said.

"What do you mean?" Taryn asked.

"Two kills in one night?" Troy asked. "We've got a real problem on our hands."

"We don't know that Dillon's dead," Ron said. "He's just missing at the moment."

"I don't think we're going to find him alive," Troy said.

A short drive up the road confirmed Taryn's worst fears.

They found the remains of Dillon on the road next to his truck, his throat ripped out.

Chapter 11

Taryn sat in her office answering phone calls the rest of the morning.

It seemed Lester Flynn had become the town crier and let the whole town know about the latest killings.

Now, every Tom, Dick and Harry was calling the station demanding she do something.

Ron and Troy walked in as she hung up the phone for the hundredth time.

"Ron," she said, a note of defeat in her voice. "Call a town meeting for this evening. Tell everyone to be at the Town Hall at six. We're going to have to address the town about these killings. Word is spreading fast and everyone is freaking out."

"On it, Boss," Ron said, as he headed out the door.

"What do you want me to do?" Troy asked.

"Go down to Town Hall and start geting it set up. Take Cheryl with you. I'll man the phones."

Once everyone had taken off to do their jobs, Taryn leaned back in her chair and drew in a deep breath, then slowly blew it out. What in the world was happening around here? What was she going to tell the townsfolk? She had no real answers yet. Dr. Middleton told her it was an animal attack, as well as a human attack. When she told the town, there would be a bunch of people taking off for the woods to go hunt down whoever, or whatever, was responsible for the killings. A lot of people could get hurt, let alone all the animals that would be shot and killed in the attempt to find the real culprit.

A familiar, dull ache was beginning to build behind her eyes again.

Popping a couple ibuprofen, she reached for her phone to call Penny when the front door of the station suddenly burst open.

Getting up out of her chair, she walked out to the front to see Benji standing there.

His red rimmed, swollen eyes attested to the fact that he'd been crying. "Is it true?" he demanded. "Is it true, Sheriff?"

"What, Benji? Is what true?" Taryn asked, walking over to him.

"Ginny Lee?" he said, between sobs. "Is she dead?"

"Yes," Taryn said. "I'm sorry, Benji. I was told you two used to date."

"Yeah, we did," Benji said. "How did she die?"

"An animal attack. Up at the cemetery."

"The same animal that killed Frank and Duke?" Benji asked.

"We believe so," Taryn said, carefully.

"I'm gonna kill it," Benji shouted. "I'm gonna kill it dead, Sheriff."

"Benji, calm down," Taryn said. "We're holding a town meeting this afternoon to address the situation. Come and hear what we have to say."

"I don't need to hear what you have to say," Benji said, spit flying from his mouth. "All you're gonna do is tell us to sit home and you'll handle it."

"I can't allow a bunch of people to go stomping around through the woods with guns," Taryn said. "That will only result in people getting hurt."

"I'm not going to hide in my house in fear. I'm going to hunt it down and kill it."

"Benji, you don't even know what you'd be hunting. How are you going to know what to look for?" Taryn asked.

"I don't know, but I just can't sit at home and do nothing," Benji said. He didn't wait for a response. He turned on his heel and stormed out the door, slamming it behind him as he went.

By now, Taryn's headache was full blown. Looking at the clock above the door, she noticed it was just before noon.

Trudging back to her office, she plopped down in her chair as her phone began to ring.

"Sheriff's office," she said, reluctantly into the receiver.

She spent the rest of the day answering calls, taking complaints and hearing demands about what the sheriff's office should do about these killings.

By the time six o'clock rolled around, Taryn was in a foul mood.

Locking the door to the station, she headed up the street toward the Town Hall. She knew better than to try to drive. Everyone in the community would turn out for this meeting and finding a parking space anywhere near the Town Hall would be impossible.

Taryn figured the walk would do her good. She needed to gain her composure and shake off the irritation she was feeling. The cool late afternoon air felt good on her heated skin. If she had had to take one more call demanding she do something, she was going to scream. What did the town think she was doing? Sitting in her office and ignoring it all?

Feeling the irritation creeping back in, she took several deep breaths and reminded herself that people were just scared and were looking for answers.

As she rounded the corner, Town Hall came into view. Sure enough, the whole town had come out for the meeting. Cars filled every parking space and were lined up and down both sides of the street.

Climbing the steps, she pushed open the door and walked in. Everyone was milling about and the din of noise from everyone talking at once was almost deafening.

Taryn scanned the crowd looking for Ron and Troy. She finally spotted them sitting at a table in the front of the room.

She noticed that Benji, nor Gerti, were present. The thought made her nervous. She hoped he wasn't out there in the woods searching for the killer. He was upset at the station earlier and she didn't want him going out and doing something stupid, like getting himself killed.

Making her way through the crowd, she walked around to the back of the table where Ron and Troy were waiting for her. She grabbed up a microphone that was laying there.

"Are you guys ready to get this done?" she asked them.

"Sure thing, Boss," Ron said.

Troy nodded his consent.

Flipping the little switch on the microphone, she held it up to her mouth and spoke into it.

"Could everyone please take a seat," she said. "We're ready to begin now."

The noise level rose as chairs screeched across the floor as people took their seats.

Finally, when everyone was seated, Taryn cleared her throat and began. "I know everyone is concerned with the recent events in the area. We will try to answer all your questions and listen to your concerns, as well as lay down some guidelines."

A soft murmur rose from the crowd, but Taryn ignored it and pressed on. "Let me start by saying that I know a lot of you have heard rumors as to who or what may be killing folks in the area. We do not have a definite answer to this yet. Dr. Middleton, the local medical examiner, is suggesting that it is possibly a man with a pet wolf."

The murmur around the room grew and a man from the back stood up and shouted over the noise. "A man and a wolf? Are you telling us that some maniac with a pet wolf is going around killing folks?"

"That's what we believe, yes," Taryn said. "The autopsies have confirmed that both human and wolf DNA were found on the victims."

"Do you have any idea who this man is?" an elderly woman on the front row asked.

"I'm sorry, but no," Taryn said. "Not at this time."

"What are you planning on doing about it?" the man from the back asked.

"We are asking for anyone who has seen or heard anything unusual to come talk to us after this meeting is over," Taryn said.

"That's it? That's all you're doing?" A young man asked.

"We don't have any leads as of yet," Taryn said. "We've been in contact with the neighboring counties to see if anyone in their towns fit the description, but so far, none do."

"So what are we supposed to do?" asked a woman holding a toddler in her lap. "I'm afraid to let my kids go outside and play. Am I supposed to keep them locked up inside all day?"

"The killings have only happened late at night, so we're asking everyone to stay indoors after dark. Don't go out unless you absolutely have to. No camping, no late night get-togethers, no roaming around in the woods at night and no hunting. I don't want anyone out there in the woods trying to be vigilantes. Let us handle it."

"It's summer," said the man in the back. "You can't expect us to sit inside all night and do nothing."

"We feel it's best, for right now anyway, if everyone would please abide by these guidelines. They're being suggested in order to keep you safe. We don't know who or what we are dealing with right now and we don't want anyone else getting hurt," Taryn said. "As of this evening, I am setting a nine o'clock curfew until we catch the culprit doing this."

"You can't do that!" shouted the man. "It's summertime. We have a right to be out enjoying ourselves."

"Sir," Taryn said, losing her patience. "Do you want to be next? Is that what you want? Do you want one of your family members to be next? Or one of your friends? If not, then please stay inside your homes starting at nine o'clock tonight." Taryn knew the man was planning on arguing with her some more, so she quickly added, "Thank you for your time, everyone. When we get more information, we'll let you know."

Taryn turned off the mic and slammed it down on the table.

Ron and Troy stood up and began walking among the townsfolk trying to soothe the angry ones and offer comfort to the scared ones.

Taryn's temper had gotten the better of her and she felt ashamed for losing it at the end, but sometimes she just didn't understand people. Why was it so hard to follow safety precautions? Why couldn't everyone just realize it was for their own good?

Penny and Cheryl walked up to her as she was folding up the chairs where she, Ron and Troy had sat.

"Rough crowd," Penny said.

"You handled it better than I would have," Cheryl said.

"I lost my cool," Taryn said. "I was trying not to do that."

"You did the best you could under the circumstances," Penny said. "Wanna go get a milkshake over at Tom's?"

Taryn was glad for the distraction, so she happily accepted the invitation.

As they sat in their booth talking and enjoying their frozen treats, the man from the meeting, as well as several other men Taryn didn't recognize, came up to their table.

"I want you to know, Sheriff," he said, looking down at her in what Taryn took as a threatening manner. "Me and the boys here are going out hunting. We're gonna bag us this killer and do your job for you."

"Sir," Taryn said, rising up out of her seat and leaning in toward him. "If I catch you out after dark or get wind of you hunting anywhere in this county, I will arrest you and charge you with everything I can."

"You do what you have to do, Sheriff," he growled, "But you ain't gonna stop us."

"Watch me," Taryn threatened. "Get out of here before I arrest you for public disturbance."

The man sneered at her and stepped back, signaling for his friends to do the same. "If you ain't gonna do your job, we'll do it for you." With that, the men left the restaurant.

"Do either of you know who that man is?" Taryn asked Penny and Cheryl.

"Never seen him before," Cheryl said.

"I heard someone at the meeting call him Clint, but other than that, no," Penny said.

Just then, Taryn noticed Vince sitting at the counter looking over at them. Taryn nodded at him, so he got up and came over.

"That guy's a real jerk, huh?" he said to the three of them.

"Do you know him?" Penny asked.

"Not personally, but I know *of* him," Vince said. "His name's Clint Brogan. He's a real hothead who likes to hang out at Roger's Bar over off of River Road."

"Is he bad news?" Taryn asked.

"Mostly just likes to run his mouth," Vince said. "He's all talk, but no action, if you know what I mean. I wouldn't take him seriously. He's full of hot air."

"Do I need to worry about him running off into the woods hunting this thing?" Taryn asked.

"I doubt it," Vince said. "He acts all tough, but he's really just a coward. He'll probably take your threat to heart and stay home, tucked in his house, quaking in his boots, scared to actually take a step outside."

"I hope so," Taryn said. "Even though I don't care much for the man, I'd hate to see him killed."

"If it would make you feel better to check on him, he lives off Mehaffey Road, up past the Sturgill's place."

"Thanks, Vince," Taryn said. "I appreciate it."

"No problem," he said. "Happy to help."

The four of them sat in the booth and talked until the sun was beginning to set.

Taryn had put in a call to Ron and asked him to print up some fliers to hang around town announcing the curfew. As she walked back toward the station where her car was parked, she noticed that he had already got them placed in several of the local business's windows.

She reached her car just as the sun was dipping behind the hills.

It must be right around nine o'clock, Taryn thought as she climbed into her SUV and started to head toward home.

Taking a detour, she decided to run passed Clint Brogan's place and make sure he really wasn't organizing a posse to go out tonight.

She followed Mehaffey Road till she passed Henry Sturgill's place. Driving a little ways farther up the road, she found Clint's place.

A single wide trailer sat back off the road at the end of a dirt driveway. A rusted out car sat up on blocks in the front yard, almost completely covered by overgrown weeds. Household trash was scattered all across the yard and broken lawn furniture was piled up on the tiny front porch.

A single light shone in what Taryn assumed was the living room, but no one seemed to be home.

Taryn turned around and decided a check on Benji and Gerti was probably a good idea, too.

By the time she reached the Willis home, it was dark. She knew she was breaking her own curfew, but she really wanted to check on Benji.

Pulling up to the house, she was just getting out of her car when Benji opened the front door and stepped outside onto the porch.

"Hey, Sheriff," he said to her. "Something wrong?"

By the looks of him, he wasn't in much better shape than when she'd seen him earlier.

"Hi Benji," Taryn said, stepping up onto his porch. "I just wanted to stop by and check on you and your mama."

"Mama's not here right now," Benji said. "She went to visit her sister over in New Lafayette."

"Will she be spending the night over there?"

"Yeah," Benji said. "Why?"

"There's a nine o'clock curfew," Taryn said. "I don't want anyone out after dark for awhile."

Benji just stared at her with his mouth hanging open.

"Benji?"

"Does that apply to me, too?" he asked her.

"Yes, it does. I don't want you out roaming around at night right now."

"I told you I was going to hunt down that monster that killed Ginny Lee."

"I know you did," Taryn said. "But I'd prefer if you didn't. I don't want to have to arrest you for breaking curfew."

"You are," Benji said, looking up at the sky. "It's past nine and you're out."

"I'm on my way home. I wanted to stop in and check on you, though. Promise me you won't go out, Benji. I don't want to see you get hurt."

"I ain't making promises I can't keep."

"Benji, please."

"Someone's gotta get the guy that did that to Ginny Lee."

"We will," Taryn said. "I didn't know you still had feelings for her."

"Well, I do...did," Benji said.

"I'm so sorry," Taryn said. "By the way, do you know Clint Brogan?"

"Clint? Sure," Benji said. "He was just over here about an hour ago. Why?"

"He was threatening to get a posse together and go hunting tonight. Is that why he was here?"

"Maybe," Benji said, hedging her question.

"If he was trying to get you to join them, I really hope you're smarter than that."

"I don't hunt with other people," Benji said. "I hunt alone."

"I'm glad to hear you won't be joining them tonight then."

"No, ma'am," Benji said. "But that don't mean I ain't going out."

Taryn just shook her head. "Since I obviously can't stop you, would you please do me a favor?"

"What favor?"

"Please, be careful. If you see or hear anything out of the normal, get home. Get home as quick as you can."

"Sure thing, Sheriff."

"Oh, and Benji?"

"Yeah?"

"Don't make me arrest you. If you go out, I don't want to hear about it."

"You know I'm going out, though. Why aren't you arresting me now?"

"I can't arrest you for saying you're going out. I would have to catch you while you were out. Don't let me catch you out."

Benji put his head down and chuckled. "You're alright, Sheriff. You're a good person. And don't worry, you'll never catch me out."

Taryn smiled and shook her head. "Good night, Benji."

"Good night, Sheriff."

Taryn turned out of the drive and headed toward home.

It was so dark tonight. No stars shone in the sky. No moon was visible. It was creepy.

Maybe it was knowing that someone or something was out there stalking the town, but Taryn felt uneasy. She felt like she was being watched all the time. A chill ran up her spine.

It was unsettling to know that when she got home she would be alone. All alone. In the house. By herself. Out in the middle of nowhere. Alone.

Mentally shaking her head, she realized she was spooking herself.

"Get a grip," she said, out loud. "You're the sheriff. You have a gun. Nothing is going to hurt you."

Her small pep talk didn't work.

As she pulled into her drive and parked, she sat in the car and looked around. No movement anywhere. Everything looked normal. But she still felt uneasy, like something wasn't right. Like she was being watched.

She swung the car door open and jumped out as quick as she could and bolted for the front door.

Fumbling with her keys, she tried to find the right one. She gawked around making sure she wasn't being sneaked up on by some unknown entity.

When the key finally slid into the lock, she turned it quickly and flung the door open, almost falling to the floor in her haste.

Slamming the door shut behind her, she slid the lock into place and leaned against the door.

Taking a deep breath, she was thankful to be safe and sound inside.

Hidden back among the trees, the figure turned and disappearing into the night.

Chapter 12

Taryn awoke to the sound of gunshots in the distance.

"Those stupid men," she grumbled to herself. "They're gonna get themselves killed."

Flopping over on her side, she looked at her alarm clock.

3:31 a.m.

Groaning, she rolled over and pulled the covers up over her head.

She knew they were out there hunting for the killer. And she knew, no matter what Vince said, Clint Brogan was the leader of the group.

Coward, or not, he had organized a hunt party and they were now, at 3:30 in the morning, out there firing off their guns and doing who knew what else.

Anger built up inside her. She would have to go pay a visit to Mr. Brogan tomorrow and if he was, indeed, out there hunting, she would arrest him for breaking curfew.

She knew if it was him, he'd brag about it. That was enough for her to slap him in jail for a night...or two.

~~~~~

Those idiots. How dare they think they can hunt me down. Don't they know their bullets can't kill me? Even when I'm in my human form, I'm invincible.

I watch them stomp through the woods from my hiding place. Several of them walk right past me and don't even see me hunkered down in the undergrowth.

They didn't realize I was the one they were hunting when they came around recruiting men for the hunt earlier this evening. They even made mention of where the hunt was going to take place.

Too easy. If any of them had been one of the ones on my list, tonight would have been the perfect setting for taking them out. I could still take one or two out just for the fun of it, but no. No hunting for me tonight. It's too much fun watching these idiots out here puffing up their chests, acting like half cocked roosters. I don't want to miss all this fun.

I hear Clint say how he's going to blast me into the next life. Fat chance, Bucko.

He passes by me so close I can smell his aftershave.

Idiot. Don't you know when you hunt that you aren't supposed to wear anything that gives off a scent?

Amateurs.

One of the so called hunters fires his gun off into the darkness claiming he sees an animal. He isn't even sure what he saw. He just randomly fired his gun at something that moved. He's going to end up killing someone.

But they won't be bringing home any trophy kills tonight.

In fact, as I made my way to Wilson's Grove where the hunt was to begin, I chased off any animal that was in the area. No sense in any poor, defenseless animal being taken out by these boneheaded, want-to-be warriors.

After stalking them through the woods for several hours, I decide to slink off and leave them to their hunt.

I cross the deserted road that leads to her house.

I watched her come home from work last night. She was out past curfew.

No worries. She made it home safely.

I think she sensed me, though. Her gaze kept darting around and she booked it to her porch and got inside quickly. Even from where I was standing in the shadows of the trees, I heard her slam the lock into place.

Doesn't she know*? Doesn't she* feel *that I would never hurt her? I just wanted to make sure she got home safely.*

It's now about 3:30 in the morning. I've been out all night following those stupid hunters around making sure they didn't come near her house.

I know she's sleeping, but I just want to see her. I want to know *she's safe. She's my only concern.*

As I approach her house, there are no lights on.

I was afraid that the dumb egg firing off his gun would have awoken her.

But everything is dark. Everything is still.

I creep along the side of the house, careful not to step on anything that might alert her to my presence.

Crap. A twig. Maybe she didn't hear it.

Reaching the back of the house, I see that she still hasn't opened the curtains or the window like she had done before.

Blast it all.

I may not be able to see her after all.

But I have to try.

I inch my way along the house until I'm standing outside her bedroom window.

I lean in and try to peer around the curtains.

Awww, the curtains weren't closed all the way. There's a thin sliver between the panels. I press my eye to the tiny opening and peer in.

There she is. She's bundled up under the covers, but I can see her shape laying there.

She is so tiny, but so strong. What a woman. I've never admired a person so much.

Love? Yeah, I guess I do.

She shifts under the covers and before I have time to back away, she pulls them down off her head and catches me looking in at her.

I back away quickly and take off running.

She wasn't meant to see me. I don't want her to know I'm watching her.

As I run off into the woods, her scream follows me.

I'm sorry, Taryn. I never meant to scare you.

~~~~~

A rustle of leaves outside her bedroom window. The snap of a small twig.

Someone was outside her bedroom window.

Better not be those hunters, Taryn thought as she shifted under the covers, trying to pull them down off her head where she had pulled them up earlier.

Finally managing to free herself, she gazed at the window at the foot of her bed. There was a small opening between the curtains and as she stared at it, she saw a dark shadow moved swiftly past. The shadow was big enough to cover the whole window.

Before she realized what she had done, Taryn let out a scream so loud it hurt her own ears.

Jumping from the bed, she grabbed her gun off the nightstand and rushed over to the window.

Throwing back the curtain, she aimed her gun at the glass and yelled, "Get out of here!"

She stood trembling in her pajamas holding her gun out in front of her for several moments before she let out the breath she was holding and dropped her arms to her sides.

Did she imagine it? It was dark outside. Maybe it was just the shadow of her curtains. But curtains didn't dart off when you screamed. Someone was there. Taryn knew it in her gut. Someone had been standing outside her bedroom window watching her sleep.

Jerking the curtains closed and making sure no gap was left, she quickly got dressed and went out to her living room.

She knew she wouldn't be getting any more sleep tonight.

Picking up her phone, she punched in Rhobby's number. On the third ring, she quickly hung up. What was she doing? She couldn't call Rhobby. That wouldn't do her any good. She was just scared and didn't want to be alone.

"You're a big girl," she told herself. "You don't need Rhobby here to chase away the monsters. You have a gun and you know how to use it."

Easing herself onto the couch, she pulled the blanket off the back and cuddled down into the cushions. Flipping on the television, she turned to an old classic movie channel. Maybe if she watched tv for awhile, she would be able to calm down enough to go back to bed. Maybe.

Taryn woke to the sound of her phone ringing.

"Hello," she said groggily, after fishing around on the couch trying to locate the device.

"Taryn?" said Rhobby's voice through the phone. "Are you ok? I saw you tried to call last night."

"Oh, I'm sorry," Taryn said. "I must have sat on the phone and butt dialed you or something." She hated to lie, but in the light of day, her fear of shadows during the night seemed a bit ridiculous and she didn't want to admit to him that she had been scared and he was the first person she had thought to call.

"Oh," he said, sounding disappointed.

Taryn didn't say anything, but waited to see if he was going to say anything more.

"Would you be interested in meeting up with me later for dinner or something?" he asked her, a hint of hope in his voice.

"Rhobby, I don't think that's a good idea."

A deep sigh on the other end of the phone let Taryn know that he had already known the answer before he'd even asked it.

"Why don't you ask Norma Sue?" Taryn bit out. The stress of the last few days was beginning to wear on her, but she regretted the words as soon as they were out of her mouth. "I'm sorry. That was uncalled for," she said. "I've been under a lot of stress lately and I didn't mean to take it out on you."

"Taryn, when are you going to forgive me for that?"

"I don't know. Maybe never."

"I gotta go," Rhobby said, sounding defeated. "I gotta get ready for work."

He hung up before she could say another word.

Throwing the phone down on the couch she huffed off to her bedroom to get dressed.

Sitting down on the end of the bed, she pulled her socks on.

As she sat there, her gaze went up to the window. Had she really seen a shadow through the slit in the curtains or was her imagination playing tricks on her. With the strange killings and talk of shape shifters and werewolves, she had to admit she was letting some of it get to her. She was creeping herself out.

"One way to find out," she said out loud to herself. "Gotta go look and see if there's anything out there that would suggest someone was standing outside my window last night."

After getting her uniform on, she slipped her feet into her boots and stepped out onto the front porch. The sky was a brilliant, clear blue. A soft breeze blew across her face as she took in her surroundings.

Nothing seems out of place this morning. Nothing seemed to cause any tingling up her spine or chills to snake through her veins.

Stepping off the porch, she headed around to the back of the house where her bedroom window was.

As she walked, she scanned the ground for any evidence that someone had been there.

The path around the house was hard packed dirt. Too hard for anyone to leave any tracks. Small twigs and branches were laying across the ground and leaves from the overhanging trees were scattered about, but no visible signs of a person having walked through here.

Reaching the window, she examined the ground under it, but the ground seemed undisturbed.

She leaned in to look closely at the window, but nothing she saw gave her reason to believe someone had been there.

"See?" she scolded herself. "You're freaking out about nothing. You're spooking yourself."

Making her way back to the front of the house, she told herself she needed to start watching comedies or reading a funny book before bed to get her mind off all the unpleasant things going on lately. Maybe if she did, she wouldn't keep scaring herself and her mind would stop conjuring up shadows outside her window that didn't exist.

~~~~~

When she got to work, she threw the door open to the station and stomped inside.

"Something wrong, Boss?" Ron asked.

"Yeah. Everything," Taryn said, harsher than she had intended. "Sorry. I didn't sleep well last night, due in part to gunshots being fired in the woods near my place."

"You're kidding," said Troy. "Someone decided to go against curfew and go out hunting anyway, huh?"

"Of course," Taryn grumbled. "There always has to be some jerk who just can't abide by the rules."

"Any idea who it was?" Ron asked.

"Oh, I have a pretty good idea, alright," Taryn said. "Clint Brogan."

"What are you going to do?" Troy asked.

"I'm going to take a run out to his place and have a talk with him," Taryn said.

"Want me to come along?" Ron asked.

"Yes," Taryn said. "He tried to act intimidating and tough toward me at Tom's last night. I'd prefer some backup in case things get out of hand."

"I heard he was going around town last night gathering up guys to go on the hunt with him," Cheryl said.

"I wouldn't doubt it," Taryn said. Turning to Ron, she motioned toward the door. "Let's get some coffee and donuts from Pandy's and then head out that way."

Taryn let Ron drive while she woofed down her crème buff and gulped down her coffee. She figured she needed the caffeine to keep her awake. Last night's lack of sleep was already catching up to her. The sugar rush from the donut wouldn't hurt either.

They arrived at Clint's house a little after nine o'clock. Taryn reached over and laid on the horn.

"What are you doing?" Ron asked.

"He kept me up last night firing his gun, so I'm going to wake him up by blowing the horn. Fair is fair, right?"

Ron chuckled as he stepped out of the car.

Clint opened the trailer door and stumbled out onto the porch. "What's going on out here?"

"Clint Brogan," Taryn spoke loudly. "Were you out hunting last night?"

"Why, no, Sheriff," Clint said, rubbing his eyes. "You told me there was a curfew, didn't you?"

Taryn glared at him. "I know you were out. You're too stupid to obey a simple curfew."

"Maybe I was, maybe I wasn't," Clint said, sneering at her. His limp, greasy hair clung to his head and the clothes he had on looked like he'd slept in them.

"If I find out that you were, I will be back," Taryn threatened.

"It's not my fault you can't, or won't, do your job," Clint taunted. "But since you won't, then it's up to me and some of my boys to do it."

"So," Taryn said. "You admit you did go out last night?"

"So what if we did," Clint said. "We didn't find nothing. We didn't kill anything."

"Ron, you know what to do," Taryn said.

"Clint," Ron said, walking up to him. "You're under arrest for breaking curfew."

"You can't prove I went out," Clint said.

"You just admitted that you did," Taryn said. "You heard him, didn't you, Ron?"

"Sure did, Boss."

"Maybe some time sitting in a cell will make you come to realize the error of your ways," Taryn said.

"Ok, now, wait a minute," Clint said. "What if I promise not to go out again? Will you just let me go with a warning?"

"Not a chance," said Taryn. "You threatened me last night and I told you what would happen if you went out."

"Oh, come on, now," Clint bellowed. "I heard you were a nice cop."

"I am as long as you don't break the law," Taryn said, opening up the back door of the cruiser to allow Ron to help Clint into the backseat.

Once Clint was in and buckled up, Taryn slammed the door.

"Ohhh, that felt good," Taryn said under her breath to Ron.

"Tell me about it," Ron said. "A couple days sitting in jail should cool his heels."

After putting Clint in one of the cells in the back of the station, Taryn stopped up at Cheryl's desk.

"I need to get some stuff done in my office this afternoon," she told her. "Please don't disturb me unless it's an emergency, ok?"

"Sure," Cheryl said. "Rough day?"

Cheryl had the uncanny ability to see through Taryn's lies sometimes.

"Yeah, you could say that. Please just give me a couple of hours to get some stuff done and be alone for awhile."

"No problem," Cheryl said.

Taryn hadn't wanted to admit to Cheryl or the guys that her nerves were shot and she was in desperate need of some down time. With the killings, the town meeting, the hunters out last night and her problems with Rhobby, she was feeling out of sorts and needed some time to compose herself.

After sending Ron and Troy out to patrol the town, she quietly closed her office door and plopped down in her chair.

Hot tears streamed down her face as soon as she sat down. She just let them come.

She didn't know why she was letting everything get to her. She was usually a strong woman who could handle her job, her home life and everything else without much problem. So why was she having such a hard time lately?

Rhobby.

It was Rhobby, of course.

She didn't want to admit it even to herself, but it all came crashing down around her as she sat there crying.

She knew she was still in love with him. She knew she always would be. He had been the love of her life and still was.

She missed his hugs. She missed the smell of his skin when they snuggled up together at night. She missed the sound of his laughter. She missed him being there when she got home from work. She missed him. Period.

She never told him, but she had called Norma Sue several weeks ago and asked her if it really was over between her and Rhobby. Norma Sue had told her that she had ended it with Rhobby awhile back because she believed that Rhobby wasn't in love with her, but, was in fact, still in love with Taryn. They had gotten into a big fight over it, so she left town and didn't plan on coming back.

Taryn should have taken comfort in that, but she didn't. Her mind kept running over the fact that if Norma Sue came back to town, Rhobby might go running back to her, leaving her brokenhearted all over again. She was just too scared to take the risk.

As she sat there crying, her heart began to ache even more. Who had she called last night when she was scared?

Rhobby.

Who was it that she wished was there the last time she had gotten scared.

Rhobby.

Every time he called or came around, it seemed to break down her resolve even more. It was getting harder and harder to tell him no.

A dreaded realization was beginning to dawn on her. She was thinking of taking him back. Giving him another chance. Taking the risk.

Oh, she wouldn't just let him move back in, but the idea of accepting his invitation for a date was beginning to really appeal to her.

No wonder she was such a mess. She was letting her guard down and felt vulnerable. But, life was all about risks, right? You never know what might happen if you don't take the chance.

A heavy weight seemed to lift off her shoulders as she accepted the truth.

She wanted Rhobby back.

Drying her eyes, she took several deep breaths and picked up the phone.

"Here goes nothing," she said to herself as she punched in Rhobby's number.

~~~~~

Taryn stood in front of the mirror and scrutinized her appearance.

She had taken a shower after work and slipped into her favorite pair of jeans and a casual, yet stylish, soft pink shirt.

Her curls were still wet, so she simply used some combs and piled them on top of her head. Rhobby always said he liked it when she wore her hair that way.

She wasn't much into makeup, but she applied a small amount of mascara to her lashes and smeared a strip of pink lipstick across her lips.

Smacking her lips together, she quickly grabbed some toilet paper and wiped the lip stick off. She felt awkward with it on, like she was a teenager going on her first date.

Rhobby was her husband. Ex-husband, but still. She wanted him to be impressed with the way she looked, but she didn't want to look ridiculous or out of character for herself.

She sat on the couch and fiddled with the remote on the tv waiting for him to arrive.

Glancing at the clock, she realized he should be there any minute now. Her hands were clammy and she kept biting her bottom lip.

Why was she so nervous? She was beginning to feel ridiculous for getting dressed up for him. He had seen her in everything from her uniform to her old, ripped up house clothes. He wasn't going to care what she was wearing. Would he?

She was just starting to get up and go back to her room and change when she heard his pickup pull into the drive.

Chapter 13

Taryn greeted Rhobby at the door.

She noticed that his hair was slightly damp and his shirt was freshly pressed.

She felt a stab of relief that she wasn't the only one who was nervous. He had obviously taken the time to make sure he looked nice, too.

"I'm glad you called," he said.

"I'm still scared about all this, but I want to give it a try,. No promises, though," Taryn said. She felt it was best to be up front with him. She didn't want him thinking they were just going to pick up where they'd left off.

"You look nice," he said. "It's been awhile since I saw you dressed up."

"Thank you. You look nice, too."

Rhobby stepped closer and leaned in and gave her a quick, superficial hug. It felt awkward, but Taryn hugged him back as best she could. He was so familiar, yet so foreign to her now. She wanted to fall back into his arms and let go of all the hurt and pain, but she knew she had to take this one step at a time or risk getting hurt again.

She took in his appearance more closely now that he was standing so close. He was clean shaven and she could smell his aftershave. Nice, she thought. She had always liked the way he smelled. His jeans fit him well and the shirt he wore was tucked neatly into his pants.

Taryn had almost forgotten how sexy and handsome he was.

Almost.

Smiling up at him, she stepped from in front of the door and invited him in.

"Uh, Taryn," he said. "I thought maybe we could go for a walk. Help break the ice, you know?"

"Oh, sure," Taryn said, a little embarrassed. "Just up the road, or did you have somewhere else in mind?"

"Up the road is fine. It's a beautiful evening," he said, looking up at the sky.

Taryn had asked him to be at her house by seven. That gave her plenty of time to get cleaned up after work and get a quick bite to eat before he arrived. He hadn't said anything about going out for dinner, so she figured tonight would be a night to reacquaint themselves, instead of enjoying a meal together.

Shyly, she slipped her hand through his arm as he led her off the porch and down the driveway.

They slowly headed up the road. At first, Taryn didn't think Rhobby was going to talk. Just as the silence was beginning to get a little uncomfortable, he spoke up. "I want you to know I never loved Norma Sue."

Taryn looked down at the ground. She knew this was going to be a painful talk, but she braced herself and looked up at him. "Why did you do it, then?"

"I was stupid," Rhobby said. "You were working all the time and I got lonely. I got tired of being alone all the time. It was no excuse."

"My job hasn't changed," Taryn said. "There are times when I have to work late or I get called out at all hours of the night. What if you get lonely again?"

"Taryn, I realize the fault wasn't yours. Being lonely is no reason to run off to someone else. I was being selfish. I'd like to think I've done some growing up over the last year."

"But what if you get lonely again?" Taryn pressed. "Are you going to go find someone else again?"

"If I get lonely, I'll get a dog," Rhobby said. "I realized something through all this. I love you, Taryn. Only you. I've been miserable since you left. I don't want anyone else. Just you."

Taryn felt tears threaten, but she refused to let them flow.

Blinking several times, she gently squeezed his arm, unable to speak. Her throat felt tight and it burned from trying to hold back the tears.

"I know it will take time and work to get 'us' back together, but I'll do whatever I need to do to make it happen," Rhobby said.

Taryn found her voice and whispered, "I want 'us' back, too. Please just be patient with me."

"I'll give you all the time you want," Rhobby said. "As long as you're willing to work on it, you take all the time you need."

He leaned down and placed a kiss on the top of her head. It was such an endearing, familiar gesture that she finally couldn't hold the tears back anymore.

"Hey," Rhobby said, concerned. "Are you crying?"

Taryn used to the back of her hand to wipe away the tears that had fallen down her cheek. "Yes," she said. "But they're tears of hope."

They walked farther along road and talked about their day. Taryn could only handle so much emotion at a time and decided to change the topic for awhile to help calm her nerves.

She told him about the killings. About what Dr. Middleton had told her about both human and wolf DNA being found on the victims. She told him about the hunters being out in the woods last night and how she thought someone had been outside her window.

"No wonder you've been so stressed lately," Rhobby told her. "You've got a lot going on right now."

"Too much for such a sleepy little town," Taryn said.

"Any possible suspects yet?"

"None," Taryn said. "Not one. We don't have a single lead."

Rhobby pulled her hand through the crook of his arm even tighter. "I don't like the idea of you being out here in the woods all by yourself with all this going on."

"What do you suggest?" Taryn asked. She was hoping he wasn't suggesting he move back in. Not yet. They still had a long way to go before that could happen.

"How about a dog?"

Taryn felt relief flood through her. A dog. Whew. She was glad he had suggested that instead of what she feared he was going to ask.

"I don't think a dog would be a good idea," she said. "I'm gone too much of the time and I wouldn't want to have it locked up in the house all day or be chained outside."

"Yeah, you're probably right," Rhobby agreed. "What about a home security system?"

"I can't afford that on my salary," Taryn told him.

"We'll come up with something," Rhobby told her.

The sun was sinking low on the horizon and long, deep shadows were beginning to creep across the road in front of them. Crickets began their nightly chirping and small flashing specks of light from fireflies could be seen dotting the edge of the woods along the road.

"I think it's getting close to curfew," she told Rhobby. "We'd better be heading back."

Glancing at his watch, he lifted his eyebrows as he looked down at her. "It's past nine," he said. "We broke curfew."

"We'd best get back quickly then before someone sees us," Taryn said, chuckling. "It wouldn't be good for anyone to catch the sheriff out after curfew."

They had walked about a mile out the road and it would take them several minutes to get back if they hurried, but Taryn didn't want the night to end. It was the first time in a long time that she felt happy. Truly happy. It was so nice being with Rhobby again and she was in no hurry to get back and have it end. She knew that once they reached her house, he would leave for the night. She just wasn't ready to say goodbye yet.

"Let's walk back through the woods," she suggested.

"What? Why?"

"That way, no one will see us if they happen to drive by."

"No one should be out now. Not if they obey the curfew," Rhobby said.

"True, but a lot of people will ignore the order," Taryn said. "I'm just not ready to go back yet."

Rhobby looked down at her and smiled. "I'm not either," he said. "I've really enjoyed spending time with you tonight."

Taryn took him by the hand and pulled him into the woods.

"What about the killer?" he asked, suddenly nervous.

"We're together," Taryn said. "I have my gun on me. It's not that far to my house from here."

Rhobby reluctantly followed her deeper into the woods. What little light remained from the day didn't reach the interior of the trees. Deep, dark shadows loomed around them. Low hanging tree branches swaying in the unseen breeze. The smell of damp earth and rotting wood permeated the area.

Taryn suddenly regretted her decision. It was dark and eerie back in the trees. Every scurrying animal, every rustle of a tree leaf seemed to send her senses into overdrive.

"Rhobby," she said, with a slight tremble in her voice. "Maybe this wasn't such a good idea after all."

"We're here now," he said, squeezing her hand in a comforting effort. "Let's just hurry and get back to your house."

They stepped deeper into the woods and soon found an animal trail that allowed them to move through the trees with less effort.

The sun had completely dropped down behind the trees now, throwing them into total darkness, making their progress slow and tedious.

"I'm really starting to think this was a bad idea," Taryn said, gripping Rhobby's arm tightly between her fingers. "I can't see anything and it's creepy back in here."

"It's ok," Rhobby said. "We'll be back at your place soon."

As they walked deeper and deeper into the woods, moonlight was beginning to peek through the tops of the trees offering a silvery glow to the spots on the ground where it was able to penetrate the thick trees.

They stepped into one of these silvery patches when Taryn jerked on Rhobby's arm to get him to stop.

"What it is?" he asked, turning to face her.

"Listen," was all Taryn said.

"Listen to what? I don't hear anything."

"Exactly," Taryn said on a shaky whisper.

"What's wrong?"

"Where did all the crickets go?" Taryn asked. "Where did all the normal night noises go?"

They stood still and listened. No crickets, no birds, no small woodland creatures could be heard. An eerie stillness fell over the area. The only sound Taryn could hear was her own breathing.

"Rhobby," she said, barely above a whisper. "Something's out here with us."

Rhobby gently placed his hands on her arms and pulled her to him. "It's ok," he said, softly. "You've got your gun, right?"

Taryn nodded and mumbled, "Yeah."

A fear unlike anything she had ever felt before washed over her. She could feel the hair on the back of her neck stand up and her blood suddenly turned to ice. She couldn't seem to draw in a breath of air. Her whole body trembled in fright.

Rhobby felt her body tighten, so he pulled her into his arms and hugged her close to his chest. "Time to get out of here," he said.

Taryn started to step back from Rhobby's embrace just as something huge and dark loomed up behind him. She saw it over his shoulder, but she never heard it coming.

Everything happened so fast, she didn't have time to react or pull her gun.

A grotesque expression crossed Rhobby's face as he was jerked out of her arms and hurled to the side. A wrenching scream tore from his throat as he landed several feet away.

Taryn felt something hot and wet splash across her face. She knew it was Rhobby's blood. The metallic smell of it filled her nostrils.

Unable to move, she dropped to the ground as a huge, black monster stepped in front of her. Its enormous back paws stomping down on either side of her, it reared its head back and howled. The low, deep sound reverberated through the woods and echoed off the hills in the distance.

Sheer terror paralyzed Taryn, making it impossible for her to move. The werewolf's massive body loomed over her as she laid on the ground looking up at it. Red glowing eyes glared menacingly down at her. A long snout curled back to reveal long, razor sharp fangs. Long, massive, muscular arms reached out for her, the talons extended. Blood dripping from the claws at the end of it's massive hand.

The last thing Taryn registered was the monster stopping in the middle of its impending attack and lurching backward away from her. It looked at her for a moment, confusion crossing it's features, then turned and bolted off into the darkness.

Taryn watched in horror as the monster disappeared out of sight. Her whole body was trembling and she couldn't breathe. Her heart was pounding so hard, her chest hurt. A wave of dizziness washed over her almost causing her to pass out.

Finally catching her breath, she rolled over onto her side and saw Rhobby laying on his back several feet away. A lone, agonizing groan escaped his lips.

Quickly getting to her knees, she crawled over to him.

He was alive. The werewolf hadn't killed him. She could hear his labored breathing and see his chest rising, even in the dark.

Reaching him, she began frantically checking him over for wounds.

After a thorough search, all she found were deep claw marks across his chest.

His shirt was torn to shreds over the spot where the wounds were. Blood soaked the fabric and ran in rivulets down his side to soak into the ground.

Needing to staunch the flow of blood, Taryn quickly removed her shirt and pressed it to the wounds.

"Rhobby?"

"Yeah…," his voice was weak and muffled.

"Can you move?" Taryn asked. "We need to get out of here."

"I think so," he said. "Taryn?"

"Yes?"

"Was that a werewolf?" Rhobby asked.

"Yes," Taryn said. "It was."

"I thought so."

With Taryn's help, Rhobby got to his feet. He was weak from losing so much blood, but he was able to stay on his feet.

Throwing his arm across her shoulders, Taryn began guiding him back to the animal trail that would lead them out of the woods.

Blood from Rhobby's gaping wounds ran down his chest and onto Taryn's shoulder and side. She was startled at the amount that seemed to flow from the deep gashes. She knew if she didn't get him to a hospital soon, he would die.

Not wanting to scare him, she tried to hurry him along, but the going was slow. He was losing blood at an alarming rate and he was getting weaker by the minute. His weight was beginning to take a toll on her and several times, she stumbled and almost fell.

Quickly regaining her footing, she pressed on, almost dragging him at times. She knew her strength was coming from adrenaline, otherwise, she would not have been able to support his weight. Fear of losing him, kept her going.

Casting nervous glances all around her, she watched every tree branch sway, every shadow that crawled along the forest floor.

The woods seemed to press in on them from all sides. It had gotten darker. The moon had slipped behind some clouds and it was getting increasingly difficult to follow the trail, but the normal woodland noises had returned. Crickets chirped, lightning bugs flashed their yellow lights and small animals could be heard scurrying across the ground. Taryn knew as long as they heard these sounds, they were safe.

They seemed to walk for hours before Taryn saw a break in the trees up ahead.

"We're almost there," she panted.

Breaking from the trees, Taryn knew it was just a short jaunt up the road to her house.

Rhobby had started stumbling and dragging his feet. Taryn didn't know how much farther he could go before he totally collapsed.

"Just a little farther," she coached him. "You can do it."

Finally, her porch light came into view. With a sigh of relief, she forced herself to half guide, half drag Rhobby up the drive to her SUV.

Leaning him against the side of the vehicle, she rushed into the house and grabbed her purse and keys.

By the time she got back to the SUV, Rhobby had slid to the ground, unconscious.

"Oh no," she said. "Come on, Rhobby. Wake up. I need your help. I can't lift you into the car by myself."

She placed her hands under his arm and tried lifting him. He was just too heavy. She watched helplessly as he slumped back down to the ground.

Tears began running down her cheeks. "Come on, Rhobby," she yelled. "Don't do this to me. I need your help. Please."

She leaned down and tugged on him again.

Somewhere off the in the distance she heard the terrifying howl of the wolf. It seemed to be coming from all around them. It echoed off the hills and through the trees. The low, deep sound resonating through her very bones.

Fear gripped her. Her breathing quickened and her heartbeat raced. Sweat broken out on her brow at the thought that the monster might still be close by.

With an unnatural strength, she heave-hoed until she had Rhobby in a standing position. Throwing open the door of the SUV, she shoved him in as best she could. He flopped onto his side with his head falling toward the driver's door. Lifting his legs, she shoved them in and slammed the door shut.

That howl could have come from anywhere. It unnerved her the way it seemed to surround her.

Running around to the driver's side, she flung open the door and dove in.

Rhobby's head was blocking her from getting into position to drive, so propping it up on her lap, she shoved the car into gear and backed up.

Not waiting for the vehicle to come to a complete stop, she threw it into gear and stepped on the gas. Dirt and gravel flew out from under her tires as she pulled out of the drive and tore off down the road toward the hospital.

The hospital was a good twenty to thirty minutes away.

Glancing down at Rhobby, she caught her breath. Even in the dim light from the dashboard, he looked pale and ghostly.

"Rhobby, remember when we first met?" she asked him. She hoped that by engaging him in a conversation, she might be able to comfort him. It gave her comfort as well, knowing he might be able to hear her even though he was unconscious. "That was the best day of my life."

She talked to him the whole way to the hospital, telling the story of how they met and regaling him with funny anecdotes of their first few years of marriage together.

When she pulled up to the emergency room entrance, she threw the car into park and dashed inside.

"I need help out here," she yelled, when she had entered the hospital. "Please, I need help!"

A nurse came over with a gurney and rushed out to the vehicle with Taryn.

He helped lower Rhobby out of the car and onto the gurney, then rushed off with him, leaving Taryn to stand outside the hospital doors alone.

Parking the car in the nearby parking area, she raced back inside and approached the front desk.

After being told she would have to wait, she took a seat in the waiting room and leaned her head back against the wall.

It was then that she realized she didn't have a shirt on. She was sitting in the hospital waiting room topless.

She looked down at her blood smeared body as a shiver ran through her. She was covered in Rhobby's blood.

Suddenly a wave of nausea overtook her and she leaned over the arm of her chair and heaved onto the floor.

A nurse came over and offered her a glass of water while an orderly cleaned up her mess.

"Is there someone you would like to call to come sit with you and bring you a change of clothes?" the nurse asked.

Taryn looked at him trying to clear her head. "Uh...yeah," she told him. "I have my phone. Thank you."

She reached into her purse and pulled out her phone.

Scrolling through her contacts, she found Penny's number.

It felt like hours and no one had come out to tell her how Rhobby was doing. Penny still hadn't arrived and Taryn's nerves were shot.

Pacing around the room with her arms folded over her bra in an attempt to cover herself, she glanced toward the nurse's station for the hundredth time. No one seemed to pay her any attention.

An elderly couple sitting across the room kept looking at her. She knew they must think she was crazy, running around without a shirt on.

Feeling self-conscious, she moved to the other side of the room and turned her back to them.

Just when her patience reached its limits, Penny came through the door. Holding a t-shirt in her hand, she took one look at Taryn and rushed over to her. "Oh my goodness, what happened?"

Taryn gratefully pulled the t-shirt over her head and sat down. She wasn't sure how much to tell Penny. It truly was an unbelievable story.

Finally deciding on the truth, she told Penny what had transpired that evening.

"A real werewolf?" Penny said, leaning in so the other people in the room wouldn't hear her. "That's unbelievable."

"I know," Taryn said. "I didn't believe it myself until I saw it with my own eyes."

"Why didn't it kill Rhobby...or you?"

"I have no idea," Taryn said, feeling her skin crawl at the memory. "I think it was going to, but it stopped when it looked at me."

"What are you doing to do?" Penny asked.

Taryn didn't get a chance to answer. The nurse who had helped her get Rhobby into the hospital approached her and knelt down in front of her. "Ma'am," he said. "Can I talk to you privately for a moment?"

Taryn looked at Penny, then nodded to the nurse.

He led her around a corner where they could be alone. "The doctor would like to talk to you about your husband. We need to know what happened out there," the nurse said. "His wounds are severe and all he keeps telling us is a werewolf attacked him."

Taryn ignored the fact that he'd said 'your husband'. Now wasn't the time to pick bones. "He's awake? He's going to be ok?" she asked, instead.

"Yes, ma'am," the nurse said. "He's awake and he's going to be fine, although, with a lot of stitches and time."

Taryn closed her eyes and let out a long, slow breath.

"Follow me," the nurse said. "You can see him now. The doctor is still in the room with him."

Taryn followed the nurse down a long hallway and through a set of doors. Turning left, he walked down to the second door and ushered her in.

"Mrs. Givens?" the doctor asked.

"Yes," Taryn said. "How is he?"

"He has deep gash wounds that go all the way to the bone. It took a lot of stitches to sew him up and we gave him a blood transfusion, but he'll recover," the doctor said.

Rhobby was laying on the bed with an IV inserted into the back of his right hand. He was deathly pale, but smiling at her.

She rushed over to the bed and leaned down and hugged him. "I'm so glad you're ok."

"I've been better, but the doc here says I'll live," Rhobby said, weakly.

"Mrs. Givens," the doctor said. "Can you tell us what happened to your husband? The loss of blood has made him a little delirious. He keeps telling us he was attacked by a werewolf."

Taryn looked at Rhobby and frowned. If he continued to talk like that, they would probably send him up to the psych ward.

"We were out in the woods and we were attacked by a black bear," Taryn said. "Came across it and must have scared it. It all happened so fast."

"The wounds he sustained are pretty severe. A normal bear couldn't do that."

"Well, it was a pretty big bear."

"Ok, I'll put it in his file," the doctor said, clearly not convinced by her story. "He's lucky the bear didn't kill him."

Taryn closed the door behind the doctor and went over to Rhobby. "You can't tell people you were attacked by a werewolf. They'll think you lost your marbles. Just tell people it was a bear until I can figure this thing out."

Rhobby looked at her and nodded. "Ok, I guess you're right."

A nurse walked in and informed them that Rhobby was being moved to a room upstairs. Taryn was distressed to find out that he would have to stay in the hospital for a few days. The doctor thought the wounds were too deep and severe for home care and would need several days to heal before he could tend to them himself.

Taryn got the room number and stepped back out to the waiting room to let Penny know what was going on.

"Are you staying here tonight?" Penny asked her. "Surely, you aren't going home alone?"

"I'm going to stay here tonight, but I need to go home and shower first," Taryn said. "Would you come with me?"

"I have a better idea," Penny said. "You can come to my house and shower and change clothes. I have plenty of things you can borrow. I don't think going back to your place out in the middle of nowhere is a good idea right now."

Taryn agreed. She didn't want to admit that going home scared the crap out of her.

~~~~~

After a quick shower at Penny's. She slipped into a t-shirt and a pair of sweatpants that Penny had laid out for her. They were a bit big, but Taryn didn't care.

Once back at the hospital, she made arrangements for a cot to be brought into Rhobby's room for her.

By the time she had fussed over Rhobby and made herself comfortable on the cot, she realized she had not called Ron or Troy. That would just have to wait till morning.

She laid back on the stack of pillows that were propped up on the cot and listened to the hums and whirs of the machinery that was attached to Rhobby.

The events of the evening finally caught up to her.

A werewolf. A real life werewolf.

What was she going to do? How do you kill a werewolf. Something Troy said seemed to try to surface to the forefront of her mind, but refused to reveal itself. It seemed to stay hidden in the gray area of her mind.

She closed her eyes and exhaustion finally overtook her. She had so many questions, but they would just have to wait till morning.

Chapter 14

Must kill. Tonight.

The blood thirst is becoming so strong. It's been a couple of days and I can't hold off any longer.

I...need...blood.

I...need...meat. Raw meat.

I pull my list out of my sock drawer. Only a few people left.

Tonight, it's…

Whose supposed to be tonight?

Looking at my list, I see the name. Oh…

How could I not know whose next?

What's wrong with me? I've never had a problem remembering who my next victim is. I've memorized the list, for Pete's sake!

I don't stand in front of the mirror tonight when I change. I don't need to. It's quick now. Like flipping a switch.

I rush out into the night. It's not quite dark yet. The cool air hits me in the face, but it doesn't cool down the fire burning in me.

Where am I going again? Oh yeah...

I stop on the dirt road and look around. No one's out tonight. The stupid curfew.

I sniff the air.

A deer. In the field next to me.

I don't want a deer. I want human flesh and blood.

I amble down the road, not sure of where I'm going again. I just want to kill.

Something.

Anything.

I walk for awhile. Then I hear it.

Humans.

In my woods.

Oh, good!

No need to wonder who I'm after tonight.

Someone has made it very easy for me.

I duck back into the woods and covertly move toward the sound of the humans. They are talking, laughing.

I'm very aware of the fact that my presence has silenced all the creatures of the forest. It was gotten so still. I wonder if the humans have noticed.

I inch my way closer.

Ahhh...there they are. Just up ahead. I can see them, even in the dark. They're huddled together.

A man and a woman.

I stalk them first. Circling slowly around them to plan my best avenue of attack.

They don't hear me. I'm able to move about with little, to no sound. They'll never know I'm here till it's too late.

Ahhh, the woman smells good. She will do. I need to satiate my lust for blood. She will do just nicely, indeed.

But first, I must get the man out of the way. He has moved in close to the woman.

I step up behind him and I see the woman look over his shoulder. She sees me.

Time to move in.

I thrust my arm out and wrap it around the man and dig my claws into his chest as deep as I can. I don't want him getting up and trying to stop me when I go for the woman.

Jerking my arm, I throw the man off to the side. I can feel his flesh rip beneath my claws. I love the feeling. I smell his blood as soon as I tear his flesh open.

Ahhh...a feeling of deep satisfaction comes over me. I will come back to him once I finish with the woman.

She has fallen to the ground. She hasn't run off.

Good. This makes it so much easier on me.

Stepping over to her, I place a foot on either side of her in case she decides to run. She won't get away from me, though. She couldn't outrun me if she tried.

She smells so good. So...familiar. Something in my brain warns me to stop.

Why? Why does she smell familiar? Who is this?

No matter. I need blood. Her blood.

I lean down to look into her face. I want to see the terror, the fear.

The smell of fear is like a drug to me.

I see her face.

I want to rip. I want to tear, but…

Wait…

Something in me stops me.

What? Why can't I kill her?

I'm ready. I've got my arms reaching out to grab her and sink my teeth into her tender flesh.

Why can't I bite her?

My mind is messed up.

I'm confused.

I stare down at her and awareness comes over me.

It's her.

I can't kill her.

I have to get a hold of myself. I can't hurt her. *What's happening to me? I'm losing control.*

I want so bad to rip her. To kill her. To taste her blood. I'm overwhelmed with the need of it.

But it's her.

Confusion swamps my mind.

Jumping back, I take off running. I run and run and run.

I have to get away from her. *I don't want to hurt* her.

I run through the woods not caring if I make noise. I have to get away from her. *Far away from* her.

Reaching my house, I collapse onto the ground just outside the door.

I'm panting. I'm out of breath. I'm angry.

What happened tonight?

What's wrong with me?
I almost killed her.
That just cannot happen again.
Getting to my feet, I throw my head back and let out a long, low howl.

Sorrow fills me. I am afraid now. If I had killed her, *I would never forgive myself.*

Something is wrong. Something is happening to me.

I need to go see the old crone in the woods.

She is the only one who can help me.
Soon...I must go soon.

Chapter 15

Taryn awoke when the nurse came in to check on Rhobby.

"Good morning," he said, as he checked the clipboard hanging at the foot of Rhobby's bed.

"Morning," Taryn said, groggily, rubbing her eyes. "What time is it?"

The nurse checked his watch and said, "It's just after 8."

"Thanks," Taryn said, getting up off the cot.

She waited until the nurse was done with Rhobby before she leaned over and gave him a kiss on his cheek. "Good morning," she whispered close to his ear.

"Good morning, Beautiful," Rhobby said.

"How are you feeling?"

"Like I was attacked by a werewolf." He tried to laugh, but his face scrunched up in pain and he laid his hand across his chest where the bandage was. "Ohhh, not a good idea to try to laugh. I'm really sore."

"You're going to be sore for awhile, I imagine," Taryn said.

"Taryn?" Rhobby asked, suddenly serious.

"Yeah," Taryn said.

"Do you know much about werewolves?"

"Uh, no. Why?" Taryn asked.

"I was clawed by one," Rhobby said. "Does that mean I'm going to turn into one?"

"No," came a voice from the doorway. "You'd have to get bit by one to turn into one."

Taryn turned to see Ron and Troy coming through the door.

"Hey guys," she greeted them. "I'm sorry I didn't call. I haven't had the chance yet."

"Hey, Boss," Ron said. "No need to apologize. Penny called to let us know what happened."

"But we want to hear it from you," Troy said.

Rhobby maneuvered himself into a sitting position while Taryn propped pillows up behind his back.

"Guys, I'm not sure you're going to believe this, but...," Taryn started.

"It's a werewolf, isn't it?" Troy asked.

"Keep your voice down," Taryn warned. "I don't want the hospital staff to hear this."

"I told you," Troy said, smugly.

"Well, I personally, am not happy you're right," Taryn said.

"You're lucky you both weren't killed," Ron said. "What happened?"

"We were out walking and it got late. I didn't want anyone to see us out past curfew, so we decided to take a shortcut through the woods. We were about half way back to my place when we were attacked," Taryn said.

"You should have known better than to be in the woods right now," Ron said. "You know about the animal attacks. Why would you risk it?"

"I guess I never thought it would happen to us," Taryn said. "It was only a little after nine. The attacks all happened much later in the evening."

"So how did you manage to not get killed?" Troy asked. "Don't get me wrong, I'm glad you didn't, but no one escapes a werewolf attack. How did you?"

"I honestly don't know," Taryn said. "It grabbed Rhobby and flung him off to the side. Then it stood over me and was about to attack, but it looked at me kind of funny, then took off."

"That's weird," Troy said.

"Tell me about it," Taryn said. "You should have been there. It was like it got all confused or something."

"Well, I'm just glad you two are ok," Ron said. "How bad are your wounds, Rhobby?"

"Doc said I needed over a hundred stitches and I lost a lot of blood, but I'll recover. I'll just have a few nasty scars on my chest," Rhobby said.

"Better a few scars than to be dead," Ron said.

Ron and Rhobby began a game of '*show me your scars*', so Taryn pulled Troy off to the side.

"You mentioned something before about a way to kill a werewolf," Taryn said. "What was it?"

"Silver," Troy said. "You need silver."

"Like a bullet?"

"Exactly."

"I wish I would have paid more attention when you were telling me all the werewolf lore," Taryn said.

"There isn't much to tell," Troy said. "Legend has it that a man can only turn into a werewolf on the full moon, but ours can obviously turn at will. It kind of breaks the rules, you know?"

"Will a silver bullet kill our werewolf?

"In theory," Troy said.

"Where would I go to find one of these silver bullets?" Taryn asked.

"You'll want to see Lyle Coburn over on Locust Run Road."

"That old gun shop?" Taryn asked.

"That's the one," Troy said.

"Can't you go get one for me?" Taryn asked.

"Nope, Lyle and I had a run in a couple years back," Troy said. "He wouldn't be happy to see me."

"He knows I'm the sheriff," Taryn said. "Will he help me?"

"Considering what you are there for, yes."

"Why do I have a bad feeling about this?" Taryn asked.

"Just be cool," Troy said. "Don't go in there acting like you're going to arrest him and you should be fine."

"If you know they are doing something illegal, why haven't you arrested them?" Taryn asked.

"They help us out sometimes with cases, if we agree to turn a blind eye to what all they do there," Troy said.

Taryn looked sideways at Troy. "We're going to have to have a talk about that later."

"I figured, but for now, Lyle has what you need, so don't look a gifted horse in the mouth."

Taryn shook her head and walked back over to the bed where Ron and Rhobby were still comparing injury stories.

Rhobby was starting to look a little gray skinned and tight around the mouth, so Taryn knew he was beginning to feel pain again and probably needed more meds.

"Ok, guys," she said. "Time to let Rhobby rest."

"Are you coming in to work today, Boss?" Ron asked.

"No," Taryn said. "If it's ok, I'm going to take today and tomorrow off to be here with Rhobby. Can you two handle things without me?"

"No problem," said Troy, as he winked at her. "We know you have a lot to do. By the way, are you guys back together?" He pointed his finger between Taryn and Rhobby. "Because if you are, congratulations."

Taryn looked at Rhobby and smiled. "We're working on things," she said.

"Well, we're happy for you," Ron said.

"Thanks guys," Taryn said. "If you need me, you got my number."

After Ron and Troy left, Taryn turned to Rhobby and noticed he had a grimace on his face and a bead of sweat was forming on his forehead. "You're in pain, aren't you?" she asked him.

"Yeah, it's pretty bad," Rhobby said, tightly.

"I'll go find the nurse," Taryn said. She headed out the door to go find the nurse's station.

Within minutes, the nurse had arrived and administered enough medication to make Rhobby very drowsy. Before he dozed off, he took Taryn's hand. "I don't want you going back to your house alone tonight."

"I have to go back eventually," Taryn said. "I'm scared about it, though. I won't deny that."

"Stay here with me," Rhobby said, his eyelids beginning to droop. "I want to know you're safe."

"I'll stay again tonight, but I'll have to go home tomorrow night," Taryn said. "I'll see if Penny can stay with me."

"I'd prefer you didn't go back at all till the werewolf is killed. You're in danger out there."

"I'm going to get a silver bullet," Taryn said. "Troy says that's the only way to kill it."

"Taryn," Rhobby said. "Please be careful. I don't want to lose you."

Rhobby laid his head back on his pillow and within seconds was sound asleep.

Taryn was glad the medicine knocked him out. She couldn't begin to imagine how bad his wounds hurt. The gashes had been deep and even with the stitches, they were red and raw looking.

Kissing her fingertips, she laid them on his chest. "I love you, Rhobby Allen Givens," she whispered. "I don't want to lose you either."

Chapter 16

I've waited impatiently all day for this, but it's finally time to go.

I wanted to go earlier, but work kept me late today.

No matter. Under the cover of darkness is better anyway. I don't want anyone seeing me out here. They might get suspicious.

I don't change into my wolf form tonight. There's no need to. I'm not on the hunt. After what happened last night, I'm still a little leery about changing. I don't want to lose control like that again. That simply cannot happen again. That's why I'm here.

Parking my car out of sight along the old service road, I get out and look around me. It doesn't look like anyone has been back in here recently.

The old, dirt road is overgrown with weeds, making it hard to get a car back in here.

But not impossible.

If someone had driven back in here over the last couple of days, the tire tracks would still be visible.

I sniff the air to make sure, though. No human scent in the air. Good.

As I make my way along the hidden path through the thick bramble of weeds and overgrowth, I notice that my senses seem overly strong tonight. I can hear the smallest of *critters scampering along the ground from a long way off. I hear insects that my normal human self would never be able to hear. My skin feels prickly and sensitive to the slightest touch.*

Something is wrong. My senses shouldn't be this strong. Not in my human form.

I walk for what feels like hours until I see a small pinprick of light coming from a single candle in a tiny window.

I've arrived.

Stepping out into the clearing that surrounds the old crone's house, I feel anger rise up from my inner most being. This was supposed to be a gift, but it's starting to feel more like a curse. What went wrong?

I was so excited to get what I came for last time that I blew off most of what she'd told me. Now I wish I'd listened.

Stepping up to the door, I raise my hand to knock, but before I can, the door slowly swings open on it's own.

It always creeps me out when it does that.

"Come in," came the gravelly voice of the old woman.

"You knew I was coming?" I ask.

"What are you here for this time," she asks, ignoring my question.

"Something's wrong with me," I say. "I got confused last night. I couldn't remember

what I was doing or who I was after. Why? What's happening to me?"

The old crone is sitting in her rocker in front of the fireplace, just like last time. The small kitten I had brought her is sleeping on a small, padded bed next to her.

Turning her head to look at me, she motions for me to come closer.

The room is stifling hot. She has a small fire burning in the fireplace with a pot hanging over it. A gurgling, bubbling sound seems to be emanating from it.

The pungent, sweet smell of drying herbs fills the room, mingled with an odd, earthy smell. It isn't necessarily a pleasant scent. It seems too strong and it's making my head feel like it's filled with cotton.

I step closer to her. The heat from the fire is stifling. I suck in a lungful of air that seems to burn my lungs and chokes me.

"You didn't listen," she says, as she leans forward and stirs whatever is in the pot.

"I'm listening now," I say, a little impatiently.

"How many times have you changed forms?"

"A few. Why?"

"How many times?" she asks again, firmly.

"I don't know, four or five," I say. "Maybe six."

"Don't you remember what I told you?" she asks. "I warned you that the more you change, the more you would become wolf-like. You would begin to lose your human self, eventually becoming nothing but the wolf."

"After only four or five times?" I ask, incredulously. "I figured it would take a lot longer for that to happen. I still have a few people on my list that I want revenge against. Are you telling me that if I continue turning into the wolf, I will lose the human side of myself altogether?"

"I warned you. I told you that could happen," she says, coldly. "You should have spaced out your killings. Not done them all within a few days of each other."

I stare at her, feeling my anger rising even higher. "Then do something!" I demand, taking a step toward her. "Make it stop."

"How bad has it gotten?" she asks. "Tell me what you're experiencing."

"I can turn into the wolf really quickly now, without any pain," I say.

"Go on," she says. "What else?"

"Last night, I kept forgetting who I was suppose to be going after. I ended up roaming around until I heard voices. I attacked a couple for no reason. They weren't even on my list."

I don't tell her about Taryn. She is a secret I'm not willing to share with anyone. Not even with the old crone.

"Did you kill them? Even though you weren't specifically after them?" the old woman asks.

"No, but I almost did," I say. "I felt confused and disoriented. Like I was losing control. I ended up running off."

"You will become more of the wolf as the moon gets fuller."

"Are you trying to tell me that I can't stop this? That I'm going to become fully a wolf and no human side of me will remain?"

"Yes," the old crone says. "As the moon gets fuller, the more wolfish you will become. On the night of the full moon, you will no longer have a human side left."

"Then do something," I demand again. "Make it stop."

"I can't," she says. "I told you it was irreversible. I told you the risks. I warned you this could happen. You knew all this, but wanted it anyway. Now, it's too late. You will begin to lose more and more of your human self every time you change."

A deep rage wells up inside of me. No! How can this be? Why didn't I listen to her when I agreed to do this? All I wanted was to get even with the people who hurt me. I never thought I'd turn into the wolf permanently.

"You can fix this," I growl at her. "You made me like this, so you know how to reverse it."

"There is no reversing it," she says. "You've gone too far. You're past any help I could have offered you. I wouldn't have been able to stop it anyway, though. I could have only slowed it down."

"Then slow it down!" I shout, balling my hands into fists at my side.

"You're too far gone," she says, getting up out of her rocker. "There's nothing I can do for you now. You need to leave."

I know I am making her nervous.

Good.

I need help and she's the only one who can help me.

I take another step toward her. A threatening step. My hands are balled into fists, my back is ramrod straight and I curl back my lip to show her I mean business.

The little kitten that's been asleep, suddenly jumps up out of its bed and winds itself around her legs.

As I lean my face in toward her to yell at her, the kitten arches its back, its hair standing up on end. It spits and hisses at me, then lets out a long, low, growl.

Feeling irked at its behavior, I raise my foot to kick it out of the way, when the old crone strikes me across the face. Hard. I'm so stunned, I just stand there for a second staring at her.

"Don't you dare threaten my cat," she hisses at me. "Get out!"

"I'm not going anywhere till you help me," I say, between gritted teeth.

"Get out and don't come back here," she yells, pointing at the door. "Go!"

A rage like nothing I've experienced before comes over me. I feel heat rising up my face and my heartbeat quickens.

"I...need...your...help," I grind out.

"I told you to leave," she says, heading for the door.

I feel myself change without consciously doing so.

I'm not in control. Anger has taken over.

All I feel is the urge to kill. I ache with it. My bones hurt in want of it. The need for blood pulses through my veins.

I cannot fight it. I will not fight it.

The look of terror on the old crone's face sends a flash of deep satisfaction through me and quickens my pulse.

She tries to get to the door, but I block her path before she can even take a step.

I feel hot drool dripping down from my lips. My hands clench and extend.

I can smell her fear.

It excites me.

Lunging forward, I sink my claws into her shoulders and rip downward, shredding her skin to the bone. She lets out a shriek and stumbles backward. I can see her mangled flesh under the torn dress.

I want more.

Lunging forward again, I dig my claws deep into her chest once more, jerking her toward me. I plunge my teeth into the side of her neck, ripping off a huge chunk of flesh. Blood squirts out and gushes down her neck and shoulder. I feel the hot, sticky gore run down my jowls and the taste sends me over the edge.

I mindlessly plunge my teeth into her neck and shoulder over and over and over again, savoring the salty, metallic taste of her blood.

I continue to rip and tear at her flesh with my teeth and claws.

I'm in a frenzy.

I can't stop till I've shredded her skin to ribbons and her blood covers me.

Finally feeling sated. I drop her bloody, torn body to the floor.

Sitting back on my haunches, I throw my head back and howl. A low, guttural howl that reverberates through my entire body.

As I sit there, I feel myself change back into my human self.

I'm covered in her blood. Soaked in it.

I look around the room.

Her blood is splattered everywhere.

I look down at her broken and bloody body. Deep claw marks are gouged into her flesh. Her skin is in ribbons. Her face, neck and shoulders are nothing more than a bloody pulp.

Holy cow...I did this?

I'm suddenly afraid. I know I turned into the wolf, but I don't remember attacking her. I don't remember doing all this carnage. I only remember getting mad and changing. What happened after that I have no memory of.

I'm losing control. It's happening way too quickly. Before long, there will be no more me left.

Looking down at my clothes again, I quickly start ripping them off of me. I can't wear these home. I can't get caught with blood all over me.

Twisting the clothes up into a ball, I throw them into the fire. At first, they just sizzle and smolder, but soon, the fire overtakes them and they ignite, sending up blue and orange flames. I watch until they are nothing more than ashes.

As I watch the fire burn down, I realize I'm standing in front of the fireplace naked, covered in blood.

I rush over to the sink and began dousing my arms and face in a bucket of water she has sitting there. It's cold, but it doesn't matter. I just need to get her blood off of me.

Grabbing a small towel that is hanging on a peg, I quickly dry myself.

I turn at a sound on the other side of the room.

The kitten.

Poor thing. I'll have to take it with me. I can't leave it here alone.

Carefully walking over to it, I lean down to pick it up. It hisses and spits at me again.

Reaching under its belly, I scoop it up and cuddle it against my chest. It yowls, but doesn't struggle to get down.

Looking around the small cabin, I realize I can't leave it like this. What if another one of her 'clients' comes along and finds her dead? Torn apart. Brutally. Someone might report it to the sheriff's office.

Not likely.

Most people would never admit to coming here. It isn't exactly the place decent people come to. It's a place of last resort when someone feels they are all out of options.

I must burn it down. That's the only option. Burn it to the ground.

Wrapping the towel I'd used to dry off with around my hand, I lift a small log out from the fireplace. The end is still glowing red.

I walk around the cabin and touch the burning, red end of the log to every cloth surface I can find. I touch it to the ends of the dried herbs. I touch it to the blanket on the back of the rocker. I touch it to the kitten's bed.

After several minutes, the fire spreads to engulf the whole cabin.

Holding the kitten close to me, I duck out the door and dash across the yard to stand on the other side of the clearing and watch as the structure is completely swallowed up in flames.

I know this fire will not be seen by anyone. It will burn itself out without ever being detected. The cabin sits so far out in the woods away from civilization that no one will even see the flames or smell the smoke.

I stand and watch for a long time. I watch as the roof collapses. I watch as the walls cave in. I watch until it is nothing more than a burning pile of rubble.

A deep sadness fills me. She was my last hope. She was the only one who could save me. What was I going to do now? Who could I go to for answers? Who would help me? I was truly on my own now.

Tucking the kitten into the crook of my arm, I head back through the woods to my car.

When I reach it, I place the kitten on the passenger seat and crawl behind the wheel.

Firing up the engine, I head back down the old road. I don't bother to turn my headlights on. I can see perfect without them anyway. I guess that's part of me becoming more wolfish. My eyesight is perfect in light or darkness.

I glance over at the kitten. "What am I going to do with you? You wouldn't be happy with me. You'll always be afraid," I say to it. "I need to find you a good home. Somewhere where you will be well loved and cared for."

I sit silently for several moments thinking, when I suddenly know where I will take the tiny feline.

Taryn. She will take really good care of the little guy.

With my mind set, I drive home.

Pulling up into my yard, I leave the kitten in the car while I run inside and put on some clothes, then grab a box and an old towel.

Stuffing the towel into the bottom of the box, I gently place the kitten inside.

I run back inside and grab a Styrofoam bowl and a bottle of water.

Once I have everything I need, I jump back into the car and drive over to Taryn's house. I know she probably won't be home. I really messed Rhobby up and she's probably at the hospital with him.

I hope so anyway.

I don't want her to see me drop the cat off.

I look at the clock on the dashboard and see that it's almost dawn. I was out in the woods for hours. I still have to go to work today.

It's going to be a long day with no sleep.

I slowly pull up into Taryn's driveway.

No SUV.

She's not here.

Good.

I pull the kitten and his box out of the car and carry them up onto the front porch.

Lifting the lid, I fill the Styrofoam bowl with some water from the bottle and place it in the corner of the box.

Petting the little guys head, I close the lid by folding the flaps over on top of each other to make sure he can't push it open and escape.

I rush back to my car and quickly drive away.

I need a quick shower, then it's off to work.

I don't have time to think about what I did tonight. I'll have to worry about that later.

Chapter 17

Taryn left the hospital just before 8:00 a.m.

She was nervous about making the trip to see Lyle Coburn. She had heard rumors that he was a rough character and a shrewd business owner, but he had never gotten himself arrested for anything since she had been sheriff, so she had never actually met the man.

As she drove down the dirt road leading to her house, her mind couldn't help but drift back to the night of the attack on her and Rhobby.

A werewolf. Not a legend, but a real live werewolf.

In her mind's eye, she could still see the gigantic stature of the beast. The blood red eyes, the long, sharp claws. She could still hear the howl ringing in her ears.

A shiver ran up her spine.

Not wanting to go home by herself, even though it was early morning and the sun was up, she knew she had to. She had to get a shower and change clothes. She was, after all, still wearing Penny's t-shirt and sweatpants.

Pulling up into the drive, she noticed something sitting on her porch next to the front door.

A box.

Carefully stepping out of the vehicle, she looked all around her.

Everything was just as she'd left it. Nothing was messed up or out of place.

"What were you expecting?" she asked herself, as she climbed the stairs to the porch. "It wouldn't have come here. Stop freaking yourself out."

She cautiously approached the box. What was in it and who left it here?

She nudged it with her foot and heard a small thump come from inside. A tiny meow followed.

"Ohhh," Taryn gasped, as she quickly unfolded the flaps and peered down into the box. "A kitten!"

She reached down inside and pulled out a tiny, black kitten. It couldn't be more than six to eight weeks old. Holding it close to her chest, she noticed a strange smell coming from its fur.

"You smell like fire and burnt herbs," she said to it, wrinkling up her nose.

Leaning over the box while still holding the kitten close, she searched around for a note, letter or anything to let her know where the kitten had come from.

The only thing in the box was an old towel and a Styrofoam bowl full of water.

"Who left you here?" she asked the kitten. "How long have you been sitting in that box?"

Unlocking her front door, she carried the kitten in and gently set it down on the floor.

It sat down and looked up at her pathetically, its little body wobbling. It meowed up at her and she couldn't resist picking it back up again.

"Ok, you can come with me to lay out my clothes."

She carried the tiny cat back to her bedroom and set it on the bed while she picked out the clothes she would wear after her shower.

"You need a bath, too," she told it.

Grabbing a couple of towels from the linen closet, she filled the bathroom sink up with warm water and gently placed the kitten down in it.

She thought it would fight and claw to get out of the sink, but it sat quietly in the lukewarm water and let her rub a small dab of shampoo into its fur.

After scrubbing the cat until the burnt smell was gone, she rinsed it thoroughly and wrapped it in one of the towels.

Placing the kitten and the towel in a corner, she jumped into the shower and washed off as quickly as she could.

After pulling on a pair of jeans and a casual top, she gathered up the kitten and headed back out to the living room.

A quick call to the vet and she bundled the kitten up in a towel and placed it back in the box and set it on the passenger seat of the SUV.

The vet's office was two miles outside of town. It sat along the bank of the river with a view of the water.

Dr. Patty Wiseman, the veterinarian, met Taryn at the door.

"So this is the little abandoned kitten, huh?"

"Yep," Taryn said. "I have no idea if it's a boy or a girl. I was hoping you could check him or her out to make sure there are no health issues and get the first shots done."

Dr. Wiseman took the kitten from Taryn and turned it with it's butt toward her and lifted the tail. "You've got a little boy here," she said. "I'm guessing it's no more than six or seven weeks old. Awful small for its size, though. Must have been the runt."

"Will that affect it's health?" Taryn asked.

"Not likely. It just means he'll be a small cat," Dr. Wiseman said. "If you'll leave him here, I'll do a thorough exam and give him his first set of shots."

"Thank you," Taryn said. "I really appreciate it."

"What are you going to call the little fellow?"

"I don't know," Taryn said. "I haven't thought of a name yet."

"He's as black as ink," Dr. Wiseman said.

"That sounds like a good name," Taryn said. "Inky."

"Inky, it is," Dr. Wiseman said. "You can pick him up later today."

"Thanks again, Dr. Wiseman," Taryn said, reaching over to scratch Inky's head.

After leaving the vets office, Taryn headed for the station. Even though she had taken the day off, she wanted to check in and talk with Ron and Troy.

Pulling in to her normal parking spot, she was glad to see that both Ron's and Troy's vehicles were there.

She opened the door to the station and stepped inside. Cold air hit her in the face with a blast.

"Geez guys," she said. "It feels like the arctic in here."

Cheryl jumped up out of her seat and came running around the desk and threw her arms around Taryn. "I heard what happened," she said. "I'm so glad you are ok."

Taryn patted Cheryl's back. "Me too. It's a night I certainly won't forget."

"Was it really a werewolf?" Cheryl asked, with a shiver. "Ron and Troy told me."

Taryn looked over at the two guys. "You aren't running around telling everyone that, are you?"

"No, Boss," Ron said. "Just Cheryl. We figured she needed to know since she works here, too."

"That's fine," Taryn said. "But if anyone else asks, tell them it was a bear. I don't want a mass hysteria on my hands along with everything else."

"I thought you took the day off today," Troy said. "What are you doing here?"

"I wanted to talk to you guys about all this," Taryn said. "Cheryl, you may as well hear it, too. I want the curfew notice to be put out again. Call the newspaper and the radio station. Have them put it out there *today*. Tell them we have a rogue bear in the area and no one is allowed out after nine o'clock. Anyone caught out after nine will be arrested. No exceptions. Ron, make up more fliers and hang them on every telephone pole and store window you can. I don't want anyone out after dark."

"You got it, Boss," Ron said.

"Also," Taryn said. "I hate to do this to you, but I'm going to need the two of you out there patrolling at night to make sure everyone is staying inside. I'll join you tomorrow night."

"Are you going to see Lyle Coburn today?" Troy asked.

"As a matter of fact, yes," Taryn said. "That's the reason I took the day off. I'm headed that way after I make a run to Tucker's for some cat supplies."

"Cat supplies?" Cheryl asked. "Since when do you have a cat?"

"Since this morning, apparently," Taryn said. "Someone dropped one off in a box on my front porch. I found it when I went home this morning."

"Any idea who would dump a cat off on your porch?" Ron asked.

"No idea," Taryn said. "It's actually a tiny, black kitten. I just dropped it off at the vets before I came here."

"Are you going to keep it?" Troy asked.

"I guess so," Taryn said. "I never thought I'd get a cat, but it's so adorable and I really could use a companion, being out there all alone and all."

Cheryl wriggled her eyebrows at Taryn. "I heard you and Rhobby are back together."

"We're working on things," Taryn said, with a smile.

"Well, I'm happy for you," Cheryl said. "I hope everything works out."

"Thanks," Taryn said. "By the way, anything going on this morning around here?"

"Nothing we can't handle," Troy said. "Get out of here. This is supposed to be your day off. If we need you, we have your number."

Taryn laughed. "Ok, ok," she said. "I'm outta here."

Taryn left the station and headed to Tucker's to get the cat supplies she needed.

Pushing a shopping cart full of supplies down an aisle, she saw Benji Willis coming toward her.

"Hey Benji," she said, when he approached her. "How're you doing?"

"Question is, how are *you* doing, Sheriff?" Benji asked.

"I'm guessing you heard about Rhobby and me being attacked?" Taryn was getting concerned at how fast news traveled. At this rate, rumors were bound to get started and she didn't want the wrong information to get out there.

"Yeah," he said. "Sheila, over at the hospital told me. Glad you and Mr. Givens are ok."

Sheila Talbert was one of the night duty nurses at the hospital. She and Benji had dated for awhile, but Taryn knew they had remained friends after the breakup. She had not been the nurse attending to Rhobby, so Taryn knew the rumors were already starting. Such was life in a small town, Taryn thought. There was no such thing as privacy. Everyone knew everyone else's business.

"What did you hear?" Taryn asked.

"Sheila said Rhobby was attacked by a bear," Benji said. "I wasn't sure whether or not to believe that. I spend a lot of time in the woods and I haven't seen any signs of one around here lately. I was shocked to hear that you guys were attacked by one."

"Well, I assure you," Taryn said. "It shocked me, too."

"Are you sure it was a bear?" Benji pressed. "I mean, if one was around, wouldn't other people have seen it, too?"

"It was a bear," Taryn said, firmly. "Trust me. I saw it."

"Ok," Benji said. "I was just making sure. I guess I'll need to keep a close eye out when I'm in the woods."

"Benji," Taryn said. "I'd really rather you didn't go out in the woods right now, ok?"

"I can handle a bear, Sheriff," he said. "I know what to do if I encounter one."

"This wasn't an ordinary bear, Benji. It was vicious. It attacked us without warning. Please stay out of the woods for now."

"No can do, Sheriff," Benji said. "Unless it becomes illegal to be out there, then I'm gonna be out there."

"You need to listen to the good sheriff here," said a deep voice over Taryn's shoulder. "She's just trying to keep you safe."

Taryn swung around to find Vince standing behind her. It unnerved her a bit that she hadn't even heard him coming.

"What's it to you?" Benji asked Vince. "If I want to run around out in the woods, I don't see what the big deal is. I spend more time out there than I do at home."

"Benji, for now, please just stay out of the woods," Taryn said. "Just for a few days, ok?"

"Whatever," Benji sighed. "I'll see you later, Sheriff. Bye Vince."

Benji walked off and disappeared around the end of the aisle.

"Let me guess," Taryn said. "You heard about the attack on Rhobby and me, too?"

"Yeah," Vince said. "What happened?"

Taryn told him what happened, leaving out the part about it being a werewolf and replacing it with a bear.

"Wow," Vince said. "You two were lucky it didn't kill you."

"I know," Taryn said. "That was the scariest night of my life."

"So, do you think that bear is what's been killing people around here?"

"I'd have to say yes," Taryn said.

"What are the plans for catching and killing it?"

Taryn wasn't about to tell Vince that she was heading over to see Lyle Coburn to buy a silver bullet. She would never be taken seriously in this town again if that got out.

Instead, she simply shook her head and said, "I don't know yet."

"Well, I hope you find it soon," Vince said. "No more innocent people need to get killed."

"I have Ron putting out a new curfew order," Taryn said. "With strict enforcement."

"Good idea," Vince said. Looking down in her basket his raised his eyebrows and looked at her. "Thinking of getting a cat?"

"Already got one," she said. "Someone dropped one off on my porch last night."

"Seriously? Are you going to keep it?"

"Yep," Taryn said. "I dropped it off at the vets this morning to have it checked out."

"I never figured you for a cat person," Vince said. "I always saw you as a dog lover."

"I am, but if you saw this cute little guy, you'd understand why I can't give him up," Taryn said. "He's so tiny and as black as night."

"It's a boy? What are you going to call him?"

"Inky," Taryn said. "I got the idea from Dr. Wiseman.

Vince laughed, which made Taryn laugh. "Do you have a better idea?" she asked.

"No," Vince said. "Inky is a good name for a black cat."

"Well, I'd better go," Taryn said. "I have more errands to run and the day is getting shorter."

"Well, at least you won't be alone now," Vince said. "I imagine it will be a little scary being out there all by yourself after the attack."

"Yeah, it sure will, but what choice do I have?" Taryn asked. "I don't want to be scared to live out there alone. I have to get past the fear."

"I could come stay with you for a few nights if it would make you feel better," Vince offered. "On the couch, of course. That way you wouldn't be alone."

"I appreciate that," Taryn said. "But Penny is going to come stay with me."

"Good," Vince said. "I'm just glad you won't be alone."

"Me too," Taryn said.

After checking out, Taryn threw all the supplies into the back of the SUV and sat down in the driver's seat and took a long, deep breath, blowing it out slowly.

She knew she couldn't delay the trip to Lyle Coburn's any longer.

She felt strange about it, though. What was she supposed to say? *I need a silver bullet because I saw a werewolf the other night and I want to kill it?* She would look like an idiot.

Troy had told her that Lyle could help her. Did that mean he had sold silver bullets to other people before? She shuddered to herself. She hoped not. One in the area was enough. There was just one, right? The thought that there could be more caused a wave of fear to wash over her. She had only imagined one, but what if there were more?

Quickly shaking off the thought, she shoved the SUV into gear and pulled out of the parking lot.

Chapter 18

The drive out to Coburn's Ammo and Arms Shop seemed to pass by too quickly.

Taryn grimaced as she pulled into the small, gravel parking lot.

The building was a moldy shade of gray with black iron bars on the windows.

Stepping out of her SUV, she was relieved, yet somewhat concerned at the same time that there was only one other car in the parking lot. Relieved that she wouldn't have to wait long to get help, but concerned that she was walking into a shop that she was unfamiliar with and didn't know what to expect. She would have felt better if more people were around in case things got ugly. That way, she wouldn't be alone with Lyle Coburn.

She gripped the solid metal doorknob and turned it, shoving the door open. The door was heavy and made a scraping sound as it slid across the gritty floor.

The atmosphere in the shop was exactly what she had expected. The air was smoke filled and stale. Guns of all sorts lined the walls and behind the counter, several shelves were loaded down with different boxes of ammo. The yellowed windows allowed little outside light to filter in, so the room was dark and gloomy.

Looking around, Taryn didn't see anyone at first, so she took a step farther into the room.

"Can I help you?" came a rough voice from behind the counter.

Taryn blinked her eyes. The heavy smoke filling the room was burning her eyes and nose. She stifled a cough as she stepped up to the counter.

The man who stood behind it was tall, heavily tattooed and smelled of old smoke and body odor. His dark, greasy hair was plastered to his head and he had a cigar hanging from his lips.

"Can I help you," he asked again, impatiently.

"I was told to come see a Mr. Coburn about some special ammunition," Taryn said. Her throat was on fire from breathing in the cigar smoke, so her voice was a little hoarse. "Are you Lyle Coburn?"

"Who sent you?" Lyle asked, unpleasantly.

"Troy," Taryn said. "Troy Garrett. He said you would be able to help me."

Taryn didn't notice the other man sitting off to the side of the counter until Lyle looked in his direction and motioned his head toward the door, signaling for the man to leave. The man quickly got up and walked out the front door, pulling it closed behind him.

"So Troy sent you, huh?"

"Yes, sir," Taryn said. "I need special bullets."

"How is Troy these days?" Lyle asked, ignoring her request.

"He's fine," Taryn said. "He said to tell you hello."

"He did, did he?" Lyle sneered. "Well, tell him Lyle said hello right back."

"I will be sure to do that," Taryn said. "Now, about those bullets."

"You're the sheriff, ain't ya?"

"Yes, sir, I am."

"Now why would I want to help *you*?" Lyle asked.

"Listen," Taryn said, hardening her voice. "I'm not here to cause you any problems. You've never caused me any issues with the law and you've never been arrested or even brought in for anything since I've been sheriff. In fact, I've never even heard of you till recently. So I really don't care what kind of operation you run here. I'm not here for any of that. All I'm here for is something I was told you have that I need. So are you going to help me or not?"

A slow, dopey smile crossed Lyle's face. "I like your tenacity."

Taryn stared hard at him, but didn't say anything else.

"What exactly is it that you need?" Lyle asked, after scrutinizing her for a moment. "And what makes you think I have it?"

"A silver bullet," Taryn said. "Troy told me you would be able to help me out."

Lyle squinted at her and wrinkled up his nose. "A silver bullet? You want a silver bullet?"

"Yes," Taryn said.

"What for?"

"I...uh...just need one," Taryn said, afraid to tell him the whole truth. "Please."

"What...do...you...need...it...for?" he asked, emphasizing each word. "I won't help you if you don't tell me what you need it for. I don't just go around taking odd requests without knowing the reason for them."

"I...uh...we have a werewolf killing people around here."

Lyle threw his head back and laughed. "Oh, we do, do we?"

"I saw it," Taryn said, barely above a whisper.

"Say what now?" Lyle asked. "You say you saw it?"

"Yes," Taryn said, softly. "I saw it with my own two eyes."

"Well now," Lyle said. "I'd say that's a good reason to want a silver bullet then."

"Haven't you heard of the killings going on around here?" Taryn asked.

"I keep to myself," Lyle said. "I don't pay much attention to what goes on around here. I mind my own business."

"So...do you have one or not?" Taryn asked.

"Yeah," Lyle said. "I've got one."

Taryn's hopes rose as he stepped out from behind the counter, but instead of walking over to the shelf of ammo, he went over to the front door and slipped the lock and dead bolt into place, then flipped the 'open' sign to 'closed'.

Taryn's heart sank and she gulped down a lump that suddenly formed in her throat. Was he going to hurt her? Kill her? She took a step back as he walked past her to a dirty, old couch that sat up against the far wall.

"If you tell anyone about what I'm fixing to show you, I'll make you real sorry," he threatened.

Taryn gulped again. "I already told you, I'm not interested in what you do here. I'm only here for one thing."

Lyle reached down and grabbed the cushions off the couch and tossed them onto the floor. Then grabbing a small rope handle, he lifted the plywood that sat in the frame. Taryn was astounded to see it was a trap door.

Leaning down to get a closer look, Taryn saw that a set of steps led down into a lower room.

Lyle stepped back and motioned for Taryn to go first.

Squelching down a stab of fear, Taryn stepped into the frame of the couch and began the descent down the steps into the lower room, followed closely by Lyle.

Once they were down, Taryn gazed around the room. Shelves lined all four walls and chests and footlockers were spread across the floor. The only light came from a single, dingy bulb hanging in the middle of the room. Under the light was a small rectangular table.

Boxes of what appeared to be regular ammo filled the spaces on the shelves, but somehow Taryn figured they were not what they appeared to be.

As if to prove her right, Lyle reached over and grabbed a box labeled 9mm hollow points off of one of the shelves.

"I'm guessing you want 9mm, right?" he asked. "Isn't that the standard issue gun for cops? A 9mm Glock?"

"Yes," Taryn said. "Yes, it is."

Lyle opened the box to reveal fifty rounds of silver bullets inside, all shiny and new.

Taryn stared at the rounds and her mouth dropped open. "How often do you sell silver bullets?"

"I like to be prepared for any scenario," Lyle said, pulling one from the box and handing it to her.

The small, silver bullet felt heavy in her hand. She turned it over and over, looking at every angle of it. "It is real silver, right?"

Lyle snatched the bullet from her hand and shoved it back into the box. "Of course," he growled. "I don't sell anything but the best."

"I didn't mean to suggest otherwise," Taryn said. "I've never done this before and I just want to make sure I'm getting the right stuff. I don't want to shoot a werewolf only to make it mad. I want to kill it."

Lyle looked at her with his brow furrowed. "You really saw one, didn't you?"

"Yeah, I did," Taryn said. "Up close and personal."

"How did you get away?" Lyle asked, curiosity lacing his voice. "Why didn't it kill you?"

"I have no idea," Taryn said. "How much for a bullet?"

"Lady," Lyle said. "You're gonna need more than one."

"Why?"

"What if you miss?"

"Oh," Taryn said. "Good point. How many do you suggest I get, then?"

"The whole box."

"Why the whole box?" Taryn asked. "That's fifty bullets."

"You're gonna want your deputies to have some, too, right?"

Taryn was ashamed to admit that she hadn't thought of that.

"Uh, yeah, of course," she said, feeling heat rise up her face. How embarrassing, she thought, that someone like Lyle would have to remind her to get some for her men.

"Three hundred dollars," Lyle said.

Taryn eyes got wide and her mouth gaped open. "Three hundred dollars? Are you kidding me?"

"No, ma'am," Lyle said. "And that's a discount because you're a friend of Troy's."

"I don't have three hundred dollars," Taryn almost shouted at him. "

"Then you don't get any bullets," Lyle said, turning around to slide the box back onto the shelf.

"Wait," said Taryn. "Do you take MasterCard?"

"Why, yes I do," Lyle said, with an ugly smile on his face. He grabbed the box of bullets back off the shelf and tucked them under his arm. "Follow me upstairs and I'll get you rung up and you can be on your merry little way."

Taryn groaned inwardly. What a snake, she thought. If she didn't desperately need those bullets, she would be tempted to slug him in the face with her fist.

When they reached the main floor, Lyle quickly put the couch back together and flipped the sign on the door to 'open' again and stepped behind the counter.

After ringing her up, he wrapped the bullets in a brown paper sack and handed them over the counter to her. "Pleasure doing business with you," he said. "If you ever need any special items again, be sure to look me up. Oh, and by the way. You'll need to shoot the beast in the heart, if possible. It'll kill him quicker that way."

Taryn stopped and looked at him. "What if I don't?"

"It'll still kill him, but not immediately."

"Like, how *not immediately* are we talking?"

"If you shoot him anywhere but the heart, it could take several minutes for him to die."

Taryn stared aghast at him for a moment, but didn't respond. Her mind was going in circles and she just wanted to get away from this place and this horrid man.

Quickly tucking the bag under her arm, she dashed out of the shop and into the fresh air.

The acrid smell of smoke clung to her clothes and her eyes continued to water for several minutes. Coughing a couple of times to clear her lungs, she opened the car door and slid in.

Lyle's words were beginning to sink in. Great! Not only did she have to get close enough to the werewolf to shoot it, but she also had to make sure she hit it in the heart. This was just getting better and better all the time, she thought.

As she drove down the road, she thought she'd better check to see if the bullets would actually fit her gun. Just because Lyle said they would, didn't exactly make Taryn trust him.

Pulling over in the old stone church's parking lot, she opened the box of bullets and pulled one out. Sliding her Glock from under her shirt where she had it concealed in a waist holster, she dropped the clip out and squeezed the bullet into it. Slamming the clip back into the gun, she stepped out of her car.

The old church was deserted today. The pastor's office was no longer located within the building, so most days it was empty unless there was a wedding or funeral going on.

As Taryn stopped and admired the beautiful architecture, the stone walls and stained glass windows offered comfort to her. She had never seen such a beautiful church before. It had weathered so many storms, but still stood strong. It had seen many happy moments and many sad ones, too.

Looking around to be sure she was alone, she stepped behind the church and lifted her gun to shoulder height.

If she wanted to be sure the bullets would work with her gun, she'd have to fire it to make sure.

The blast from the barrel was deafening in the quiet, peaceful surroundings.

Taryn lowered the gun with a nod. It worked perfectly.

Picking up the silver casing, she stuffed it into her pocket and got back in her car.

Just as she was getting ready to leave, she saw Lester Flynn coming down the road toward her.

He walked up to her window and leaned down to look in at her.

Rolling the window down, she said, "Hi Lester."

"Was that you shooting down here?" he asked.

"Yes, it was," Taryn told him. "I was trying out a new kind of bullet."

"I was just coming down the road from mowing the cemetery and heard the shot."

"Sorry about that," Taryn said. "I didn't mean to scare you."

"New kind of bullets, huh?"

"Yep," Taryn said. "I should have waited to get home before trying them out. I hope I didn't give you too big of a fright."

"No, not too bad," Lester said. "Glad it was you, though and not some hoodlum out doing damage to the church."

"Well, hope you have a good day, Lester," Taryn said. "I need to get to the station."

"Can I ask you something, Sheriff?"

"Sure."

"Are they silver?"

"Is what silver?" Taryn asked.

"Your new bullets?"

Taryn was shocked. She looked at Lester, but the look on his face was serious.

"What makes you think I'd have silver bullets?" Taryn asked cautiously.

"That's what you'll need to kill a werewolf," Lester said.

"What makes you think we have a werewolf around here?" Taryn asked.

"What else could kill folks like what's been done around here? I ain't believing none of that nonsense about it being a man and his pet wolf. That's just hogwash. It's a werewolf. I'm sure of it."

"Lester," Taryn said, shaking her head. "You're a wise man."

"I know," Lester said. He turned and walked back up the hill toward the cemetery.

Taryn drove to the station and pulled in just as Ron and Troy were pulling in.

"Hey guys," she called to them when she stepped out of her vehicle. "Can I see you both inside for a moment?"

"Sure, Boss," Ron said.

"You got them, didn't you?" Troy asked.

"Inside please," Taryn said, looking around to make sure no one heard them.

Once in her office, she pulled the box of bullets out and set them on her desk. "Here they are," she said. "Cost me three hundred bucks." She said this glaring at Troy.

"Hey," Troy said. "It's not my fault what he charges."

"You bought a whole box?" Ron asked. "Why?"

"Don't ask," Taryn said. "Lyle Coburn isn't exactly one to negotiate."

Cheryl stepped into the office and saw the box on the desk. "Are those..." she started to say, but didn't finish.

"Yes," Taryn said. "They're silver bullets. You might want to take a few yourself."

Cheryl leaned over and plucked five from the box. "Thanks," she said. "I hope I never have a reason to use them, but I feel safer having them."

Ron and Troy each grabbed several and Taryn closed the box and stuffed it back into the paper bag. "I don't want any of you going out at night without those," she said. "Do you hear me?"

"Yes, Boss," Ron said.

"No worries here," Cheryl said.

"No problem," said Troy. "You coming out with us tonight after all, Taryn?"

"Not tonight," Taryn said. "I'm going back to the hospital to see Rhobby, then I have to pick up my new kitten."

"Anywhere special you want us to patrol?" Troy asked.

"You let Clint Brogan out, right?" Taryn asked.

"Yeah, this morning," Ron said. "We warned him if he was caught out again, we'd haul his sorry butt right back in here."

"Well, make sure you do a couple of drive-bys past his place. I wouldn't put it past him to go out again," Taryn said. "And take a drive past Benji and Gertie's place, too. Benji has made no bones about the fact that he intends to go out regardless of the curfew. I just don't want to see him get hurt."

"You got it," Troy said. "We'll take a swing by your place, too, if you want us to."

"Please," Taryn said. "I'm a bit leery of going home and being there by myself right now."

"Isn't Penny going to stay with you?" Cheryl asked.

"Yes, but she doesn't get off work till late," Taryn said.

"I could come over for awhile and keep you company," Cheryl offered.

"No," Taryn said. "I don't want you out if you don't have to be. Penny's staying the night at my place. You'd have to drive home in the dark if you came out and I'm not willing to allow you to do that. I'll be fine till Penny gets there."

Taryn gave further instructions to Ron and Troy then headed over to the hospital to see Rhobby.

Rhobby was sitting up in bed when she walked into his room. "Hey, Babe," he said, when she sat down on the edge of his bed. "I missed you."

"I missed you, too," Taryn said, and meant it. "How're you feeling?"

Rhobby pulled back the bandage that covered his wounds and Taryn gasped.

The angry, red cuts were swollen and raw looking. The stitches were holding the wounds together, but the skin was puckered up and blood oozed out around them whenever he moved. "Doc said it will take some time to heal."

Taryn traced her finger gently around one of the wounds. "Rhobby, I'm so sorry," she said. "I never should have suggested we cut through the woods."

"It's not your fault," he said. "I'll heal. I'll be ok."

Taryn leaned over and rested her head on his uninjured side. "I bought silver bullets today," she told him.

"Where did you get them from?"

"Lyle Coburn's shop out on Locust Run Road."

"I hope you were careful, Taryn," Rhobby warned. "He's got a bad reputation."

"So I've heard," Taryn said. "If I'd had any other choice, believe me, I would have taken it."

Taryn curled up on the bed next to Rhobby and told him about the kitten and her trip to Lyle's.

After awhile, she glanced down at her phone and noticed the time. "I gotta go," she said, regretfully. "I have to run by the Dr. Wiseman's and pick up Inky."

"Is Penny still coming over to stay with you?"

"Yes," Taryn said. "She'll be over once she gets off work."

"Good," Rhobby said. "I don't want you there all by yourself."

"I don't want to be there all by myself, either," Taryn said. "But, at least I have those silver bullets. I won't be defenseless now."

Kissing Rhobby on the top of his head, Taryn reluctantly crawled off the bed. "I'll stop in tomorrow to see you," she told him. "I hope the doctors can get those wounds squared away."

"I'll have some pretty ugly scars once they heal," Rhobby said, wrinkling up his nose. "I hope they don't gross you out."

"Haven't you heard," Taryn said. "Girls think guys with scars are sexy." She winked at him as she walked out the door.

Chapter 19

Taryn sat in the waiting room at Dr. Wiseman's and waited for her to bring Inky out to her.

When Dr. Wiseman came out carrying Inky in her arms, Taryn's heart felt light and happy. What an adorable little kitten. He was so tiny, but his meow filled the whole room.

"How is he?" Taryn asked, taking the small black bundle from Dr. Wiseman's arms.

"He is in perfect health," Dr. Wiseman said. "He got his first set of shots and his rabies tag will be taped to your receipt. He's a bit too small for a collar just yet."

"Great," Taryn said, snuggling Inky under her chin. "What about neutering? When can we schedule that?"

"Not for a few more weeks," Dr. Wiseman said. "He needs to be quite a bit bigger first. I'll have Trish at the front desk, schedule an appointment for you."

"Thank you so much, Dr. Wiseman," Taryn said.

"You're welcome," Dr. Wiseman said. "Good luck with him."

Taryn set him on the front seat next to her as she drove home. She was pleasantly surprised that he hunkered down against her thigh and slept the whole way.

It was late afternoon as Taryn pulled into her driveway. The sun was still up, but the impending darkness of night was only a couple of hours away.

Apprehension filled her as she realized it was the first time she would be alone here since the attack.

Maybe she should go into town and wait till Penny got off work.

No. She was a cop. She had a gun. She should be able to handle herself in case of another attack.

Yeah, well, that hadn't helped last time, did it? Everything happened so fast, she hadn't had a chance to react. Would she be able to next time?

Next time?

She sure hoped there wasn't a *next time.*

Nervousness came over her as she grabbed up Inky and stepped out of the car.

Was she going to feel creeped out being here on her own? You betcha! But she knew she had to get over that fear. She couldn't continue to live here if she was always afraid. This was her home. She loved it here.

She scanned the property several times before stepping up onto the front porch. She looked over toward the woods, but didn't have the sensation that someone was watching her this time.

Letting out a long sigh, she went inside and closed the door, locking it securely behind her.

Running around the house, she flipped on every light, including the outside lights.

Somehow, that made her feel safer.

Settling down on the floor with Inky, she turned on a comedy show and waited for Penny to arrive.

~~~~~

Darkness is coming soon.

I can feel the need to kill rising up in me. It builds like a fever that washes over me in waves. It builds and builds until I can't concentrate on anything but the desire, the need to kill.

Strong. It's so strong. It's beginning to overpower me.

Will I have control tonight? Or will the wolf take over?

I only have a couple of nights left until I am no longer human.

Only a couple.

The full moon will be my undoing.

I must kill as many people off my list as I can before that happens.

I am afraid. I've never been afraid before. But I am afraid now. I don't want to lose the human part of me completely, but I know it is inevitable. The wolf part of me grows stronger with every passing day. What will happen when nothing but the wolf remains?

I want Taryn to know. I want her to know who I am before it's too late. But how? I can't reveal myself to her just yet, but still…she needs to know. She needs to understand.

I look down at the list in my hand. There are several more people on it. Will I be able to finish my task before my human self no longer exists?

An idea comes to me as I read down through the list. I will go to my next victim's house before I change. That way, I am already at the location in case I lose my self and don't know what I'm suppose to do or where I'm supposed to go. My wolf side will only care about killing. And this way, he will be in the exact spot I need him to be to kill the next person on my list.

I feel the night urgently pressing in on me. It's time to go. If I wait much longer, I may not make it to my destination. The wolf will take over and do as he pleases, instead of doing what I please.

Stripping out of my clothes, I bolt out the door of my house, sticking close to the woods so as not to be seen.

The person on my list tonight is Lexi Andrews.

Ahhh, yes. Lexi.

I am going to enjoy this kill. How dare she laugh at me when I asked her out. How dare she snub her nose at me. The embarrassment and humiliation of it still burns me up. She thinks she is so much better than me, but she is wrong. I can still hear her high pitched giggle as she looked at me like I was some loser who wasn't worth her time. Then what does she do? She turns around and shacks up with that jerk Scott Higgins. Like he is better than me? Ha! He's nothing but a high school drop out. He can't even keep a job, yet she had no problem hooking up with him.

Her blood is going to taste so good. I can already taste it.

Her house is not far away. If I hurry, I can be there just after dark.

The moon is bright tonight. There is a glowing, silvery halo shimmering around it. It's beautiful, but it reminds me again that it will be full in two nights time.

The night is breezy and cool. The smell of earth and wood permeate the air around me. The soft, mossy ground is like a sponge under my feet.

Up ahead I see the house. The woods surrounding her home shield it from view from the road. No one will see me sneak up. No one will see me kill her.

Several lights are on throughout the house.

Good. She's home.

With any luck, Scott is with her.

A two for one night! Lucky me!

As my resentment and anger built within me, I feel the wolf emerging.

No, not yet. Please.

I want to at least see the horror on her face when she realizes she is going to die.

I push the anger down. I can't afford to let the wolf out yet. I must grapple for control until it's time to exact my revenge.

I creep up to the large living room window and peer in. The curtains are parted just enough for me to look between them. I am standing in full view, but they don't see me.

Lexi and Scott are both sitting on the couch watching tv. I am looking at the backs of their heads. The blue glow from the screen illuminates the room.

The tv suddenly flashes to a white background and I see my reflection like a shadow on the screen.

Lexi gasps and quickly turns toward the window, but I have ducked down just before she sees me.

I dart to the wood line, just out of view as Scott pushes the curtains back farther and gazes out into the night.

Time to turn into the wolf.

I look down at my body as black hair sprouts out all over my skin. I feel my nose extend and long, sharp fangs drop down out of my gums. I watch as long, razor sharp claws push out from the tops of my fingertips. My legs lengthen and contort until they resemble that of a dogs. I feel my ears stretch and twist into long, pointed triangles.

I look down at myself and realize how magnificent I am. How powerful. I am perfection.

I take a step toward the house and realize I am still me. *I don't know how long I will stay in my right mind, but I fully intend to make the most of it.*

I steal up to the house. I don't want to look in the living room window again, so I make my way down to the far end of the house.

Time for a little fun.

Dragging my claws into the vinyl siding, I gouge deep scoring lines along the side of the house for several feet. The screeching sound it makes causes my hair to stand on end, but it excites me.

I hear thumps and bumps coming from inside the house. Suddenly the front door swings open and Scott pops his head out and looks around.

He sees me. Fear etches across his face and he freezes.

I snarl and take a step toward him.

He rushes back inside and slams the door.

Ohhh, this is getting fun!

I rush at the door and slam myself against it, jarring the frame.

I hear them scream. I hear their footsteps stomp down the hall to the bedroom.

Turning, I rush to the end of the house where I see the lights go out from the window.

Do they think they can hide by turning off the lights? Don't they know I can smell them?

Peering into the window, I see them huddled on the bed. I lift my arm and rake my claws down the glass.

Ssccrreeeeeeeeecccchhhhh.

Lexi screams. Scott shouts something unintelligible.

I am revved up now. I feel my heartbeat quicken. Blood pounds through my veins.

I pound the side of the house with my fists. The force of it causes the windows to rattle and shake.

I throw back my head and let out a long, drawn out howl. I feel it come from deep within me.

From inside the house, I hear the cocking of a gun. I laugh to myself.

They don't know their measly bullets will not kill me.

I howl again and pound on the side of the house, harder this time.

I hear Scott's footsteps run down the hall.

I beat him to the front door.

As he throws it open, I am already there. Waiting.

His eyes meet mine and I see the blood drain from his face. He knows it's too late. He knows he is dead.

I smell his fear. I want blood. I need blood. I must have blood.

I am gone.

The wolf has arrived.

~~~~~

Lexi sat on the couch next to Scott. It was only around ten o'clock, but she was getting bored.

"I hate this stupid curfew," she said.

"What would you be doing if you could go out?" Scott asked. "Not like there's much to do around here."

"It's just the idea of not being allowed to go out that's driving me nuts," Lexi said.

She turned her attention back to the tv and watched as talk show host interviewed the celebrity who was a guest star on the show.

Lexi leaned her head against Scott's shoulder as the program switched to a commercial.

Just as the screen flashed white, the shadow of a man's head and shoulders crossed the screen.

Lexi gasped and jerked around to look out the large living room window that faced the road. The curtains were only partly closed and she could see out into the front yard.

"What?" Scott asked. "What's wrong?"

"I just saw someone looking in the window," Lexi said, breathlessly. "Through the part in the curtains."

"No one's out there, Lexi," Scott said, jumping to his feet and going over to the window. "See?" he said, as he pushed the curtains aside and gazed out into the yard. He turned his head from side to side, but didn't see anything.

"Oh...well...I thought I saw someone, ok?" Lexi argued.

"Who would be out prowling around anyway?" Scott asked. "With the curfew in place, no one is supposed to be out running around."

"I know," Lexi said. "It must have just been something on the tv."

They cuddled up on the couch again and before long, a loud metal screeching sound could be heard coming from outside the house.

"What in the world?" Scott asked.

"I told you someone was out there," Lexi said.

"Just, shut up, alright," Scott demanded. "I'm going to take a look."

"Scott, don't," pleaded Lexi. "Something isn't right about this."

"It's just someone out there jerking us around," Scott said.

"What if it's not?" asked Lexi. "What if it's the killer?"

Scott swung around and gave her a disgusted look. "Just shut up, would ya?"

Lexi huffed out a breath, but didn't say another word.

Scott threw open the door and looked around.

As his gaze fell to the side of the house, terror licked through his veins. The deep, red, glowing eyes that met his were not human. He was looking into the face of a monster.

Quickly slamming the door shut, he turned to Lexi.

All of a sudden a thundering crash hit the door, rattling the frame.

Scott let out a yell and jumped back from the door as Lexi screamed.

"Get back to the bedroom!" Scott yelled at Lexi.

"What is it, Scott?" she demanded, still standing in the middle of the floor.

"GO!" Scott shouted at her.

Still not moving, Scott grabbed her by the arm and dragged her down the hallway to the bedroom. He flung her onto the bed as he rushed over and flipped the light off.

Jumping into the middle of the bed with her, Scott put his arms around her and pulled her close.

Lexi was crying now. "What's going on?" she whispered. "What's out there?"

"I don't know what it is," Scott said. "Hush now, I don't want it to hear us."

Lexi looked over at the window and froze. Red, glowing eyes stared back at her from the darkness.

As she watched, a huge, black arm raised up and long, deadly looking claws grazed down the window, sending a raw, grating sound through the room.

Lexi screamed. Scott shouted for the beast to go away.

A horrifying howl shattered the stillness of the night.

Suddenly, loud, hard thumps could be heard along the side of the house under the window.

"It's going to kill us," Lexi sobbed. "We're gonna die."

"No, we're not,"Scott said, sliding off the bed and reaching for his gun from inside the closet. He cocked the barrel and checked to make sure there was ammo in it.

Another howl sounded. Then more pounding on the side of the house.

Lexi ducked her head and put her hands over her ears. "Make it stop!" she cried.

Scott tore down the hallway to the front door.

Lifting his gun, he threw the door open.

He realized his mistake immediately.

He didn't have time to aim and fire the gun. The monster lunge toward him with lightning fast speed, knocking the gun out of his hands.

Scott stared in horror as the beast curled back its lips and growled a low, menacing sound.

Trying to step back, Scott felt a searing, white hot, pain in his chest as long, curved claws were thrust into him.

Somewhere in his terror frozen mind, Scott felt a ripping sensation across the front of his body. Looking down as if in a dream, he saw his flesh being torn from his body. Muscle and bone were exposed, before the gush of blood poured down the front of him.

He looked, disbelievingly, into the eyes of the most horrific creature he had ever seen.

He watched as if in slow motion as the beast opened its mouth wide and closed it down over his face.

The crunching and splintering of bone exploded in his ears, as his eyes bulged and filled with blood.

Dropping to his knees, Scott barely noticed as his nose and upper lip were ripped from his face. Blood seeped into the open cavity of his mouth and began to run down the back of his throat, choking him.

Scott spluttered blood from his mouth for a moment, then fell face first to the ground.

The werewolf lifted its massive back leg and brought it crashing down on the side of Scott's head.

Scott never felt it.

A scream split the air.

Bursting through the front door, the monster crashed through the house and down the hall, tearing the bedroom door off its hinges and flinging it out of the way.

In one bounding leap, the beast was on top of Lexi, pinning her to the bed.

She screamed as she looked up into the face of the monster. Blood dripped from its jowls and shreds of skin hung off its fangs. She could smell the pungent metallic smell of Scott's blood on its breath.

She screamed again as long, curved claws tore into her chest, ripping her shirt and shredding the flesh beneath.

Pain exploded through her body. Gasping and unable to breath, she started swinging her arms at her assailant.

Grabbing handfuls of its thick, black hair in her fists, she jerked and pulled.

The beast threw back its head and howled.

She watched in horror as the monster snapped its eyes back to hers, then crushed his teeth down into the top of her head.

She felt her scalp being ripped away from her skull. Blood ran down the back of her head and pooled onto the bed beneath her. She could feel the sticky, hot texture coat the back of her head.

The monster reared back, snagging her scalp with its teeth, ripping the skin from her head and face.

Lexi felt no pain. Only the realization she had was that she was dying.

She remotely felt claws ripping and tearing the flesh from her neck and chest before darkness came over her and she was gone.

~~~~~

Heaving breathing.

The taste of hot, sticky, wet blood in my mouth.

Wetness soaking the front of me.

I sit back on my knees and let the fog clear from my mind.

I'm back.

Looking down, I see the mangled, bloody body of Lexi laying beneath me.

Her face is gone. Just a bloody, boney mess remains.

Good. I hope she suffered. Maybe now she will know what it felt like for me when she laughed and scoffed at me for asking her out.

I feel no remorse. No sympathy.

Scooting off the bed, I follow a bloody trail out to the front door.

Scott is laying face down on the ground in a pool of blood.

Yes! Looks like I got them both real good.

I look down at my feet and realize I am standing in a pool of Scott's blood.

This is not good. I am human again. I can't leave any evidence of my human self here.

Slipping my bare feet into a pair of Scott's sandals that are sitting by the door, I run to the bathroom and grab a towel that is hanging on the rack.

I check the hallway on my way back to the front door to make sure I haven't left any other evidence.

I haven't.

I mop up the bloody foot tracks I left and tuck the towel under my arm. I can't leave it behind.

Feeling immensely satisfied with the work I've done here, I smile to myself as I trot back off into the woods and make my way back home.

Chapter 20

It was just after ten when Taryn heard tires crunching on the gravel outside and knew Penny had finally arrived.

She opened the door just as Penny stepped up onto the porch.

"Glad you made it," Taryn said, quickly ushering her inside. "I was beginning to get worried."

"Sorry," Penny said. "We had a crate of milk spill over in the storeroom and I had to stay and help clean it up."

"I'm just glad you're finally here," Taryn said, giving Penny a hug. "I never used to think it was creepy out here all by myself, but now..."

"I understand," Penny said. "The drive out here was spooky. I kept looking around, afraid I'd see the werewolf come charging out of the woods at me."

"You didn't see anything, did you?" Taryn asked. "No one out? No big, scary monsters lurking in the woods?"

"No," Penny said. "But I'll admit, the drive out here freaked me out a bit. I was glad you opened the door when I arrived. I'd hate to be standing out there on your porch waiting with those woods so close. You wouldn't hear anything coming till it was too late."

Taryn shuddered. "Don't remind me."

Penny glanced down and saw Inky sitting on a blanket Taryn had laid down for him. "Whose this adorable little guy?"

"That's Inky," Taryn said. "Someone dropped him off on my porch this morning."

Penny looked up at her with a scowl on her face. "Seriously? Who would do that?"

"I don't know, but I'm kinda glad they did," Taryn said. "He's been keeping me company while I was waiting for you to get here."

With the late hour, Taryn and Penny decided it was time for bed. Penny opted for the guest bedroom next to Taryn's.

"You know," Penny said. "If I get scared, I'm coming to your room and bunking with you."

"Trust me," Taryn said. "If I get scared, I'll be coming to get you."

The women laughed as they each headed for their own room.

Taryn set Inky on the bed and changed into her pajamas. He curled up next to her pillow and began purring.

"I think I'm going to love having you around," Taryn told him, as she scratched behind his tiny ear.

The moon wasn't full yet, but it's silvery glow filtering through the closed curtains illuminated her room in a soft blue hue.

Crawling into bed, she curled up on her side facing Inky. She presses her face into his soft fur and sniffed. He began to purr.

Closing her eyes, she started to drift off to sleep.

Somewhere out in the night, she heard the faint sound of a howl.

Instantly awake, a shiver ran down her spine. She recognized that howl. It was the same one she'd heard the night she and Rhobby were attacked.

It was out there somewhere in the darkness.

The werewolf.

Sitting up in bed, she listened.

Her heart began to pound in her chest. Please don't let it come here, she chanted over and over again in her head.

Switching on the bedside lamp, she reached over and grabbed her gun. She dropped the magazine out of it and began popping the regular 9mm bullets out onto the bed.

Grabbing the box of silver bullets, she pulled them out one at a time and began stuffing them into the magazine. It held fifteen rounds, so she filled the whole thing with the silver bullets.

Ramming the magazine back into the gun, she cocked the barrel.

Suddenly, another howl sounded from somewhere out in the night.

Footsteps thumped across the floor outside Taryn's room.

Suddenly, Taryn's door was flung open and Penny burst in. "Did you hear that?" she asked, breathlessly.

"Yeah," Taryn said. "Looks like you're sleeping in here with Inky and me."

"Yes, I am," Penny said, grabbing the corner of the blankets and lifting them up to crawl in. "Move over."

Taryn scooted over to allow Penny to crawl in next to her.

The two women laid silently in bed for a long time listening for any more howls, both hoping and praying they didn't get closer.

Taryn said a small prayer for Ron and Troy who were out patrolling the hollow. Wherever they were, she hoped they were safe and sound and nowhere near where the howls were coming from.

She knew that somewhere, out there in the darkness, another attack had just taken place. She knew there was nothing she could do to stop it and nothing anyone could do for the victim. It was too late. They were already dead.

Praying for daylight to come quickly, Taryn slipped the loaded gun under her pillow.

She didn't sleep at all that night. She laid awake listening for any sound that would alert her to the werewolf's presence outside her house.

Thankfully, none came.

~~~~~

Taryn rolled over and grabbed Penny by the shoulder and gently shook her. "Time to wake up, Sleepy Head," she said. "I have to get up and get ready for work."

Penny stretched and yawned. "What time is it?"

"6:30," Taryn said, slipping from the bed. "You're more than welcome to stay in bed as long as you like, but I have to get up."

"Sounds good to me," Penny said, rubbing her eyes. "I didn't sleep a wink last night, did you?"

"No," Taryn said. "Not after hearing those howls."

"It was the werewolf, wasn't it?"

"Yeah, it was," Taryn said.

"Someone got killed last night, didn't they?" Penny asked.

"Yeah," Taryn said. "My job today will be to try to figure out who."

"I don't envy you that job," Penny said.

"I don't envy me the job, either," Taryn said. "What time do you have to go into work today?"

"I'm off today," Penny said. "Do you want me to stay here and watch Inky?"

"Sure," Taryn said. "If you aren't afraid to stay here."

"The werewolf never attacked anyone during the day, right?" Penny said, an edge of fear lacing her words.

"No," Taryn said. "I think everyone is safe during the day."

"Then I'll stay here and keep an eye on Inky for you," Penny said.

"You're planning on spending the night with me again tonight, right?" Taryn asked.

"Yep," Penny said. "That's the plan."

"I can't thank you enough," said Taryn. "You don't know how much I appreciate it."

"What are friends for?" Penny asked.

Taryn finished getting ready for work. She hated the idea of leaving Penny there alone at the house all day by herself, but none of the attacks had happened during the day. She gave Penny strict instructions, though, that if anything happened or she had any bad feelings, to get out of the house and get to town as quickly as possible.

Taryn jumped in her SUV and headed to the station with a heavy heart. Someone was killed last night. But who? They would have to do a search of the hollow until the victim was found.

It was going to be a long day. Time to get to it.

~~~~~

Taryn walked into the station and immediately called Ron and Troy to her office.

"Boys, we've had another killing last night," she said, without preamble, as she pulled the chair out from behind her desk and sat down.

"You heard the howls, too?" Troy asked.

"Yeah," Taryn said. "The way sound travels in the hollow, though, there's no telling where it came from. We'll have to do a house to house check."

"That's over five hundred homes," Ron said. "Do you want to split up and search? We could cover the area quicker that way."

"No," Taryn said. "We don't know what we'll encounter. Let's stick together. We'll ask everyone we run into if they heard anything or if they know of someone who's missing."

Taryn heard the front door to the station open and Cheryl start talking to someone.

"Let's go see what going on," Taryn said, getting up out of her seat.

Stepping out of her office, Taryn saw Lester Flynn standing in front of Cheryl's desk.

"What's going on, Lester?" Taryn asked.

"There was another killing last night," he said, his voice a little shaky.

"Do you know who was killed?" Ron asked.

"No," Lester said. "But I heard the howls."

"Do you know what direction they were coming from?" Taryn asked. "Could you tell if they were close to your place or not?"

"Sounded like they were coming from up the river past the old church," Lester said. "Not many houses out that way, but there are a few."

"Well, that will help narrow down the search area," Troy said, looking at Taryn.

"Thank you, Lester," Taryn said. "I appreciate you coming in to tell us. We all heard the howls, too. We just couldn't tell where they were coming from."

"You need to kill it, Sheriff," Lester said. "Soon, before it kills more people."

"I know, Lester," Taryn said, taking him by the arm and leading him to the door. "We're doing our best."

After Lester left, Taryn turned to Ron and Troy. "Well, let's get going before someone stumbles across the kill sight. I'd really rather that didn't happen."

The drive out past the old church was a solemn one. They all knew they were going out there to find a dead body. Taryn had called Dr. Middleton and told him to be ready for a call once they found the victim.

As they drove along the road that paralleled the river, Taryn felt her heart sink. There were only three properties out this far. Cyndi Byers, Randy Newell and Lexi Andrews. One of them was probably the victim.

Stopping at Cyndi's house first, they found her and her three kids safe and sound. When asked if she had heard or seen anything last night, she told them that they had stayed up most of the night watching action movies and the tv had been turned up loud so she could hear it over the kids running and yelling through the house. She had not heard or seen anything unusual.

Next was Randy Newell's place. He was a single man who lived all alone. He told them that he had gone to bed early with a headache and had not heard anything out of the ordinary, either.

As they got back in the car and headed toward Lexi Andrews' house, Taryn looked at Ron and Troy, dread filling her bones. "You know there's only one house left," she said. "Lexi's. It's a ways back in the woods and far enough away from her neighbors that if anything happened out there, no one would have heard anything."

Ron simply nodded.

Troy suddenly pointed out the windshield, "There it is," he said, indicating a weed infested, gravel driveway that turned off to the left.

Turning into the drive, a heavy dread filled Taryn. She knew before she even saw Scott's body laying on the ground in front of the house that they had found the right place.

"Ron, call Dr. Middleton," Taryn said. "Tell him to bring the meat wagon."

Chapter 21

Taryn.

I must let Taryn know. Now.

I'm running out of time.

It won't be long till someone figures out it's me anyway.

I've called off work for the last two days. I can't risk going in. I'm losing control so quickly and I don't want to turn into the wolf while I'm there.

After tomorrow night, it won't matter anyway. The wolf will be the only thing that exists.

I have to let Taryn know who I am. I have to make her understand. But how?

A letter.

Yes, I'll write her a letter.

I'll leave it on her front door so she'll find it when she goes home.

I need her to know why I'm killing all these people. I need her to know why I don't want to hurt her. She needs to understand. She needs to know I would never hurt her on purpose. Never.

I run to my kitchen and grab up a notepad and pen.

Getting comfortable on the couch, I begin writing.

My Dearest Taryn,

I'm running out of time and I need to tell you who I am...and what I am.

Let me start from the beginning. I grew up in Switcher's Hollow, the same as you. I live here, went to school here, work here.

You are not going to want to hear this, but your father strayed once. Only once, but that was all it took to conceive me. Our father went back to his wife and daughter and pretended like I didn't exist.

You were 5 when I was born. I learned of your existence just a few short months ago when my mother passed. As I was going through her things, I found my original birth certificate. My father was Bud Lewis. He was your father, too. Along with my birth certificate, I found a letter my mom left for me. It told how she met our father one night along a dirt road just outside of the county. She had a flat tire and he stopped to assist her. They ended up having a one night tryst in the back of her car. I was born nine months later. When she told him about me, he told her I wasn't his and he didn't want to see her again.

She did the best she could raising me, but I needed a father.

I was small and skinny and very awkward when I was young. I was mercilessly picked on by kids at school. They told me my mom was a tramp and that's why I didn't have a father. I was beat up, kicked around and tormented all through school. When I graduated, I joined the military. Once I came back, I had buffed up, gotten tough and made myself the town's "golden boy" by being polite, helpful and kind to everyone. No one remembered the geeky, awkward boy from school.

But I remembered every one of them.

Frank Forrester was my first victim. When I was around ten or so, I went to see him about helping out around the farm so I could earn a little extra cash. But instead of helping me, he fired his shotgun at me. He peppered me with so much buckshot I thought I'd be scarred for life.

Duke Forsythe was next. He humiliated me in front of everyone in high school gym class. I got my revenge, though.

Ginny Lee Maloney came third. She set me up as a thief at Barrett's Drug Store. I thought my new reputation of "golden boy" was going to be ruined, but Mr. Barrett must not have told anyone. Ginny Lee ended up paying for that mistake.

Lexi Andrews was fourth. She humiliated me and made fun of me for asking her out. Like she was so much better than me. Well, she isn't laughing now, is she?

By now, you know I'm a werewolf. I chose to become one on purpose to get the revenge I deserved. I won't go into details about how I accomplished it. You don't need to know all that.

What I didn't count on, though, was the wolf eventually taking all control from me. I am quickly losing my human side and by the next full moon, I will no longer be human at all.

I realized I was losing control the night I almost attacked you. Thankfully, my human side was able to recognize you and stop before I did you harm.

You are the one person I would never want to hurt. You are my sister. I care about you. You are the only family I have left.

I want you to know all this.

I want you to understand that I would never hurt you.

I've watched you from time to time. You caught me looking in your bedroom window one night. You also knew I was watching you from the woods that one night, too. Never with the intention of hurting you. Never. I just wanted to get to know my sister.

By the time you get this letter, I will be only one night away from being fully wolf.

I will never have the chance to know you as a sister. I will never have the chance for family holidays, birthdays or get togethers. But I want you to know, that I am glad you are my sister. I am so proud of you. You are a good person and I truly admire you.

I won't give you my name. I don't want you to think badly of me. I have more people to kill before I lose all control. Once I am the wolf, I will kill at random. I will no longer be able to choose my victims.

Watch out! I don't want you to fall prey to my animal side. I will no longer be able to stop myself if I come across you. I will no longer know who you are.

I wish you all the best.
I love you.

Your brother,
The Wolf

P.S. Hope you like the kitten.

I fold the letter neatly and stuff it into an envelope.

I scrawl Taryn's name across the front and tuck it into the back pocket of my jeans.

I will take it out to her house after I swing by Tom's for lunch.

I don't want to risk her stopping home for lunch and catching me while I'm leaving this on her door.

I jump in my vehicle and head into town.

Chapter 22

Taryn plunked herself down in the chair in her office.

Two more people dead.

Not just dead. Mangled. Butchered. Torn to shreds.

The werewolf was getting more vicious in its attacks.

She laid her head in her hands and closed her eyes. They needed to find out who the werewolf was and fast. She didn't want more gruesome deaths on her hands.

Word was going to get out about this and she knew there would be a mass panic in the town over it.

Shaking her head, she let out a long sigh.

Glancing up at the clock on the wall, she saw that it was almost noon.

Her body felt weary and heavy. Her muscles ached. Her spirits were low and she just wanted to hide in her office all day, but she knew she couldn't do that. And to top things off, she had to go out on patrol with Ron and Troy tonight.

Dragging herself up out of her chair, she walked out to Cheryl's desk. "I'm going to Tom's for lunch. Wanna go?"

"Sure," Cheryl said. "You look like you could use some company."

"I don't want to be alone right now, that's for sure," Taryn said. "I called Penny to come down and join us, too."

"Good," Cheryl said. "The more the merrier."

They opted to walk the short distance to the diner. The sun was shining, it was hot and Taryn needed the fresh air.

By the time they got there and were seated, Penny came in.

"Where's Inky?" Taryn asked. "Did you leave him at the house?"

Penny winked at Taryn and opened up her bag. Inky stuck his head out and meowed.

Kimmie walked over just at that moment and saw the tiny kitten. "Oh my," she said. "How adorable. I'll get him a little saucer of milk." She hurried off without taking their drink orders.

"Well, I see who gets all the special treatment," Taryn said, laughing as she reached over the table and rubbed her hand over Inky's head.

A couple of minutes later, Kimmie rushed over with a small saucer full of milk. "Here you go," she said, handing it to Penny.

Penny set the saucer on the seat next to her and lifted Inky out of her purse. He lapped up the milk, purring the whole time.

"Taryn," Penny said. "You look like someone put you through the wringer."

"I feel like that, too," Taryn said, pinching the bridge of her nose between her thumb and forefinger.

"I'm telling you, something's wrong," Oliver Jones voice drifted over to them from his spot at the counter. A short, robust man in his late sixties, he owned a small construction business at the edge of town. "He hasn't been to work in two days."

"I hear that's fairly normal for him, though," said Clive Thomas, a lifelong friend of Oliver's. "I don't know what you're worried about. He'll show up when he needs money."

Penny leaned in across the table. "I wonder what that's all about."

"Doesn't Benji work for Mr. Jones?" Cheryl asked.

Taryn strained to hear the rest of the conversation, but the men dropped their voices and she couldn't hear anything else they said. "I'm going to go make sure everything is ok," she said. "The last thing we need is a missing person."

Sliding out of her seat, Taryn walked over to the counter where the two men were sitting. "Afternoon, Oliver. Hello Clive," she said. "I couldn't help but hear you say someone hasn't shown up for work in two days. Might I ask whom you're talking about?"

"Hello, Sheriff," said Oliver. "It's that Benji kid. He hasn't shown up to work for the last two days. I tried calling him, but his momma just tells me he ain't home. I'm one step away from firing him."

"He hasn't called you to tell you he wouldn't be there?" Taryn asked, a little concerned.

"No, ma'am," Oliver said. "He just ain't showed up and hasn't returned my phone calls, neither."

"I'll take a drive out there this afternoon and check on him," Taryn said.

"Thank you, Sheriff," Oliver said. "He may be worthless most of the time, but when he bothers to show up at work, he does a good job. I'd hate to lose him, you know?"

"I understand," Taryn said.

Just as Taryn turned to walk back to her seat, Lester Flynn walked in with Andy Clemmons. "Something's got to be done, I tell ya!" Lester said in a loud voice. "There's been too many killings and not enough police work."

"I hear ya," said Andy. "What are we supposed to do? Hide in our homes until they decide to find this guy?"

"It ain't no guy," Lester said, his voice becoming louder as he talked. "It's a dad-gum werewolf."

Taryn made her way over to him quickly. "Lester," she said. "You need to calm down. You're gonna start scaring folks. I don't need you coming in here spouting off about werewolves."

"Well, it's true, Sheriff!" Lester bellowed at her. "When are you going to be honest with these folks and tell them the truth?"

"Lester, please," Taryn said. "We're doing everything we can. Now, please keep your voice down and stop all this."

"No, ma'am, I won't," Lester said, raising his voice even more. He stepped into the middle of the diner and cleared his throat. "Ladies and gentleman, we have a werewolf on the prowl. Don't let the sheriff here tell you otherwise. We had another killing last night. I heard the howls. Just ask Sheriff Givens here what happened last night."

All eyes turned on Taryn. Heat rose up her cheeks and she stepped forward, hoping to dispel the terror she saw on everyone's faces. "Yes, it's true, unfortunately," she said. "We had a couple who were killed last night down past the old church on River Road. However, please don't let Lester scare you. We are doing everything in our power to keep you safe."

"What have you done, Sheriff?" Andy demanded. "Do you have any suspects? Any leads at all?"

"I wish I could say that we did," Taryn said. "But, at the moment, we have no leads. But we are diligently working on it."

"How many people have been killed so far?" Lester demanded. "Six? How many more have to be killed before you and your deputies find some answers?"

"I understand you are all scared," Taryn said. "We put the curfew in place for your protection. We are doing nightly patrols. We are trying our best to find the perpetrator."

"Well, that's not good enough, Sheriff," Andy said. "We need answers. We want to feel safe in our neighborhoods. In our homes."

"I understand that, Andy," Taryn said. "I want answers, too. I want to find this guy as bad as you do."

"What are we supposed to do?" Lester asked. "Leave town? Go somewhere else till you catch this monster?"

"Actually," Taryn said. "If you have somewhere to go till this is over, that would probably be a good idea. The less people I have to worry about, the better."

"Sounds like a good idea to me," Andy said. "I'm going home and packing me and my family up and heading across the river to stay with my momma till you figure this out."

"Good, Andy," Taryn said. "I think that's for the best."

"We don't all have a place to go, Sheriff," a woman in the corner booth stood up and said. "What are we supposed to do?"

"Stay inside at night," Taryn said. "Lock your doors and close your windows."

"Sheriff," Lester's voice boomed around the room. "You gonna tell them it's a werewolf that's been doing the killings?"

"Lester," Taryn said, a warning in her voice. "Knock it off."

A murmur of voices rose around the room.

"Folks," Taryn said. "Please calm down. We don't need a panic. Please let Ron, Troy and me handle this. If you would just stay in your homes and not go out after dark, you will all be fine."

"How do you know that, Sheriff?" Lester demanded. "How do you know we'll all be safe. A werewolf can break down doors and bust through windows."

A loud murmur erupted around the room at his words.

Several people got up from their booths and headed for the door.

"Where are you all going?" Lester demanded. "Don't you want to hear this?"

A man in his early fifties grabbed his wife by the arm as he was leaving. "No," he said. "We're going home and packing. We aren't sticking around to become werewolf bait."

Several 'yeahs' and 'us too' followed the man's statement as several people walked out the door.

Taryn felt a headache begin to pound in the back of her head.

Turning to Lester, she walked up and stuck her finger in his chest. "If you stir up a ruckus and cause a panic, I'll haul you in for disturbing the peace, you got it?"

"I'm scared, Sheriff," Lester said. "I want everyone to know what's really going on around here. They have a right to know what they're up against."

Taryn couldn't fault him for his reasoning. The townsfolk did have a right to know. She was sincerely glad that several families had decided to skip town the for time being. It would put her mind at ease to know that at least a few families would be safe.

"I know, Lester," she said. "You're right, but there is a better way to handle it."

"Like what?" Lester asked.

"Maybe we need to hold another town meeting," Taryn suggested.

"Too late," Lester said. "I've already been out this morning warning everyone. Most have decided to leave town."

Taryn walked back to her table and slid into her seat. Penny and Cheryl were staring at her with their mouths open.

"So the whole town knows it's a werewolf now," Penny said. "That can't be good."

"Do you think a bunch of the men will go on another hunt?" Cheryl asked.

"I sure hope not," Taryn said. "They wouldn't stand a chance against that monster out there."

Taryn laid her head down on her folded arms on the table. "What a mess," she mumbled.

She jerked her head up when she heard Inky hiss and yowl.

Penny picked Inky up and cuddled him under her chin as Vince approached their table.

"Afternoon ladies," he said, reaching out to scratch Inky's head. The kitten spit and puffed up his fur. "I guess he doesn't like me very much. He probably smells Walter Rigley's dog on me. I stopped by there this morning to drop off a tool I borrowed and Pluto rubbed all over me."

"How are you?" Taryn asked him.

"Question is," Vince said. "How are you? You look like someone in need of a long nap."

"Thanks," Taryn said, sardonically.

Vince laughed. "No insult intended," he said. "You just look worn out."

"That's because I am," Taryn said. "Did you catch the hullabaloo a few minutes ago?"

"Sure did," Vince said. "Sounds like Lester is trying to stir up trouble for you."

"He's just scared," Penny said.

Taryn noticed Vince's attire. Cut off denim shorts and an old, ragged t-shirt. "Not working today?" she asked him.

"Nope," he said. "Got the day off. Have some business to attend to."

"Speaking of business, "Taryn said. "I better be getting back to the office. It doesn't look like I'm going to have a chance to visit Rhobby today. I guess a phone call will have to do."

Taryn slid out of the booth, but before she could go too far, Vince caught her arm. "Can I talk to you for a minute?" he asked.

"Sure," Taryn said. "What's up?"

"Outside, please," Vince said, looking around. "Too many ears in here."

Curiosity picked, she followed him out the door and around the corner.

"What's up, Vince?" she asked, a slight frown on her face.

"Is it true, you believe a werewolf is the culprit behind the killings?"

"I have reason to believe that it's a rogue animal, yes," Taryn said cautiously.

"Be careful, would you?" Vince said.

"Sure," Taryn said. "I'm always careful. I have to be. It's my job."

"I don't want to see you get hurt, is all," Vince said.

"I appreciate that, Vince," Taryn said, feeling a bit uneasy. "What's this all about?"

"Just one friend looking out for the other," Vince said.

As Taryn watched him, his body seemed to stiffen and a strange look crossed his eyes. "Vince? Are you ok?"

"Yes," Vince said, his eyes seeming to become unfocused. "I'm hungry...so hungry." He swayed a little on his feet. Taryn reached out to steady him. When her hand touched his arm, his skin felt cold and clammy.

"Didn't you just eat?" she asked him.

"I need bloo...I mean...I need...meat...hungry," Vince stammered.

"Vince, what's wrong?" Taryn asked, concern washing over her. "You don't look well. Maybe you better go inside and sit down."

"NO," he almost shouted. "Just need...to go...home. Not feeling...well. You...better...go," he said. He quickly turned on his heel and raced off.

Taryn watched him go. What in the world was that about? Was he diabetic and having low blood sugar issues? She'd seen people have similar problems when their sugar was low. She hoped it was something like that and not a sign of something more serious.

Still feeling a bit concerned for him, she turned down the sidewalk and headed toward the station.

Cheryl came in a few minutes later, followed by Penny.

"What did Vince want?" Cheryl asked.

"He wanted to know if I believed it was a werewolf that was killing people," Taryn said.

"What did you tell him?" Penny asked.

"I told him I believed it was a rogue animal," Taryn said. "I didn't know what else to say. He got all weird acting after that, then took off."

"Weird, how?" Cheryl asked.

"Like he was confused or something," Taryn said. "Is he diabetic, do you know?"

"I don't know," Cheryl said. "But that could explain an episode of confusion, I suppose."

"Well, I have enough to worry about," Taryn said. "I can't add more to it. Vince is a grown man. If he's having a medical issue, he needs to address it."

Taryn excused herself to go call Rhobby. She felt horrible that she wasn't able to go over and visit him, but with everything going on, she felt it best to stay at the station till it was time to go out on patrol this evening.

Hearing Rhobby's voice on the phone made Taryn miss him even more. He told her the doctor said he was beginning to heal and thought he would be released in the next few days. Taryn couldn't wait.

They talked for an hour before Taryn hung up the phone and laid her head on the desk to take a little rest.

~~~~~

I must hurry. I must leave the letter for Taryn before she gets home.

Time is running out.

Must...hurry.

I drive out to her place. No one is there.

I drive past several times before I stop. I want to make sure no one will see me.

I pull my car into the drive and jump out as fast as I can.

Must hurry.

Wedging the envelope in the crease of the door beside the doorknob, I wriggle it to make sure it is secure.

It is.

Turning, I run back to my car and spin tire getting out of there.

I can't be caught.

I'm speeding down the road at breakneck speed.

I don't pass anyone.

Once I hit the main road, I slow down.

I know the wolf is getting stronger. I feel him trying to break through my subconscious.

He is ever lurking in my mind now. He is ever forcing against the bonds that hold him.

Soon...very soon he will break free and I will have no more control.

I'm home now.

I must rest for now, but there is too much to do.

I only have a short time left.

Oh Taryn...if only we could have known each other under different circumstances.

If only…

~~~~~

Taryn jerked awake when Ron walked into her office.

"Sorry, Boss," he said. "Cheryl said it might be a good idea to wake you up. She said you wanted to take a ride out to see about Benji?"

Taryn quickly sat up straight and rubbed her hand through her hair. "Oh yeah," she said. "I forgot. He hasn't shown up for work for the last two days and Oliver said he hasn't heard anything from him. I thought it might be a good idea to go check on him."

"Want us to ride along?" Ron asked, indicating himself and Troy.

"You can," Taryn said. "I need Troy to run to Pandy's and get us some donuts for the patrol tonight. No need in driving around for hours without something good to eat."

Ron laughed and went out to convey the message to Troy. Taryn heard them laughing.

She sent up a prayer of thanks for both men. She also said a prayer for their safety. She didn't know what she would do if either of them were hurt. She could never find anyone to replace them.

Grabbing her gun and strapping it around her hips, she joined Ron out in front of Cheryl's desk.

"We're heading out," Taryn said to Cheryl. "Did Penny say she was heading back out to my place?"

"Yeah," Cheryl said. "She was going to swing by her place and grab some clothes, then head back over."

"Good," Taryn said. "By the way, Troy is going after some donuts. Help yourself, but remember, the crème buffs are mine!"

Cheryl laughed and saluted Taryn. "Yes, ma'am," she said, still chuckling.

On the drive out to Benji's, Taryn was quiet. She leaned her head against the window, but didn't start up a conversation with Ron.

Noticing her solemn mood, Ron asked, "You ok, Boss?"

"No," Taryn said. "I'm scared, Ron. What if we don't catch this thing? What if it kills more people?"

"We'll catch it," he said. "Don't worry."

"I don't know how to be not worried," Taryn said.

"I know," Ron said. "But we have our silver bullets and we'll be out patrolling most of the night. With any luck, we'll find him and blast him to kingdom come."

"I hope you're right," Taryn said.

When they pulled into the drive at Benji's place, Gerti met them on the porch. "What's this about, Sheriff?" she demanded, before Taryn could even get out of the patrol car.

"Hi, Gerti," Taryn said. "We're just here to check on Benji. Is he home?"

"Maybe," Gerti said. "What do you want him for?"

"He's not in trouble if that's what you're worried about," Taryn said. "Oliver told us he hasn't shown up to work for a couple of days and we just wanted to make sure he was ok."

"He's fine," Gerti said.

A loud metallic clank came from around the back of the house.

Taryn quickly took off in that direction when Gerti yelled after her. "Leave him be," she hollered. "He's just working on something, is all."

Taryn threw Gerti an irritated glance, but ignored her words. She walked around to the back of the house, followed by Ron.

Tall, overgrown weeds choked out any grass that might have grown there. An old car sat up on blocks in the far corner. But what caught Taryn's eye was the big, metal cage that stood half erected in the middle of the yard. Benji was standing in the middle of it, trying to fasten a long bar to the top of the structure.

"Benji," Taryn said. "What in the world is that?"

Benji jumped, not having heard them come up behind him.

"Uh...hi Sheriff Givens," he said, seeming nervous. "It's a...cage."

"For what?" Ron asked.

The cage was over eight feet tall and nearly six feet wide. It was deep enough for several people to fit into it. Thick metal bars made up the sides and top and a steel metal plate made up the floor.

"It's...uh...just something I'm making...for...uh...hunting," Benji said.

Gerti came stomping around the side of the house and marched herself up next to Benji.

"He ain't doing nothing wrong," she said.

"Gerti," Taryn said, patiently. "No one is accusing him of doing anything wrong. We're just here to check on him."

"Check on me?" Benji asked. "Why?"

"Oliver said you haven't showed up for work for a couple of days and he hasn't been able to reach you," Taryn said. "With all the killings and such going on, we just wanted to make sure you were ok."

Well, that's sure nice of you, Sheriff," Benji said. "But, I'm just fine."

"Why haven't you gone to work?" Ron asked. "Or at least called Oliver to let him know you wouldn't be in?"

"I forgot to call him," Benji said. "I was busy with...this." He nodded toward the cage.

"What is that for, Benji?" Taryn asked.

"It's a cage," he repeated.

"Yes, I can see that," Taryn said, impatiently. "But, a cage for what?"

"That's none of your business," Gerti thundered. "He's allowed to build a cage if he wants to."

Taryn looked at Gerti, on the verge of losing her temper. "Gerti, why don't you go inside and make us all a nice glass of iced tea and give me a minute to talk to Benji."

Gerti huffed, but stormed off back around the house, mumbling as she went.

"Now," Taryn said, turning back to Benji. "Tell me about this cage."

"Ah Sheriff," Benji whined. "It's nothing, seriously."

"What in the world would you have a huge cage like this for?" Taryn asked.

Benji hung his head and began wringing his hands together. He mumbled something under his breath that Taryn couldn't hear.

"You know I'm not going anywhere till you tell me," Taryn said.

"It's to catch the monster that's killing everyone," Benji finally spit out.

"Uh huh," Taryn said. "And just how do you plan on catching anything in that?"

"I'll use bait," Benji said.

"What kind of bait?" Ron asked.

"Squirrels, coons, rabbits," Benji said. "Whatever I can catch."

"And where exactly do you plan on setting up this trap?" Taryn asked.

"Right here," Benji said. "In my yard."

"Not a good idea," Ron said. "You have no idea what you're up against."

"Sure I do," Benji said. "A werewolf."

Taryn shook her head, anger rising in her. "The curfew is still in effect. Don't let me catch you out or I will haul you off to jail. We'll be out patrolling tonight and we plan on making several trips past your place. If I see you even stick a toe outside your door, I'll slap cuffs on you so fast your head will spin."

"Wow, Sheriff," Benji said, rubbing his jaw. "Why are you so worked up today?"

"I'm tired of people in my town getting killed, that's why," Taryn said. "Stay...inside. Do you understand me?"

"Yes, ma'am," Benji said, realizing that arguing with her wasn't going to get him anywhere.

"I don't want to see you get hurt, Benji," Taryn said. "Stay inside."

"You got it," Benji said.

Gerti came around the side of the house carrying a couple glasses of tea.

Taryn grabbed one of the glasses and downed the contents.

Handing the glass back to Gerti, she didn't say anything, just turned on her heel and walked off.

She didn't wait for Ron, as she trudged back to the patrol car. Her nerves were on edge and she was fighting back tears of frustration. Why couldn't people just follow the rules. It was for their own safely, after all.

Slamming the door shut, she waited till Ron got in the car before she broke down.

"You ok, Boss?" he asked.

"Yeah," Taryn said. "I just needed to let off a little steam."

The drive back to the station was a quiet one. Taryn didn't feel much like talking and Ron respected her need for silence.

Arriving back at the station, Taryn was in a foul mood. The run in with Benji had only furthered her fear that the people of the town would go to any lengths to try and catch the killer. What other idiotic stunts were they likely to encounter on their patrol tonight?

She and Ron stepped out of the vehicle and started toward the front door of the station when a small group of people rushed toward them from across the street.

"Sheriff," said a young woman cradling a toddler on her hip. "Is it true what Lester Flynn said? Is there a werewolf out there? Is that what's been killing people?"

Taryn pushed down the irritation that was beginning to bubble to the surface. "We know we have a rogue animal on the prowl," she said, hoping that answer would satisfy the crowd.

"Is it a werewolf?" another woman asked.

"We know it's an animal," Taryn said. "We know it hunts at night. That's why we put the curfew in place. If you stay indoors and lock your doors and windows, you should be fine."

"You didn't answer her question," said a young man in his twenties. "Is it a werewolf?"

"Folks," Taryn said. "Please go home. Stay inside. Lock your doors and windows. Ron, Troy and I will be out on patrol tonight. You'll be safe. Please go home."

"Are you going to kill it?" the woman with the toddler asked. "Are you going to hunt it down and kill it?"

"That is the plan, yes," Taryn said. "Now, all you folks, please go home. Let us do our job."

Taryn was surprised to see the group of people slowly move off. Murmurs and grumblings followed them, but she was glad it hadn't turned ugly.

Stepping into the station, Taryn immediately headed for her office. She seriously needed some quiet time to relax and clear her head.

She sat down and laid her head on her folded arms.

At some point, she must have dozed off because Ron's knock on her door, jarred her awake.

"Come in," she called, groggily.

Ron shoved the door open and stuck his head around it. "Just wanted to let you know it's six o'clock, Boss."

Taryn quickly glanced at the clock on the wall. Sure enough, it was just after six. "Oh my goodness," she said. "I must have dozed off again. Thanks Ron."

"What time you want to meet down here for patrol tonight?" he asked.

Taryn thought about it for a moment, then said, "Let's say around nine."

"You got it," Ron said.

"Ron?" Taryn asked, as he disappeared around the door.

Poking his head back around the door, he asked, "Yeah?"

"Troy did get those donuts, didn't he?"

Ron laughed and nodded. "He got them."

"Good," said Taryn. "Something to look forward to."

Ron left her door open as he walked away.

It had been a long day for Taryn. She was irritated and frustrated and still rather tired. Deciding to grab take-out before heading home, she grabbed up her stuff and headed to the local fast food place.

The drive out to her place was a peaceful, quiet one. She rolled down the windows and cranked up some oldies on the radio and let the tension ease from her body.

Pulling into her driveway, she saw Penny's car parked in front of the porch.

Taryn was glad she had thought to grab a burger and fries for her best friend, too.

Stepping onto the porch, she did a quick perusal of the yard and woods around the house.

No weird vibes. No strange noises.

Good. She just wanted to eat and relax for awhile. Tonight was going to require all her attention and she didn't want to start the patrol off already feeling edgy and creeped out.

Stepping into the cool interior of her home, she dropped the bags of food on the kitchen counter and greeted Penny, who was sitting on the floor in front of the tv playing with Inky.

"Long day?" Penny asked. "You still look like you need a week long nap."

"And it's not over yet," Taryn said. "I grabbed us a couple of burgers and some fries."

"Awesome," Penny said. "I was fixing to raid your frig."

"Good luck with that," Taryn said, chuckling. "I haven't been able to make it to the store for the last few days. You would have starved."

Taryn and Penny ate their meals while they watched an old sitcom.

After cleaning up their dishes, Taryn picked up Inky and rubbed her cheek across his soft fur. "Penny," she said. "I don't want you to stay here tonight while I'm gone."

"Why?" Penny asked.

"It's too far out from anything," Taryn said. "I'll be out till the early morning hours and I wouldn't feel safe with you here all alone. I want you to pack up Inky and the two of you go to your place for the night. Once my patrol is over, I'll join you there."

"Whew," Penny said. "I would have stayed here, but I'm so glad you said that. I would feel much safer in town."

"I'll pack my bag and you can take it with you when you leave," Taryn said.

She grabbed up her clothes for the next day and stuffed them into a small suitcase.

Gathering up Inky's stuff, she crammed it all into another bag and set it by the front door.

"I want you leave now while it's still daylight," Taryn told Penny. She glanced down at her watch. "It's a little after eight already. It'll be dark soon."

"Sounds good to me," Penny said, grabbing Inky and cradling him against her chest."

Taryn walked Penny out to her car and helped load everything into the back seat.

"Oh," Penny said. "I forgot to tell you. There was an envelope stuffed into the crease of your door when I got here. I laid it on the table for you."

"What is it?" Taryn asked.

"I don't know," Penny said. "I didn't open it."

"Ok, I'll get it when I go in," Taryn said. "You and Inky have a good night. I'll see you sometime after we finish the patrol."

Penny gave Taryn a hug. "Be safe tonight, ok?"

"I will," Taryn said. "I'll have Ron and Troy with me so I won't be alone."

Penny drove off leaving Taryn standing in the driveway watching after her.

When she walked back into the house, Taryn remembered the letter Penny had told her about.

It was laying on the end of the table with the rest of the mail that Penny must have picked up out of the mailbox.

Picking it up she noticed that the only thing the envelope had on it was her name scrawled across the front. Turning it over in her hand, she looked for any more writing, but there wasn't any. Dropping it back down onto the table, she figured she would have to look at it later. She only had a few minutes before she had to leave for the station.

Chapter 23

It's almost dark. Time to head out for another kill.

I look at my list. I can't seem to concentrate on the names. They are just a blurry bunch of scribbles.

No matter. The need for blood is driving me tonight. I don't care who I kill. I just want blood. I want to taste the hot sticky goo run down the back of my throat. I want to feel flesh being torn beneath my claws. I want to hear the screams and groans of my victim as I claw and tear the life out of them.

Ooohhhh, yes!

I feel the need to kill building stronger and stronger within me.

I blink my eyes and I have changed into the wolf. It is becoming so easy now. It takes no effort at all.

I stand in my bathroom looking at my magnificent form. I am the perfect killing machine.

I feel myself leaving. I am drifting off into the nothing. I can't fight it. I can't bring myself back.

I am gone. Nothing but the wolf remains.

~~~~~

It's a such a beautiful night, Taryn thought. Stars were scattered across the sky and the moon was a brilliant, shimmering ball of light, casting silvery, bluish hues across the landscape. The heat of the day had past and the cool air of the evening brushed over her skin as she stood outside the station waiting for Ron and Troy to show up.

While she waited, she made a quick call to Rhobby. She knew she would feel so much better getting to talk to him for a minute.

After she hung up, she stood by her car and slowly surveyed her surroundings. How could something so horrible, like a werewolf, come to be in such a small, peaceful little town like Switcher's Hollow? Nothing like this had ever happened here before. Why now? Who was it? Would they be able to find and kill this thing soon? She sure hoped so. This whole ordeal was a nightmare.

These thoughts were running through her head when Ron pulled in, followed shortly by Troy.

"You boys ready to go?" Taryn asked, when they approached her.

"As ready as I can be," Troy said, carrying a box under his arm.

"Those better be donuts," Taryn said, indicating the box.

Troy chuckled and pulled the box out from under his arm and handed it to her. "You betcha."

"Ron, you drive," Taryn said, heading for the patrol car. "I'll take shotgun. Troy, you're in the back."

Once everyone was in, Ron pulled out of the station and turned left to start the patrol on the far end of town.

They wove their way up and down the town's main streets, then turned off onto a road that would take them out through back roads leading them out into the surrounding countryside.

Stuffing a bite of donut into her mouth, Taryn pointed to the road that would go past Benji's house. "Don't forget to check on Benji," she said, around a mouthful of powdery dough.

When they reached Benji's, all the lights were on in the house, but no one was outside.

Taryn felt a stab of relief. She was glad to see that Benji had not broken curfew. She couldn't explain it, but she genuinely cared about Benji. She didn't want to see him get hurt. And she especially didn't want to see him get killed. He was almost like the annoying little brother she never had.

Driving farther out the road, Taryn was starting to get bored. They had been driving around for a couple of hours now and nothing seemed to be going on. Everyone is tucked safely in their homes and not one person had been caught breaking curfew. Taryn was thankful for that, but the slow, gentle hum of the car's motor was beginning to lull her. She kind of wished something interesting would happen to keep her awake.

Blinking several times to clear her eyes, she chomped down on another bite of donut.

Just as she began to nod off, Ron slammed on the brakes and skidded to a halt. "What was that?" he asked, staring out the windshield.

Taryn jerked her head up and looked out the window, scanning the darkness around them. "What did you see?" she asked. She felt a prickling sensation crawl up her arms. She wasn't sure she wanted to hear Ron's response.

"I don't know," Ron said. "Something ran across the road in front of us just out of range of the headlights."

"Grab the spotlight," Taryn said to Troy in the back seat. "Quick!"

Troy rooted around on the floor for a moment, then handed a large, black cased spotlight up over the seat to Ron.

Rolling down his window, he held the light out at arms length and flipped it on.

A glaring, wide beam of white light shone out from it. Ron swung the light back and forth slowly, illuminating the woods that surrounded the small, dirt road they were on.

"Nothing," he said, pulling the light back inside. "Must have been a deer or something."

Taryn was on edge. Something didn't feel right. There was a charge to the air. A static that seemed to light her skin on fire.

"Let's get out of here," she said. "I have a really bad feeling."

Just as Ron put his foot on the gas, something rammed the side of the car, shoving it to the side of the road.

Taryn screamed as another hard thump hit her side of the car, rocking the vehicle from side to side.

Looking out the window, she saw a pair of glowing, red eyes staring in at her.

"Go!" she shrieked, leaning over in her seat toward Ron. "Step on it!"

Ron revved the engine, but the car just spun it's tires, throwing gravel out behind it.

"Ron, go!" Taryn screamed.

The huge, black monster took one leap and landed on top of the car, crushing the hood under it's enormous weight.

Taryn and Ron stared in horror as the beast bent down and glared at them through the windshield.

"Ron," Taryn said, barely able to form the words with the panic rising in her throat. "Go! Step on it! Get us out of here!"

"I'm trying, Boss," Ron said, as he stepped on the gas again.

The monster arched its back and threw its arms out to the side and let out an earsplitting howl that shook the whole car.

The tires seemed to catch and the car lurched forward. The werewolf swung back one of its mighty arms and brought it crashing down on the windshield, shattering it.

Taryn screamed and ducked down.

Ron stepped hard on the gas and the car spun gravel and fishtailed for several feet, causing the werewolf to lose its footing. It slid off the side of the car and hit the ground.

Ron pushed the gas pedal all the way to the floor and the car jerked forward and roared off down the road, throwing gravel in its wake.

Troy sat up from where he had laid down and looked out the back window. "Uh guys," he said, nervously. "It's coming! It's catching up to us!"

"I'm going sixty miles per hour," Ron said. "How is it gaining on us?"

The air blowing through the busted windshield whistled and whined as they flew down the road.

"Go fast!" yelled Taryn. "It can't possibly catch us if we go faster!"

Troy continued to watch from the backseat. "It's still coming! Go!"

"I've got the pedal to the metal," Ron yelled. "It won't go any faster!"

They tore down the road for over a mile with the werewolf keeping pace with them. At times, even running along side the road right next to them, its evil red eyes piercing the darkness. It's huffing and puffing could be heard through the open windows and its massive, heavy paws made deep, thumping sounds as they pounded the earth.

Finally, it seemed to be slowing down and as they went around a bend in the road, they lost sight of it altogether.

"Do you think we lost it?" asked Taryn, still checking out every window to see if it was still out there.

"I think so," Ron said. "I don't know how it kept up with us as long as it did."

"I don't think we're out of the woods yet, guys," Troy said. "We made it mad. It's going to keep hunting us. We need to get somewhere safe."

"We should have shot it," Taryn said. "We all have our silver bullets, right?"

"Yeah, my clip is full of them," Ron said.

"I've got mine, too," Troy said. "It all happened so fast, I wasn't able to react."

"We're trained for this," Taryn said, feeling irritated that none of them managed to get off a shot. "We're supposed to be able to react in a situation like this."

"I've never been trained on how to deal with a werewolf, Boss," Ron said. "That was a first for me."

"I know," Taryn said. "I'm sorry. I just feel like we missed our chance to get him."

"It's not over," Troy said. "He's still out there. We might get another chance before this night is over."

"What do we do now?" Taryn asked.

"I told you," Troy said. "We need to find a place to hide. He's going to keep coming after us."

Troy just finished his statement when a large, black mass loomed up next to Taryn window.

It was back.

It lunged its body into the side of the car, causing it to swerve and veer off the road.

Grass and dirt flew in every direction as Ron tried to gain control of the car.

Spinning the steering wheel hard to the right, the car lurched back onto the road as the tires squealed and spun.

A loud thunk sounded on the trunk. Troy screamed and the sound of shattering glass exploded around them.

Ron stomped on the gas and the car's engine roared as the tires gripped into the gravel and it shot off down the road.

"Don't stop, whatever you do!" Taryn screamed. "Just go!"

They whipped down the lonely, dirt road taking hairpin turns on two wheels and throwing dust and gravel up behind them as they went.

"We need to hide somewhere," Troy said. "We can't keep this chase up. The car isn't going to handle many more hits like that."

"There's nothing out this road for miles except Wallen's Junk Yard," Taryn said.

"That'll work," Ron said, trying desperately to maintain control of the car. "We'll have to find a place to pull in among the wrecked cars and wait it out till morning."

The car was beginning to splutter and spit. The wheels on the passenger side wobbled and weaved as they flew down the road. Taryn knew the car wouldn't last much longer. They had to get to the junk yard and fast.

Troy was keeping an eye out the back window. "He's slowed down again," he told the others. "He's losing ground."

Ron flipped the headlights off. The moon was bright enough to illuminate the road enough for them to see where they were going.

After what felt like miles, the dilapidated, rusty old sign of Wallen's Junk Yard came into view.

Hundreds of rusted out, broken down vehicles of every make and model dotted the hillside. They covered the large field that surrounded the property as well. The old farmhouse where Russ Wallen and his wife, Verna lived, sat lonely and dark off to the right of the junk yard. Taryn knew they were out of town right now, so they wouldn't be in any danger if the werewolf came around looking for her, Ron and Troy.

Slowing the car down, Ron turned off the dirt road and made his way carefully down a small dirt bank, then turned and drove down a row of old cars and trucks.

The patrol car bumped and swayed over the uneven ground as Ron slowly made his way through the row of junkers looking for an open spot to pull in.

Somewhere, not too far off, the three of them heard a deep, low howl fill the night air.

A shiver ran up Taryn's spine. Would he find them hidden among all the junk cars? Would he know where they were and hunt them down? Laying her hand across the butt of her gun, she pulled it out and released the clip, then shoved it back in.

"What are you doing?" Troy asked, leaning up over the back seat.

"Just making sure it's tight and secure," Taryn said. "I don't want it to misfire when I shoot it."

Ron weaved his way up and down several rows before he found an empty spot to pull into.

It was a tight fit. The patrol car barely fit between the old Volkswagen van and the Ford pickup truck, but Ron managed to squeeze in without rubbing up against either one. The noise of screeching metal would surely give away their position.

Ron turned off the engine and leaned back in his seat. "Now we wait," he said.

"Get your guns ready, boys," Taryn said. "We're going to be ready if that thing finds us here."

They sat in the eerie silence for a long time listening to every cricket, every small animal scurrying through the trees, with baited breath.

The moon was high in the sky. Its silvery light shone down across the old junkyard and reflected off the broken glass and mirrors of the vehicles around them.

As the three of them sat in total silence, Taryn's nerves were on edge. Every little noise made her jump. She realized after several moments that she was holding her breath and the grip she had on her gun wasn't safe. Flexing her fingers, she blew her breath out between pursed lips. "How long do you think we've been sitting here?" she whispered to the men.

"About an hour or so," Troy said. He was leaning up over the seat and watching out the front windshield. "Maybe it isn't coming."

"Sshhh," Ron cautioned. "Listen."

They all got still and listened.

All the crickets had stopped chirping. No small animals could be heard scampering around in the nearby woods. Even the air seemed eerily still.

"It's here," Troy whispered. "It knows we're here. It's coming."

Taryn could feel the tension coming off Troy. A static electric charge seemed to travel between the three of them.

Taryn was scanning the area out in front of the car. Deep shadows danced along the ground, giving the illusion of something moving, but Taryn knew it wasn't the beast. The beast would attack without warning. It wouldn't show itself until it attacked.

Movement out the back window caused the three of them to spin around and look to see where the noise was coming from.

Suddenly a deafening roar brought their attention back to the front of the car.

Standing in front of them, arms outstretched, drool dripping from its jowls, was the werewolf. Its huge, black form so big it almost blocked out any light coming from the moon. Its chest was heaving with each breath it took.

Taryn lifted her gun and took aim. The monster howled and jumped out of sight behind a vehicle.

"Where did it go?" demanded Ron. "Do you see it?"

A thunderous roar surrounded around them, then something large and heavy jumped onto the roof of the car, crushing the metal and causing the top of the car to cave in on them.

Taryn screamed and aimed her gun at the roof and fired.

The bullet ripped through the metal with a loud explosion.

They waited to see if she had hit the monster.

Loud, hard thumps pounded on top on the roof. Screeching sounds, like nails on a chalkboard, caused Taryn to clamp her hands over her ears. "Shoot it!" she yelled.

Ron and Troy fired their guns at the roof. A hard thunk let them know the beast had jumped off the roof of the car and hit the ground.

Afraid to move, Taryn waited for the next assault.

After a couple of minutes, the three of them slowly sat up and looked around.

Taryn screamed as the werewolf jumped onto the hood of the car and lunged toward her through the open window.

Closing her eyes, she lifted her gun and fired. The explosion rung in her ears.

She heard a loud roar followed by a long howl. Opening her eyes, she saw blood running down the arm of the werewolf.

With a final roar, it jumped off the car and disappeared into the darkness.

"I got it!" Taryn shouted. "I shot it!"

"It didn't die," Ron said. "It ran off. You must have missed."

"No, I didn't," Taryn said. "I saw the blood."

"Why was it able to run off then?" Troy asked. "Silver is supposed to kill it."

"Lyle Coburn told me that to kill it instantly, you have to shoot it in the heart," Taryn said. "But if you shoot it somewhere else, it will take it awhile to die, but it will die."

Ron threw his head back against the headrest. "Finally, this nightmare is over," he said.

"Let's get out of here," Troy said. "I don't want to wait around to see if it comes back."

The three of them crawled out of the mangled vehicle and began walking down the road toward town.

"We're miles from anywhere," said Troy. "Are we going to walk all the way to town?"

"Looks like it," Taryn said, dragging her weary feet.

They walked for over a mile when headlights fell on them from a car approaching up ahead.

Drawing closer, Taryn recognized the car.

Benji.

As Benji pulled up next to them, he looked over at Taryn sheepishly. "Hey, Sheriff," he said. "Need a ride?"

Taryn started laughing as relief flooded over her. "For once, I'm glad you didn't listen to me," she said. "Yes, we could use a ride, please."

Benji drove the three of them down to the station. He was quiet most of the way.

"You alright, Benji?" Taryn asked. "You seem awful quiet."

"Are you going to arrest me for breaking curfew?" he asked.

Taryn looked at him and smiled. "No," she said. "Thanks to you, we didn't have to walk miles to get here. I'll cut you a break this one time. But tell me, what were you doing out this time of night?"

"I was going stir crazy," Benji said. "I needed to get out of the house for awhile. I figured a short drive wouldn't hurt nothing."

"Well, I'm glad you decided to drive out that particular road," Taryn said.

Benji leaned over and gave her a quick hug. "Thanks," he said, stepping back quickly.

"Thank you," Taryn said. "I was never so glad to see you as I was tonight."

"Did you kill it?" Benji asked.

"Yes," Taryn said. "I shot it and it ran off, but it won't have gotten far."

"Are you sure it's dead?" Benji asked, looking skeptical.

"Yes," Taryn said. "I shot it with silver."

"But if you didn't see it die, how do you know it did?"

"Because it was shot with silver," Taryn said, again. "Silver kills werewolves."

"I hope you're right," Benji said.

Taryn thanked him again and sent him on his way.

Turning to Ron and Troy, she asked, "It's dead, isn't it?"

Ron shrugged.

Troy said, "You did hit it with a silver bullet, so I guess so. If Lyle said it would take a few minutes if you didn't hit it in the heart, then it's probably laying out there somewhere dead. I sure hope it is anyway."

Taryn said goodnight to Ron and Troy, then climbed into her vehicle and headed to Penny's.

As she lay in bed that night, she replayed in her mind the events of the evening.

She knew she hit the werewolf with her bullet. She saw the blood running down it's arm. Lyle told her to make sure she hit it in the heart, but if not, it would still kill it. More slowly, but it would kill it.

Relaxing in the knowledge that she did, indeed, hit it with a silver bullet, she closed her eyes and fell into a deep sleep.

Chapter 24

She shot me.

I stand at my bathroom sink and look at the small graze mark on the outside of my arm.

It burns. But it is only a small graze.

If it had penetrated my skin, it would have killed me.

I don't blame her. She only did what she had to do.

The wolf had taken over tonight, but my human self caught little glimpses here and there of what he had being doing.

I was angry with him for going after Taryn. I hated him in that moment, but I was powerless to stop him.

Did she get my letter? Did she read it? Did she know I am her brother when she shot at me? Would she have cared?

I grab some peroxide and dab a little on my wound.

Ouch! It definitely burns.

I look at my human self in the mirror and realize that this will be the last night I am ever human again.

~~~~~

Taryn stretched and yawned. She had slept like the dead last night. It was the first time in several nights that her mind was calm enough to do so. The nightmare was over. The werewolf was dead.

Rolling over, she glanced at the clock and saw that it was ten o'clock.

Getting out of bed, she padded down the hallway to Penny's kitchen and pulled up a chair at the table.

Penny was standing by the sink making a pot of coffee, Inky tucked into the pocket of her robe.

"You're going to spoil that cat," Taryn said, a little jealous of the bond Penny was developing with the tiny kitten.

"He's just so precious," Penny said. "It's hard not to."

"Did he sleep in your bed last night?"

"He sure did. On my pillow."

The aroma of freshly brewed coffee lifted Taryn's spirits. As she took the first sip, she let the hot, brown liquid slide down her throat before she spoke. "It's over," she said, with a smile on her face. "I killed it last night."

Penny grabbed her cup of coffee and took a seat next to Taryn at the table. "What happened?"

Taryn told Penny what had transpired the night before, leaving nothing out. She felt the chill of fear run through her veins as she remembered the attacks and recounted what all had happened.

"I ended up shooting it," Taryn said. "It's out there somewhere dead."

"Are you sure?" Penny asked. "I mean, if you didn't see if die, how do you know it's really dead?"

Taryn was getting tired of everyone asking her that. "Because silver kills a werewolf," she said.

"Well, I'm just glad it's all over," Penny said. "And I'm so glad that none of you guys were hurt."

"Thanks, Penny," Taryn said. "Me, too."

"So," Penny asked. "What are you going to do today?"

"I'm heading over to the hospital to see Rhobby," Taryn said, draining the last of the coffee from her cup. "I wasn't able to go over yesterday and I'm starting to miss him."

"I'm so happy for you two," Penny said, lifting Inky out of her robe pocket. "What do you want me to do with this little guy?"

"I hate to ask, but could you keep him today while I'm at the hospital?"

"Of course," Penny said. "We're becoming quite the friends."

"He's going to end up bonding to you and be very upset when I take him home," Taryn said. "But I'm glad you're so willing to take care of him for me."

"Hey," Penny said. "What are you doing this evening?"

"Not much," Taryn said. "No need to go out on patrol again, so my evening is free."

"Why don't you, me and Cheryl get together at your house and play cards or watch old movies or something?" Penny asked. "We can celebrate the death of the werewolf."

"Sounds like a great idea," Taryn said. "I could use a fun evening to get my mind off all this stuff."

"It's a date, then," Penny said. "I'll pick up some goodies from Tucker's and we can all meet at your house around seven?"

"Seven sounds perfect," Taryn said. "I have to stop by the station, so I'll let Cheryl know. She's been itching to hang with us for awhile now."

Taryn got dressed and ran over to the station.

When she got there, Cheryl was on the phone. "Yes, I'll let her know," she said, before hanging up.

"Who was that?" Taryn asked.

"Lester Flynn," Cheryl said, rolling her eyes. "He said to tell you there's a horrible smell coming from the woods behind the cemetery and wants you to check it out."

"I'm heading over to the hospital to see Rhobby," Taryn said. "I'll take a drive out there later today. Where's Ron and Troy?"

"Ron is out on a domestic disturbance call and Troy just went to get donuts," Cheryl said.

"Oh, by the way," Taryn said. "Girl's night out at my place tonight at seven. Bring chips and pop."

"Yes!" Cheryl said. "I can't wait."

Taryn left the station and went to see Rhobby. He was sitting up in bed when she got there.

"Hey," he said, when she walked into the room. "Guess what?"

"What?" Taryn asked.

"Doc said I'm healing well and he thinks I should be able to go home tomorrow."

"Oh, that's wonderful news," Taryn said, leaning over and giving him a peck on the cheek. "How are the wounds doing?"

Rhobby pulled the bandage down and showed her. The wounds were still jagged, red lines, but the swelling had gone down and they were no longer bleeding.

"Looking good there, mister," Taryn said.

"Thanks. So tell me what's been going on," Rhobby said.

Taryn ran through the events of the night again for Rhobby.

"Sounds terrifying," Rhobby said, a crease in his forehead. "Glad you all made it out alive."

Taryn could tell the story upset him, but he knew the risks of her job.

"Does this change anything between us?" she asked.

"Not a chance," Rhobby said. "If anything, it makes me appreciate you even more."

Taryn spent several hours with Rhobby, before she had to go. She still had to check out the smell behind the cemetery Lester Flynn was complaining about and she needed to run by Tucker's to get some things for the party tonight.

"I'll be by first thing in the morning to pick you up," she told him. "What time is the doctor supposed to release you?"

"He said around ten or eleven," Rhobby said. "I'm so ready to leave this place. The food is horrible."

Taryn leaned down to kiss his cheek, but he turned his head and her lips landed on his. She thought about pulling away, but decided to give in and let the kiss happen.

Sparks flew through her mind and her knees felt weak. Oh my, she had forgotten how much she loved his kisses.

"I love you, Taryn," Rhobby said, when she pulled away and stepped back.

"I love you, too, Rhobby," she said.

She left the hospital feeling on top of the world.

She had Rhobby back. The werewolf was dead. She had a party to get ready for. Y

She was dancing on air as she stepped into Tucker's.

Dashing as quickly as she could up and down the aisles, she grabbed everything she thought she would need for the party and tossed each item into her cart. She also grabbed a few staple items she needed for the house, as well.

As she unloaded her items onto the belt at the register, an unwelcome thought occurred to her. The smell that Lester was smelling...could it be the dead werewolf?

Lost in her thoughts, she quickly paid for the groceries and went out to her car.

Digging around in her purse, she pulled out her phone. Flipping through her list of contacts, she called Ron. "Hey, are you busy?" she asked.

"Just finishing up some paperwork, why?" he asked.

"Lester called the station this morning and wants us to check out an odd smell in the woods behind the cemetery. Are you free to go with me?"

"Sure, Boss," Ron said. "You wanna meet me here at the station or out at the cemetery?"

"At the station," Taryn said. "I'll pick you up in five minutes."

The cemetery was creepy any time of day, but after what happened to Ginny Lee

Maloney out here, Taryn felt it took on a whole new level of creepiness.

The sun was out and white, puffy clouds floated across the sky. The air was warm and a sweet, floral smell drifted by on a breeze, but Taryn couldn't help but feel uneasy here.

She glanced over at the headstone that Ginny Lee was murdered by. A shiver ran up her spine. The blood that had been splattered all over the marker had since been cleaned off, probably by Lester, but the image of Ginny Lee's mangled body still remained in Taryn's mind.

Suddenly, a rotting, decaying smell met their noses.

"Ewww, what is that?" Ron asked.

"I don't know," Taryn said, pinching her nose closed. "But whatever it is, it's been dead a long time. It can't be our werewolf."

Following the putrid smell, they stepped over the wrought iron fence that surrounded the cemetery and stepped several feet back into the woods.

The smell became stronger the farther they went.

Soon, they came upon the carcass of a dead coyote.

"Well, it's not our werewolf," Taryn said, feeling a little relieved and yet a little disappointed at the same time.

"I'll call the game warden and have him come dispose of the carcass," Ron said.

"Normally, I'd say leave it here, but we'd never hear the end of it from Lester."

"Good idea," Taryn said.

They were walking back to the car when Taryn felt the odd sensation of being watched. She turned and scanned the area around the cemetery, but didn't see anything. "Let's get out of here," she said to Ron. "This place gives me the creeps."

"I bet Lester is down at the church doing yard work," Ron said. "Let's go down and tell him what we found."

Lester was weed-eating around the steps of the church when they pulled in. When he saw them approaching, he turned off the weed whacker and laid it down. "Did you find what it was causing all that stink?" he asked when they reached him.

"Just a dead coyote," Taryn said. "Ron's going to call the game warden to come take care of it."

"I was hoping it was a dead werewolf," Lester said.

"You heard about last night?" Taryn asked.

"It's a small town, Sheriff," Lester said.

"Well, the werewolf is dead, so we can all go back to our normal routines," she told him.

"Without a body, how do you know it's dead?" Lester asked.

"Because I shot it with a silver bullet," Taryn said. "That's how."

"No body, no proof," Lester mumbled under his breath as he turned and picked up the weed whacker. Without saying another word, he turned it back on and began chopping down more weeds.

On the drive back to the station, Taryn turned to Ron. "You believe it's dead, right?"

"I don't know, Taryn," Ron said. "I would assume so. We just need to find its body to be absolutely certain."

"Well, I know I shot it. I saw the blood," Taryn said. "When we get back to town, you need to put out a notice that the curfew is lifted."

"Don't you think that might be a bit premature?"

"No, I don't," Taryn said.

"Ok," Ron said. "You're the boss."

Taryn dropped Ron off at the station and drove out to her place.

She didn't understand why everyone was questioning whether or not the werewolf was dead. It took silver to kill a werewolf and she shot it with a silver bullet. She saw the blood on its arm with her own eyes. He probably just staggered off somewhere and died.

Grabbing the groceries she had picked up earlier, she went inside.

Laying the food on the counter, she turned and saw the mail and the letter still laying on the table.

Picking up the mail, she rifled through the bills and tossed them to the side. Picking up the letter, she slid her thumb under the flap and tore it open.

She read through the letter once. Then twice. The blood draining from her face.

She had a brother? He was the werewolf?

A wave of dizziness washed over her. Grabbing the back of a chair to steady herself, she read through the letter one more time.

Who was he? Did she know him? She read the words slowly again.

Suddenly, the realization of who it was came over her. She felt sick to her stomach. Her head spun and she collapsed onto the chair.

Vince. The golden boy of the town.

Vince was her brother? Could it be?

But wait. She killed the werewolf last night. It was dead. Had she killed her own brother?

Tucking the letter back into the envelope, she ran to her bedroom and slipped it under her mattress.

She didn't want to tell anyone about this. Not yet. She needed to think. She needed to find out if this was true.

Grabbing up her phone, she dialed Vince's number.

No answer.

She dialed it again.

No answer.

Sitting on the edge of the bed, she debated what to do. She couldn't be one hundred percent sure it was Vince.

And if it was, she killed him last night.

Gulping down a lungful of air, she sat there shaking as a wave of nausea came over her. She ran to the bathroom and threw up in the toilet.

Her phone rang from the other room. Sprinting down the hall to get it, she saw that it was Penny. "Hey," she said, out of breath. "What's up?"

"It's almost seven, girlfriend," Penny sang into the phone. "You ready to have a fun filled, awesome evening?"

Taryn had forgotten about the party. The letter from her supposed brother had knocked the wind from her sails and she was still reeling from it. "Uh, yeah," she said, distractedly.

"What's wrong?" Penny asked. "You ok?"

"Sure," Taryn said, trying to snap out of her dark mood. "Come on over. I'm ready."

"Be there soon," Penny said and hung up.

Taryn knew she wouldn't be able to think about it right now. She had a party to get ready for.

Her mind still in tangles, she set about getting things ready for when Penny and Cheryl arrived.

Chapter 25

Penny and Cheryl arrived within minutes of each other. They were both so bubbly and giddy, it was hard not to let their infectious attitudes sway her, so Taryn pushed the thought of the letter to the back of her mind and jumped into the evening's festivities with full abandon.

Darkness began to fall as they finished their third hand of Gin Rummy.

"I need a break," Cheryl said. "I'm gonna step outside for a breath of fresh air and stretch my legs."

"Good idea," said Penny. "I'll join you."

The women stepped out onto the porch while Taryn cleaned up the cards.

When she had slid the deck back into the pack, she joined Penny and Cheryl outside.

It was past nine o'clock now.

With the full moon rising, the night was bathed in an ethereal, otherworldly glow. A cool breeze was blowing softly through the trees and the night was alive with the sounds of nature all around them.

"What a beautiful night," Penny said, looking up at the moon. "Couldn't ask for a better one."

Taryn gazed out across the front yard, aware of the tranquil atmosphere around them. No feelings of being watched. No tingling along her spine. Just a perfect, calm summer night.

"What are we going to do now?" Cheryl asked. "The night is still young."

"Let's watch a movie," Penny said. "How about a classic black and white on one of those oldie channels?"

"Sounds good to me," Taryn said. "But no scary ones. We've had enough terror around here lately that we don't need to watch something scary."

"Agreed," said Penny, turning and walking back inside.

Cheryl followed Penny, leaving Taryn to stand on the porch by herself.

Looking over toward the woods, she stared for several moments, but no movement or noise was heard.

As she stood there, a car pulled up into the driveway.

Troy stepped out of his car carrying a bag tucked under his arm.

"I come bearing gifts," he said, lifting the bag up for her perusal.

"What are you doing out here?" Taryn asked him.

"I heard you were having a girl's night out and decided to crash the party," Troy said.

"Hey, the more, the merrier," Taryn said, stepping aside and letting him pass her to enter the house first.

The night wore on as they sat on the floor in the living room watching an old movie on the television. Taryn sat with her back to the couch with Inky curled up in her lap. It was well past midnight and she was beginning to feel the effects of the last few days as weariness began to overtake her.

She yawned and glanced up at the large picture window in front of them. She jerked straight up and stared at the window. Inky, upset about being jostled from his slumber, jumped off her lap and skittered under the couch.

"What's wrong?" Cheryl asked.

Taryn continued to stare at the window, but nothing appeared there.

"Nothing," she said. "I just thought I saw eyes staring in at us. I think I'm seeing things that aren't there. I must still be shook up about last night. Sorry guys."

"No need to apologize," Troy said. "It'll take us all a long time to get over what happened around here."

Taryn settled back down with her back to the couch and continued to watch the movie.

Suddenly, a loud screeching noise could be heard from outside the house.

"What was that?" Penny asked, quickly getting to her feet.

"I don't know," Taryn said. "Everyone stay calm. It's probably just a tree branch scraping along the side of the house."

A loud thump could be heard at the back of the house, followed by several more.

"What's going on?" Cheryl said, her voice shaking.

"Troy, did you bring your gun?" Taryn asked.

"Yeah, but it doesn't have silver bullets in it," Troy said. "Just regular 9 millimeters."

"Crap," Taryn said, reaching for her gun. "I changed out mine, too."

Rushing back to her bedroom, she fumbled around with the box of silver bullets she had put into her nightstand. Dropping a couple of them on the floor, she dropped the clip out of her gun and began shoving the silver ones into it.

Ramming the clip back into the gun, she grabbed the box of bullets and rushed back out to the living room. She tossed the box to Troy. "Hurry up," she said. "Reload your gun."

A deep, guttural howl split the night air.

Troy fumbled around trying to empty his clip and refill it, but he was shaking so bad, he was having a hard time.

Cheryl suddenly screamed and pointed toward the living room window.

Penny turned and ducked just as glass shattered all around them.

The werewolf had busted through the living room window and was standing there, his lips curled back, snarling at them.

Taryn looked up from trying to help Troy load his gun and stared at the same monster she had now encountered twice before.

She was frozen in terror. Her mind didn't want to work. She just stood there staring at the beast.

"Shoot it, Taryn!" Troy yelled. "Shoot it!"

Her brain snapping back to reality, Taryn raised her arm to shoot when the monster lunged at her and Troy.

It swung its arm out and knocked the gun out of Taryn's hand, sending it flying across the room. The monster turned and jumped on Troy's back digging its claws deep into his flesh.

Taryn heard the agonizing scream Troy let out and turned to see the werewolf lift him up using its claws and sink his long, razor sharp fangs into the back of Troy's neck, snapping his head completely off.

His head bounced and rolled across the floor toward Taryn, coming to a stop right in front of her.

Taryn stifled a scream as the werewolf turned toward her.

Dropping Troy's lifeless body, the werewolf ignored Taryn, turning instead toward Penny and Cheryl, who were hunkered down on the floor next to the tv.

"Run!" Taryn shouted at them. "Get out of here!"

Frantically looking around to see where her gun had gone, Taryn noticed it under one of the chairs in the dining room.

Diving under the table, Taryn snatched up the gun and turned to aim it at the werewolf.

To her utter horror, she saw Cheryl being grabbed by the ankle and jerked up into the air, upside down. Penny let out an earth shattering scream and dove, head first, out the broken window. Taryn heard a dull thud as she hit the ground.

Turning her attention back to the werewolf, Taryn was helpless to do anything for Cheryl. The monster was slashing at her with its claws extended while Cheryl hung helplessly in its grasp. Blood poured down her body in waves and her flesh was ripped and torn from the bone.

Taryn raised the gun and took aim. Through her tears, she watched as the werewolf threw Cheryl's lifeless body off to the side and took a step toward her.

Suddenly, she remembered the letter.

She held the gun aimed at the monster's heart, but her hand began to shake.

A honk blared from outside. The werewolf swung it's massive head in the direction the honk came from and howled.

Cheryl's body twitched. The movement caught the werewolf's attention and when its head was turned, Taryn leaped out the window. She hit the ground hard, but got up quickly.

The headlights of Penny's car snapped on and Taryn raced toward it.

Flinging the door open, Penny leaned over and yelled, "Get in!"

Taryn didn't wait. She dove into the passenger seat headfirst as Penny threw the car into reverse and floored it.

The car spun and flung gravel up into the air, but the tires gained traction and shot backwards.

Penny swung the car around, then headed down the driveway as a loud roar ricocheted through the surrounding trees.

Taryn looked back and saw the werewolf charging after them.

"Go, go go!" she shouted. "Faster!"

Penny slammed the gas pedal down and they raced down the road doing ninety miles an hour.

As they neared the old church around a the bend in the road, the car began to jerk and splutter.

"What's wrong?" Taryn asked. "Don't stop! Keep going!"

Penny looked down at the gas gauge and started thumping on the instrument panel with her fist. "No, no, no!" she shouted. "I'm out of gas!"

"What?" Taryn asked, horrified. "No, not now! Not now!"

The car gave a last splutter and died in the middle of the road.

"Quick," Taryn said, jumping out of the car. "We have to run."

"Run where?" Penny asked, getting out as well.

"The church!" cried Taryn, turning and running down the hill. "It can't cross into hallowed ground!"

Penny took off running after her.

They ran down the hill, slipping and stumbling over the loose gravel.

Not far behind them, they heard the earsplitting howl of the werewolf.

"Hurry, Penny," Taryn said, reaching out and grabbing her arm. "We have to hurry!"

They reached the bottom of the hill just as the werewolf sprang out of the trees that lined the road.

Taryn never ran so hard in her life. Dragging Penny with her, she leaped up the steps of the church two at a time.

Grabbing the door handle, she was surprised, but happy, to find it unlocked.

Throwing the door open, she and Penny burst through it, tripping over the threshold and landing on the floor.

Taryn rolled over onto her back just as the werewolf came leaping up the steps.

Using her foot, she slammed the door closed in its face.

Scrambling to her feet, she slammed the lock into place and backed up.

The werewolf didn't beat on the door. It didn't howl from outside. Was she right that it couldn't come into a hallowed place?

A horrifying thought crossed her mind. It went into the cemetery. Wasn't a cemetery considered hallowed ground?

Penny grabbed her arm, turning Taryn to look at her. "They're dead," she said through streaming tears. "Troy and Cheryl. They're dead."

"I know," Taryn said. "There's nothing we can do for them now. We have to figure out how to save our own lives."

One of the stained glass windows on the side of the church suddenly erupted into a shower of colorful shards as a rock came flying through it and skidded across the floor toward the women.

Penny screamed and ran to the pulpit, ducking down behind it.

Taryn reached into her pocket and pulled out her gun where she had stuck it before jumping out the living room window.

She gripped it tight in her hand and walked over to the front door where the light switches were and flipped on a row of overhead lights. Slowly, she walked in a circle around the room holding her gun at the ready.

Just as she got around to the main doors again, they burst open with a loud crashing sound, sending splintered wood flying through the air.

The werewolf stepped across the threshold and stood, heaving it's massive chest at her.

Taryn froze. It was inside. It came into the hallowed walls of the church.

Her mind spun in circles as she tried to think what she was doing. Fear gripped her heart as the monster took another step toward her.

"I know who you are," she yelled at it. "I got your letter."

The werewolf stopped and curled its lip back, showing its long, dagger-like fangs.

"You've Vince, aren't you?" she asked, taking a slow step backwards.

The werewolf seemed to pause, then took another menacing step toward her.

"It's me, Taryn," she said, raising her gun and aiming it at the beast's heart.

"I'm your sister, remember?"

The werewolf threw back its head and roared.

Taryn flinched, but didn't back down.

"I don't want to kill you, Vince," she said softly. "But I have to."

In a split second, the werewolf lunged at Taryn. She didn't have time to think. She didn't have time to reason. She just pulled the trigger and closed her eyes.

The blast echoed around the room, deafening her.

As the reverberating sound lessened, Taryn slowly opened her eyes.

The werewolf had been thrown backward by the blast and was slumped up against the wall next to the door.

Taryn stared at it for several moments, before tentatively taking a step closer.

The bullet had not hit its heart. It penetrated the monster through his left shoulder. Blood oozed from the wound. She could hear the labored breathing as the beast was drawing in its last breaths.

Taryn watched as the long, black hair began to suck back into its body.

She watched the claws withdraw back into the tips of its fingers.

She watched as the long snout shrunk back into its face and the long fangs disappeared up into its gums.

Slowly the form of a man began to appear.

Taryn felt tears stream down her face as the body and face of Vince began to take form.

Rushing over, she knelt down beside him.

"Taryn," he said, barely above a whisper.

"It's me, Vince," Taryn said, trying to keep her voice from cracking. "I'm here."

"You're...my...sister," he choked out.

"Yes, I am," Taryn said. She sat down on the floor next to him and pulled his head into her lap. "It's going to be ok now, Vince. It's all over."

"I'm...so...sorry," he said, as his breathing became more shallow and uneven. "I...never...meant...to...hurt… you."

"I know, I know," Taryn said, gently stroking his hair. "It's ok now."

Taryn felt a lump rise in her throat and she choked back the hot tears that continued to flood her cheeks.

"I...love...you, Taryn," Vince said. His body gave a slight shudder as his head lulled to the side. He let out a final sigh and he was gone.

Taryn sat on the floor of the church for a long time, rocking Vince's head in her lap.

Penny came over and sat down beside her, but never said a word and never tried to stop her.

The early morning rays of sunshine filtered in through the stained glass windows before Taryn gently laid Vince's head down on the floor and got up.

Looking at Penny, she said, "I need to call Dr. Middleton. He needs to come get Vince's body. And Troy's and Cheryl's."

Penny nodded her head and rubbed Taryn's back. "It's over now, Taryn," she said. "The nightmare is over."

Epilogue

Taryn arranged for Vince to be cremated. She didn't like the thought of him being buried in the creepy cemetery at the top of the hill.

Instead, she took his ashes into the mountains and stood on a cliff and let the wind carry them away.

Rhobby, Penny and Ron accompanied her on the journey.

Only the three of them knew that Vince was Taryn's brother. She hid the letter away where no one, but her, would ever know where to find it.

Taryn knew it would take many years for her to come to grips with what happened.

As far as the town knew, Vince was attacked and killed by the rogue animal, who was also shot and killed.

Taryn didn't want anyone to know that Vince was the monster who terrorized their town.

Taryn and Ron cleaned out Vince's apartment and got rid of any evidence that he was the killer. Taryn found a small piece of notebook paper crumbled up on the floor next to the couch. A list of names were written in a neat column down one side. Several of the names had been scratched out, but several still remained.

As Taryn read the names, tears filled her eyes. It saddened her to think what could drive someone to such hatred. Her heart hurt for Vince that he had allowed so much anger and resentment to drive him to become a monster just to seek revenge.

While she was boxing up his stuff, she came across his birth certificate. It, indeed, listed her dad as his father. She stuffed the piece of paper into her back pocket and hid it away with the letter he had written her.

Rhobby and Taryn got remarried a year later.

Deciding not to live so far out in the country anymore, they bought a small house in town and sold Taryn's property.

Nine months later, little Vince was born.

Inky became a treasured pet to Taryn. Knowing that he was a gift from Vince made him irreplaceable to her. Every time she looked at him, her heart warmed ever so slightly in memory of her brother.

Taryn made up her mind never to think of Vince as the monster he had become. Instead, she choose to remember him as the sweet, kind and caring man the whole town knew and loved.

"Rest in peace, dear brother," she whispered as she tucked the letter back in its secret hiding place. "I'll always love you."

About the Author

Carol Hall is an American writer who grew up in Chester, West Virginia, but now lives in the mountains of Tennessee.

Carol was inspired to write by her father who loved to tell tall tales to her and her two sisters, as well as to his grandchildren.

Carol's hobbies are reading, hiking, exploring new places and spending time with her family and friends and her three cats.

For more information or to contact Carol, please write to her at,

khiris@att.net

Other Books by Carol Hall

DISAPPEARED- Maggie Stewart loves hiking. Along with her husband and two friends, they set out on a hiking/camping trip in the mountains. Things quickly turn bad as Maggie is kidnapped off the trail by Bigfoot. Now she must fight to survive and try to escape her captors. Will she make it out or be forever lost in the mountains?

THE JOURNEY NORTH- Thirteen year old Emily Dunn is kidnapped from her home in the North and taken to the South to be sold as a slave. The year is 1864. Along the way she meets Mercy and the two become fast friends. One night, they escape their captors and their journey begins as they try to make it back to the North. Along the way they meet some new friends, but are also pursued by their captors. Will they ever make it back home?

THE INHERITANCE- Carly Montgomery just inherited the old southern plantation called Montgomery Manor from her estranged Aunt Ruth.

Upon taking possession of the house, Carly soon learns it is haunted. Strange images of a ghostly woman begin appearing to her, begging her for her help.

Carly meets Joe, the next door neighbor, and an instant romance ensues, but he is right for her? Or does the handsome police officer, Rick, hold more interest for her?

Will Carly unravel the mysteries of the mansion and help the ghost find peace or will she be forever haunted?